the

Common

Hours

DEBRA ANNE LeCLAIR

PORTALSTAR PUBLISHING, LLC

Copyright © 2024 by Debra Anne LeClair

All rights reserved, including the right of reproduction in whole or in part in any form.

ISBN: 979-8-9905823-0-9

Published by PortalStar Publishing, LLC

This book is a work of fiction. Names, characters, places and incidents either are products of the author's imagination or are used fictitiously. Any resemblance to actual events or locales or persons, living or dead is entirely coincidental.

Typesetting and Cover Design: Kerry Ellis
coveredbykerry.com

portalstarpublishing.com
debraanneleclair.com

*For all our ancestors from where
we come from to exist and express;
And especially for Somhairle Buidhe MacDomhnaill
and your need for a bard*

CHAPTER ONE

LINDSAY, 2018, NEWBURYPORT, MASSACHUSETTS, AMERICA

Sometimes, it's our mothers' secrets which send our souls scrambling. In the innermost chamber of her heart, my mother bore a desire to shift how humans live. The thing is, she possessed both the mindpower and a DNA strand to push her vision into full dimensionality.

My mom was an amazing question asker. She said it came from being a product of a mixed marriage, a Korean mother and a Scotch Irish father who only met because each had followed their curiosity and traveled out into the world. Her queries made you—helped you untwist your thoughts by turning them upside down. This embarrassed me at gatherings until I landed in college. By then, I liked entertaining the ridiculous—experiencing the expansiveness of dwelling in the opposite of what you thought was possible. My favorite game was when she'd ask friends and colleagues seated at our kitchen table, "If you could have dinner with one influential person, who would it be?" She ruled the chosen person had to be long dead and you dined with them during their time on Earth. Once I claimed Anaïs Nin and she beamed at me for the remainder of the evening. When it was my mother's turn, she'd name people you wished you'd thought of like Sacagawea and Harriet Tubman. In private, she told me more than once, Mark Twain would be her man. I didn't comprehend why that had to be a secret until the week after she died.

Her death was sudden and weird. It involved her car, but it wasn't a car accident. She had a heart attack sitting at a traffic light. She was only fifty-two, for fuck's sake. It was April 1st, the last day of my meditation retreat in New Hampshire, from where my consciousness and compassion expanded with no need to turn on the glass-and-plastic rectangle to check messages. When I got home, my mother wasn't there, but she always spent her Sundays at the Newburyport Farmer's Market.

I had only been home a half hour. Minutes after I'd dumped all my yoga clothes next to the washer and found the last peach yogurt in the fridge, a soft-spoken policewoman arrived at the door. Her mouth made sounds my brain had no choice but to decipher. I couldn't feel my face. I think it froze in disbelief. One of the most gutting things to ever happen just happened, and I couldn't turn to my mom to get through it. This time, the impossible, the ridiculous turned everything on its head, and reaching in from behind, twisted my heart, wrenching it into some unrecognizable shape, so it didn't beat right. Once alone inside, I sank to my knees and cried from my core. I stayed there until my friend Joanne found me, sitting in the threshold of the front door.

"I don't know if she suffered. What if she suffered?"

Joanne took me inside and brewed me some tea. She gave me a blanket to wear around my back because it felt raw and unprotected. And she let me be in my fits of silence until it slammed into me that I didn't know anything about making arrangements.

"I can call your dad," she offered.

My dad—oh God.

Better the words passed through Joanne's mouth. He asked to speak to me.

"I don't know what to do. Will you come help me with everything?"

His sigh dissipated into a silence that confused me with every millisecond passing. I listened hard for any sound of an answer.

"Do right by us, Dad. I'm all alone here."

"I can tell you she wanted to be cremated."

The words were like stones pelting my abdomen. She'd left me and now there would be less of her to mark she once existed.

"I can loan you the money for the funeral," he said.

It was an absurd thing to say. He knew my mother never lacked money and that she always outearned him.

"I've got access to her accounts," I said finally.

"I'm sorry, Lindsay. I could fly out of Charlotte for a day, but I might as well help from here."

I'd like to think the residue of the retreat dissolved my resentment, stopping me from going off on him, but in truth, I possessed no fire in my cells to fight it out. He had his new wife and family, kicking me down the ladder of priority, always and even now.

Joanne pointed to herself and mouthed she would help.

"I'll um—Joanne said she'll help me."

"Okay," he said, and I swear my blood dropped a few degrees. I don't remember what else I said to get off the phone. Once I saw the green phone icon change to red, I observed myself as if from a short distance, my mind realizing this would be the first night of my twenty-six years of being on the earth without a true parent. I'm still grateful that at least Joanne was there to sit on the kitchen floor with me for those first hours of trying to understand how my mother could possibly be no longer.

Three days passed and I didn't think a funeral could smell so alive. My mother's friends kept walking in with handfuls of lilacs, snipped from their own yards. They laid them around her coffin until the healing pastels swallowed up the stark white petals of the florist's roses: their chorus of scents streaming through the air. Only for this instant, life and death intermingled and lost their opposition to each other—my mother's body at peace among all the living. With her hands folded in traditional Buddhist fashion for meditation, her presence held a momentary serenity. I hoped she was communicating, "I've got your back." But another feeling began snaking through my mind; if she had my back, what was coming?"

For all the "beautiful service" comments spoken to me from mouths connected to outstretched hands, holding mine, I hoped for some sign my mother felt I honored her well. Here, her accomplishments were displayed in constant sight, like a painting that gets its own wall from where it shines its colors and layered textures under multiple spotlights. It was of some comfort to witness so many other eyes and ears remembering her essence, even for a single afternoon.

Over the few days afterward, unable to meditate, I numbed myself with reruns of *The West Wing* as I let calls and texts go unanswered after too many instances of consoling other people more than the other way around. Somehow, the drama of national and world events was easier to think about than my mom dying. On the occasion when my friends Donny and Bethany Facetimed me, they wanted to gossip. They were meaning to distract me, yet not talking about my mother felt shitty too. She was on my mind almost always.

Some relief came by surveying the vegetable garden, arranged as a labyrinth in our backyard. The delicate shoots and thickening stalks pushed through the earth in all shades of green, marking the curves of the spirals. Her prized boulder presided over the garden in the middle, where I sat. Turtles, carved of stone, appeared to be walking along the pathway. My mother liked to spend time with her spirit animals out here. Across from me, on a foot-high platform was the Buddha, resplendent in graceful robes cast in copper, his face held in the peace of pale green patina. My mother bought him way back when she was still a Catholic and initially gave him a home on the floor of her office. I thought the Buddha was the coolest guy, as my mother told me stories of him starting out life as a prince, who became truly ennobled once he left his kingdom to understand the root of suffering for all beings.

"Does he care about the kitties?"

"Yes, definitely the kitties."

"How about snakes and sharks?"

"Especially the snakes and sharks, and even spiders."

She'd often guide me through breathing, just being with the breath. My dad joined us once, but he was more fidgety than me and I could tell he didn't like it. Afterward, she called it Mommy-Lindsay time, and it made me feel like warm cookies inside.

Closing my eyes and inhaling, my palms pressed into the cool and heavy presence of the rock underneath me. I conjured my mother's soft voice singing Abba's "Fernando" while she kneeled along the winding rows of beans and carrots, her hand rake scraping an occasional stone as she pulled up weeds by their roots. Up came the familiar lump in my throat, knowing I could only hear her again by slipping into the past.

A firm knock on the garden gate startled me. I rolled off the boulder and approached the high slung gate. Unlatching the handle, my eyes met the loving smile of our spiritual mentor and my mother's sometimes research partner, Dorje Rinpoche. He bowed his shaven head and I followed, dropping my chin and bending at my hips, as I am so much taller than him.

"Glad you came around the back. These days I'd rather be with the plants than alone in the house."

With compassion shining from his dark oval eyes, Dorje remained silent, giving my words a space to land. I worried about his bare arm, the one not covered by the burgundy-and-orange monk's robes, getting cold in the chilled air of the early April morning.

"Would you like some tea?" I asked.

Dorje nodded. I was unsure of how to walk back into the house with him. I hadn't paid enough attention to the proper way to accompany a Buddhist monk when he visits your home, as my mother always took that honor. He motioned for me to lead the way and we walked, as if in a procession. Once through the kitchen door, it was easier to offer him a seat while I put the kettle on to boil.

Facing the stove, I caught my image in the blackness of the microwave and saw my hair tumbling loose from its clip. I tried to smooth the fallen pieces behind my ears before beginning with the clanking of cups and spoons.

After the steaming water was meted out and tea bags were floating, Dorje walked to the refrigerator. He stared at a thick ceramic magnet depicting an old book cover of Mark Twain's, *A Connecticut Yankee in King Arthur's Court*. He exhaled from a deep breath.

"Dorje, she'd want you to have that, from one of her spiritual teachers to another."

He took the magnet and laid it with reverence in his palm, its gloss illuminated by the sun beaming through the sliding doors. I waited for him to say something, but he seemed to let the moment pass as if it had been a wave pulled back out to the sea.

"Did she ever tell you that Mark Twain led her back to Buddhism… well, indirectly?" I said.

"She did not agree with the idea of original sin because it made it harder for people to accept themselves. She said she found greater resonance in the Buddhist teachings," he said.

"Yes, when I was in third grade, she'd read to me, or I'd read to her, and she'd always point out when one of Mark Twain's characters rejected being a sinner and instead found their own moral compass, like Huck Finn."

Dorje nodded. "Your mother lived the same way."

"She did, she definitely did," I said, replaying scenes of her coaching me to take my equal place in the world, beginning with third grade recess, playing football with the boys. After my teacher told me I might get hurt, my mother said, "People might tell you because you're a girl, you shouldn't go out there, but it's the best thing you can do."

Dorje's spoon rang gently against the insides of his cup as he stirred his tea. After a slow sip, he spoke plainly.

"We should talk about your mother's deeper work."

'Deeper' meant secret and at the mention of it my mouth went dry, but the tea was still too hot for me to take a sip.

"Please tell me you'll continue—in case there's still a chance for a breakthrough," I said.

Dorje placed his hands together, folding his fingers over as if holding his own hands.

"Lindsay, your mother did break through, more than once."

"What? No, she couldn't have…"

Reflecting my own expression, Dorje's face registered a hint of strain. I couldn't grasp this either as I had never seen him look anything other than happy, serene, or neutral. He reached into his weathered canvas satchel and pulled out a long gray envelope. Across it was my mother's familiar flourish in how she always wrote my name: the regal cursive of the L and the rest printed in well-practiced, even-spaced letters. I unsheathed the note written on a watermarked piece of paper dated two months prior.

To My Daughter Lindsay,

My wish is for you to never lay eyes on this letter, as it will only be given to you upon my passing from the earth. Understand above all else, I love you with my entire heart and spirit.

Sweetness, we've made a discovery to help all sentient beings. We found the time traveler's code and I've taken the most magnificent of journeys. I've been aching to share it with you.

You know Dorje Rinpoche is the keeper of the lost Amitabha texts. What I have not told you is that those texts contain a sacred meditation chant that opens up a neural wormhole to travel through time and space. Only women, and just a few, have the genetic predisposition. That is us Lindsay, me and you. I realize this is a lot to take in and digest, but it is my soul wish for you to carry on the work with Dorje as your guide. He will teach you all you need to learn.

With the Greatest of Love and Gratitude,
Mom

I shook the letter, as if I could shuffle the words to make it say something different.

"Can you allow this in—let your heart take hold of this gift?" Dorje said, his face becoming less clouded and more familiar.

"I can't believe she—I thought her chasing time travel was like trying to turn lead into gold. And now she wants me to—"

Then some other piece of my consciousness took a hopeful breath.

"Does this mean I can see my mother again?"

"No," he said, his eyes rounded in kindness. Tears rose in mine, and I let them slide down my face, not caring to wipe them away. My hands were too weighted down.

"Maybe she wants me to find her back in another time?"

Dorje shook his head ever so slightly, looking right into my eyes. I deflected his message in my mind, but eventually labored to speak. "How did you figure it all out?"

"Did she ever tell you Amitabha is the mythical Buddha who imparts blessings to know past lives, to alleviate suffering?"

"She had a statue she said was of Amitabha on her meditation altar. I never asked her why."

He told me about the mantra being comprised of sacred sounds. It shifts the brain waves to open up a neural wormhole from within the mind to other times and other locations.

"Your mother confirmed that consciousness can be directed to specific times and the body can follow, exactly as it's described in the teachings," Dorje said.

"You just said Amitabha is a myth."

"That is the conditioning of the modern mind. Myths are the bridge between what we believe we know and what has been collectively forgotten and now hidden from experience."

He waited, reading my face.

"In basic terms, you, the meditator, merge with the object on which you are meditating," he said.

"My mind wanders too much, and I wouldn't know what the hell I'd be doing."

"You are a healer," Dorje answered.

The word healer stopped me; it lifted me up, and for a second, I rose above the pool of doubt engulfing me below.

"Dorje, I just finished my homeopathic training. That's all I could offer."

"Your homeopathic knowledge is exactly what is needed."

So many thoughts burst into my mind—sharp pictures swarming of what would be required of me. I gazed at the small painting behind Dorje. It was of Green Tara, the Buddha who transforms suffering, and I found myself wishing she would step right into the room and into our conversation.

"Lindsay, there was a problem, an accident."

Dorje reached into his satchel to retrieve an iPad. It bore a sticker of ownership from the MIT neuropsychology program my mother headed up and where he was a consultant for her meditation studies. As he pushed the home button, the blue reflection from the screen fell across his face. He tapped it a few times and turned the tablet around for my view. It was on a page listing Mark Twain's bibliography. Even in my freaked-out state, it seemed short.

Dorje told me my mother decided her first trial should be something safe, taking care to abide fully by the laws of slipping through time and space.

"Your mother focused on a clear and specific intention in her meditation to visit Mark Twain—Samuel Clemens—where he lived in the late nineteenth century."

Dorje allowed me time to let the strange sentences sink in. Yet the science was what I could most easily grasp. My mother talked about the theorized potential powers of the brain all the time, but to actually hold presence with someone long dead...

"What went wrong?"

"Lindsay, do you remember your mother had the flu a few weeks before her heart stopped?"

"Oh God."

"She visited him before she was feeling ill but when she was contagious. It appears he died soon afterward from influenza," Dorje said pointing to the entry onscreen.

"I can give you the remedy," I said, anger and anxiety climbing up my gut.

Dorje smiled.

"But it is only you who can make the journey, once you are trained in the chant and meditation."

My weighted heart kicked against my ribs. "There is no one else?" I said in a labored whisper.

"Are there other meditating women from your mother's bloodline who have the expertise to save Mark Twain?"

No escape.

"We must get to him before too much time passes here. The news of his premature death is spreading into the collective consciousness, and there is a point that it will be irreversible. Then his death truly will be your mother's doing."

He was adamant, as any Buddhist would be, about taking care to not inflict suffering.

I nodded, peering into his eyes. Dorje intuited my need to digest it all, and he asked me to take my inner counsel through meditation. I was to meet him at the abbey later that morning, no matter what I decided.

After he left and I was alone, I walked around the house, my body spilling out from room to room, waves of fear landing against the walls and splashing along the floors. I needed to contain myself. For a few minutes, my focus pushed into ensuring the garage door was down, blinds drawn, and my phone switched off. Kneeling down onto the floor, I sat myself in the middle of the dark living room with my hand on my stomach. I willed it to settle as it writhed in acidity, just like it did the night my parents split up and when the police officer told me my mother breathed no more.

THE COMMON HOURS

Parting the drapes framing the sliding doors, I checked the labyrinth garden in our backyard, making sure it was as I left it. The mid-morning sun glinted in the eyes of my mother's plastic owl, perched and protecting the shoots and buds from predators. I was considering a venture out among the greenery to gain some grounding, but a raven landed on our boulder, formidable and so black, it shone purple in the sun. It was slow to compress its great wings; it wanted me to see it had arrived. Turning its head toward the plastic owl, it croaked out a call from deep within its chest. It fixed its eyes in my direction and soon lifted up into the sky, high above what I could see. I wished it to come back. I wished for many minutes. The raven was one of my spirit animals, and I thanked it for appearing—unsure if it was confirmation or warning.

CHAPTER TWO

The raven set me darting up the stairs and bounding across the hall, now ready to open the door to my mother's office. The room remained as if she'd simply left to stretch her legs or make a cup of tea. Several sheets of blank paper lay under a water glass, half drained; a purple highlighter rested in the crease of a neuropsychology journal. At the threshold, I paused. The walls vibrated like unorganized noise. My eyes met a mounted museum poster of Anna Freud which held a "And still she persisted" bumper sticker tucked in the corner of the frame. A picture of a brain with its circuitry lit up in neon colors and a photo of she and I all hung at a distance from each other, each having their own segment of the room complete with a bookcase or two. Mixed about the shelves were fat notebook binders and heaps of hardcovers with yellow sticky notes popping up from the pages. On an antique side table sat a century-streaked photo of our Korean ancestors, framed as if my mother knew them personally. I now wondered if she had. A handful of incense cones and a cobalt blue bottle of essential oil grasped my attention. I picked up the blend called Balance and caught a whiff of spruce and cinnamon—a familiar, motherly scent. Shaking some drops onto the diffuser pad and plugging it in, I crouched down close and waited. It was a reprieve to smell her again.

Sitting down in her padded, black desk chair, I tried to put myself into her state of mind. What seemed like a safe place to keep a diary or notes? I searched through the top compartments of her desk but only found a few stray unopened tea bags and stacks of address labels sent from various charities mixed in with junk mail and scrap paper.

I closed my eyes asking that, when I opened them, I'd be guided in the right direction. As I turned in her chair, the metal gave a weak squeal, and I sensed a gentle stir of air skim across my arms and face from the open window.

Yet I remained still. Was it not time to see or was I afraid? I refocused my mind on my question, and after inhaling to my lungs' capacity, I held it and let the breath go all at once. My eyes opened and fixated on the closet.

Inside, a multitude of long hanging dresses greeted me. There was a sparkly dress I remembered her wearing on a distant New Year's Eve. She and my dad were in awesome moods that night as they went out. Her voice was almost sing-songy as she kissed me goodbye 'until next year.'

Moving the hangers, I found a long navy cloak and the dress next to it was some kind of period costume. It was heavy and legitimate. The fabrics were old but not tired. I pulled it out with some effort and saw it had many layers, like when women wore gowns that extended far out from their bodies.

Retrieving the cloak, I laid it next to the dress on the antique Queen Anne sofa, across from my mother's desk. The cloak bore a discernible smell of metal. I took a sniff inside the closet and determined the smell belonged solely to the cloak. The seeds of an idea were crowning in my awareness. Was this her time traveler's outfit?

I endeavored to put the whole ensemble on my own body, to give it a good look. The foundational layer was of a gossamer silk, which made it a challenge to slow down and slip over my head. Once on, it skimmed over my body with a coolness that quickly transformed into a soft, comforting warmth. Once the bodice and the skirts were on me, I grew frustrated trying to get them positioned and fastened without any help. I did not do much better to secure the heavy sleeves, which were tight at the shoulder and funneled out so that at mid-arm they hung like bells. It took me some time to walk down the hall to look at myself in the full-length mirror. If anyone was watching me, they would have thought me a person in a fresh episode of psychosis as I was beyond mesmerized to see myself so transformed.

I labored to unlatch my eyes from my own image and carried the fabric with all its shushes and sheeshes back down the hallway. Once sitting back down in the desk chair, I had to make accommodations for all my skirts, only to find myself at a good distance from the desk and laptop. With stretched arms, I searched for images of women's clothing from the other centuries. Landing in the 1500s, I found a match.

"So, this was definitely about more than hanging out with Mark Twain," I said aloud.

My phone alarm chimed, and I swore, knowing it was already time to leave for the abbey. Sparks of ire rose up in me while I attempted to peel off the layers, as I shouldn't have had to do this alone. Once free, I threw on my own clothes, but paused to consider the cloak, still laying back on the sofa. Picking it up in both arms, I let it drape like the legs of a sleeping lamb. I would ask Dorje what he knew about it. Grabbing my obsidian protection stone from my knapsack, I slid it into my purse. I spotted a Kind bar at the bottom of my bag my mom gave me as I left for my retreat. It was chocolateless, so I never ate it. Now it was a sacred relic I hoped would give me courage.

Driving over, obligation, heavy with the unknown, rode in the car with me. Once through the gates of the abbey, the tension in my body spiked and continued rising as my feet crunched across the gravel walkway, which had replaced the dirt path since I was last there, a few months prior. This can't be good for the monks wearing their sandals, I thought, noticing a small stone rubbing against the skin below my ankle bone on the inside of my sneaker. I debated stopping to fish it out but decided to live with being aware of the irritation instead. Somehow, I preferred this discomfort over everything else going on in my inner slice of the world.

A smiling monk opened the immense wooden doors at the main entrance upon my approach. There were candles lit in each corner, the flames flickering as they were whipped up by the wind that entered with me. Dorje emerged at the top of the staircase, and we met at the bottom step. With veneration, he retrieved the cloak from my arms.

"Had your mother ever showed you this?" he said.

"I found it."

"And you knew to bring it here."

"Well, yeah."

He nodded and up the staircase we went. Dorje led us down the hallway, lined with close-up paintings of the Buddha's eyes and face. The lines painted in bold metallic hues juxtaposed the traces of an equable smile and eyes closed in meditation.

Dorje opened the door to an office space, rich in the fragrance of spent amber incense. Simply furnished, there were two burgundy chairs upholstered in faded cotton fabric, set between a desk and a gray, striped two-seater couch.

With both arms, Dorje motioned for me to take a seat, laying the cloak next to me.

"Dorje, why didn't she tell me?"

"I counseled her to wait."

"Why?"

"She worried that you would talk her out of continuing the work."

I felt sick. Did she see me as critical, like my father? Or did she think I couldn't handle it? Something new now seemed undone between us.

"Where did she go, other than to see Mark Twain?"

"Those were her only journeys."

I swallowed down this new confusion.

Dorje asked me about my decision to meet with him. I told him I'd thought about Mark Twain's family and how it would be for his daughters to lose their dad. I also got my mother needed me to explore this time-traveling ability. Despite what Dorje said, maybe I'd find her.

"It's for all of them," I said.

Dorje assured me my decision arose from love and compassion. A smile which emanated from his whole being steadied me into resoluteness. This was an unforeseen right path.

Beginning my initiation, Dorje opened a black, hard-backed journal.

"There are rules the time traveler has to honor. First, you cannot move in time where you might already exist, because you can't run into yourself. And you should stay away from any of the years onward from which your parents were born."

"Are there any exceptions?"

"There are none."

The friction from that rule torched up my spine and burned the back of my brain.

"How do you know there are no exceptions?"

"In Tibet, our master teacher was the keeper of the sacred Amitabha texts, and he transmitted this designation to me. In gratitude and in honor, I devote my focus to understanding all depth of their intended utility. Your mother became a fellow steward, as she brought in her own knowledge of neuropsychology to apply with reverence to the teachings. We must learn and not direct, not impose our will and attachment to an outcome."

I did not believe I could let go of my attachment to the outcome of seeing her again.

"My dear, my fondest wish for you is that, by following in your mother's path, you will usher in healing through the work itself. Your suffering will not always be like it is today—it is impermanent. Only the love is eternal."

I held a wisp of solace from the moment, but that was also impermanent.

Another directive was that you had to be clear on your intention of where you would be going. Otherwise, the traveling would not manifest or, worse yet, resort to a time or place in your unconscious.

"You visualize the time and place you intend to find yourself before you move into the meditation journey. Next, you whisper the mantra, whose syllables prime the mind's capacity to experience non-linear time," Dorje said.

He brought the journal over for me to see a portion of the sacred mantra in written form. From reading the words, I sensed a mental shift, as if they held within them the power to make all my distracting thoughts fall away.

"It is the sounds heard inside the mind which work with your intention and your genetic capability to allow you to merge with the place and time of your focus."

"Dorje, doesn't this mess around with the natural order or things? Isn't the Middle Way of Buddhism to see and accept things as they are?"

"A veil between worlds is falling away and it requires a new clear seeing into its nature. Our current reality is transient. Buddhism is interested in seeing the truth in the reality that is now emerging and manifesting."

I held my stomach.

"Shouldn't this be for a devout Buddhist nun or a Bodhisattva woman to study? How will I be able to see into the true nature of this sacred pathway when I'm barely through my Margha studies."

"You, as you are today, are the truest descendant of this knowledge, this practice."

"But how did I earn it—it can't be mine."

"It is about hearing the call and wakefully, mindfully, bringing what is already in you to the circumstance...you are here. Perhaps you can relieve the pressure by understanding this phenomenon as something that can work *through* you not *by* you," Dorje said, turning and motioning toward the depiction of Green Tara on the far wall.

I gazed at her wise and loving smile. Green Tara was compassion and liberation in thought and action and the Buddha who resonated the most with me. Dorje comprehended that well. He turned the page of the journal.

"When time traveling into the past, no time passes here because wherever you are going has already happened. That passing of time has no bearing on how time moves here, in this present moment."

I nodded in understanding.

"We do know that since this is traveling through a neural wormhole, the state of the brain dictates everything," he said. "That is why your thoughts have to be clearly focused."

"So first the brain waves shift with the mantra, and they follow my mind's intent," I said.

Dorje grinned and nodded with fervor.

"My mind will travel through my body but what happens to my body?"

"Your body goes with you as it follows through the neural wormhole. That is how your mother passed on the flu. Also, whatever your brain registers is on your person, will travel with you. For instance, it will sense you are wearing clothes; it knows you have something in your pocket, like a vial of the homeopathic remedy for the flu."

"Can I bring other stuff?" I asked.

"Yes, and you should," Dorje said, gesturing to the cloak.

"Lindsay, shall we meditate on simple mindfulness of the breath to stabilize the mind?"

"Please, yes."

I found the rustling of the buckwheat meditation cushion Dorje handed to me calming, a sound I only associate with coming into stillness. Folding my legs, I moved into my meditation posture. Dorje struck a chime. I listened as its vibration washed into me and pulsed in my heart. Where this was my focus, I shut out all visual stimuli. The sound was all there was, despite having a mind that could have, should have, been racing now.

It ends up we remained in that constellation for quite some time. Upon opening my eyes, I felt lulled, not refreshed.

In a soothing tone, Dorje asked if I was ready to try my first journey.

My senses jolted—the classic needle ripped from the record playing. I stood up but didn't know what I wanted to do. I wasn't ready.

"I will guide you. It will serve as your initiation and chance to travel in your mother's wake."

"Am I going back to some Mississippi riverboat to convince Mark Twain to take my remedy?"

"You would meet him in his writing study at his home in Hartford, Connecticut. Mr. Twain has been a happy host—he was to your mother," Dorje offered.

"And he would definitely be there, and it would be safe, and nobody would call me a witch or anything?"

"He'd offer you some tea," Dorje said.

"How will you call me back?"

"You control that aspect. You will come back when you have done what you went there to do."

"Will there be pain?"

"It may feel hard to breathe," Dorje said. "Go with a breath in your lungs already."

"What if I can't breathe?"

"The breath will always be there. But it requires more work."

I stared out the sun-filled window, as if it would offer some reassurance, but questions kept multiplying. Dorje lit some incense. As the wafts of amber sweetened the air, he showed me a picture. It was a red room and in its center was a dominating billiard table rooted near a less impressive brick fireplace.

"This is his study," Dorje said. "You are to picture it in your mind's eye as you think of August 4th, 1878."

"But what if he's not there?"

"He will be, that is one of our designated dates. His family is away on vacation, and he is writing, alone."

"When did my mother go?"

"August 3rd, 1878."

"I can go then and meet my mother. Dorje, would that not be the best solution? I would prevent Mark Twain from ever getting sick and I could talk to her, ask questions—"

I heard myself pleading with him as a cold sweat surged under my arms and heat flushed up into my face. Dorje remained silent. Not much above a whisper, he said, "August 4th."

My stomach burned under a heavy heart. After several patient moments, Dorje said, "He won't ask, but if he does, do not tell him anything about how the future impacts him, particularly about his own person or family."

"But you said he won't ask."

"He won't. But we never know."

I sought out my bag and took out my remedy kit. With shaking fingers, I opened and retrieved the vials of Gelsemium and Bryonia.

"Best to take the whole kit and hold it in your lap. And, Lindsay, call him by his real name, Samuel Clemens."

"Tell me I won't screw this up," I said.

"Remember your intent, including after you arrive."

Dorje lifted the cloak from the sofa and placed it around my shoulders. I pulled the hood up over my head. As it enclosed my body, I inhaled its metallic scent mixed in with the amber notes from the incense.

Dorje spoke the mantra evoking the connection to Amitabha Buddha. I whispered it back as he instructed. Within seconds, my attention gathered to my intended destination: seeing the red walls, the green of the billiard table, and light beaming through the open windows.

My brain felt, and this was the weirdest part—like it was falling in on itself. But it didn't hurt, despite launching through a vortex. Inside it, I traveled hot and fast until released into a chilled expanse. It was then I couldn't breathe—as if my lungs were glued shut. A grinding underneath me filled up my awareness and all motion stopped. My breathing resumed and a faint smell of metal circulated in the stillness before the scribbling of a decisive pen onto a page replaced the silence. That became everything in the darkness.

I opened my eyes to find myself sitting in a wooden chair next to a billiard table. The scribbling ceased as I met the dark and deep-set eyes of a man with tousled chestnut hair, leaning over his desk with a mouth that had fallen open under a full and dark mustache.

"Sara?" he asked as he rose from his chair. I stood as well and took a few steps to find my equilibrium as I lowered the hood of the cape.

"No, I am her daughter, Lindsay," I said and offered my hand. He shook it cautiously.

He then slapped his thigh. "Will miracles never cease?"

I was unable to look away from a person I'd seen so many times in photographs, looking now so much younger. He had an aura about him—a discernible glow. Even with his sleeves rolled up and ink on his fingers, I was spellbound to be in his presence, sharing air and conversation.

"I reckon this is your first trip?"

"Yes, testing this whole thing out. And you really know my mother?"

"We've had tea," Sam said, raising his full eyebrows in amusement. "Only yesterday."

"Only yesterday," I said aloud as I contemplated what it would be like to have had the chance to see my mother, only yesterday. Swallowing hard, I pressed on.

"Did she ever tell you, you're one of her favorite authors?"

Sam shook his head but smiled.

"I think you're aiming to flatter me," he said.

It struck me as strange my mother hadn't gushed those very words as soon as she met him. Sam motioned with his hand for me to take a seat, while he dragged over another chair so that he could sit across from me.

"Miss Lindsay, forgive the query, but she sent you on your own?"

Can I tell him? I paused, and he leaned forward. I read my sudden change in demeanor on his face.

"She has recently died," I said, my voice unsteady.

"Oh, my dear, how did she—"

"Her heart stopped. They say she didn't suffer."

He surveyed my face, his eyes remaining soft and sad, which brought up my tears. He offered me his handkerchief that, once in hand, I needed that much more. I wished so much she was there with me, so we could've made these visits together. As I let the linen soak up the emotion, I noticed Sam had his own tears. I offered the hanky back, realizing too late my makeup had stained it.

"Best you keep it," he said, plucking another from his pants pocket and smiling through his own wet eyes.

"I am so sorry to hear this saddest of news."

"Thank you, it's been hard."

Sam nodded and looked down. He ran both hands through his hair, anchoring his fingers at the back of his head as we sat in the thickening silence for several moments.

"How was the first time she visited you?"

"She appeared right over there near the fireplace. I thought she was a ghost, come here out of thin air. But her smile was sweet, which I saw as soon as she took down her hood. But I'd never seen hair cut so short on a grown woman and in such a straight line." Sam motioned both his hands at his chin.

"She loved bobs—um, that's what they call that hair style now."

"She told me that women don't like managing all that hair anymore because they've got to spend their time on face painting and such."

I laughed. Is that what she really said? I thought.

"How did you come to understand what was happening?"

"She was straight with me—laid it all out on the table."

"Why would you believe it, it must have sounded ridiculous."

"She told me in the summer of 1874 that she loved Tom Sawyer. Only three people possessed any knowledge about that book then."

My mother broke one of the rules of this time travel stuff right off the bat. Holy shit.

"What did that do for you, now knowing something you never would have before?"

Sam rolled his eyes playfully, as if he was debating with himself. It made me laugh out loud. He took a pause to open a deep brown box, lifting out an equally dark brown pipe and placing it in his mouth without lighting it up.

"Begging your pardon, Miss Lindsay, I'd like to get blowing on this but I'm aware your mother did not care for the smoke."

My father smoked—rather heavily in the years before he left.

"I don't mind," I said.

Lighting the tobacco, his face shifted to one of clear contemplation.

"I suppose there's some moral questions to be asked here, but I saw no harm in knowin' a spit of success was coming my way."

"It probably wasn't too surprising," I said.

Sam shrugged while he puffed on his pipe. As the rings rose and dissipated, to my relief, it didn't smell too bad. In fact, I liked the aroma—sweet and earthy, free of chemicals and certainly non-GMO.

"When did women start wearing trousers?" he asked, pointing up and down at my jeans.

I glimpsed down at my jeans and laughed.

"I'm not sure, sir," I said.

He waved me off.

"I wasn't testing you or nothing."

"I can tell you, it's nice for us women to have the option of a dress or pants. Makes things a whole lot easier."

Sam considered this, as he let out another long trail of smoke.

"If it didn't confuse things, I reckon that would be the case," he said.

"Is there anyone around who might see me?" I asked as an echoing of horses clopping across the way sounded into the house.

"There's George, but he's gone off to the market."

As the horses came closer, I stood at the threshold of Sam's study. Across the landing and through the windows, a black lacquered carriage stopped at the front of the home across the way. A middle-aged woman emerged in a corseted bodice and a skirt that had its own train of ruffles so layered it required a maid to manage it while she stepped to the ground. This was not a costume, not a reenactment. I turned back and took in Samuel Clemens, Mark Twain, standing by his billiard table. It hit me again that I was really here.

"Your mother took on that same look, the first time she arrived," he said.

That did me a world of good to hear.

"What did you think after she left?"

"It was a confirmation of a deep knowing that's been present most of my life. I used to dream about somebody calling on me from another time. So, it was like a trumpet blast but from a song where I already recognized the melody," he said.

"You dreamed of her—of us?" I asked, not believing I could be a piece of his rich imagination.

"Can't say it was you two, but the visitors were always women."

The rolling in of another carriage, this one closer to the house, met our ears.

"That's George. You don't have to go but you best be keeping yourself here in my study."

I closed the door and swallowed hard. "Mr. Clemens, how is your health?"

"Call me Sam and my health is fine, but today there is a small ache in my head." He straightened his posture. "And a bit in my back, but I've been hunched over my writing all morning. I do say that your mother's sojourns inspire me in my storytelling."

I dug into my bag and pulled out the homeopathic remedies. He studied me as I placed pellets of each into a tiny paper cup. Upon handing them to him, he took delight in the cup's design.

"Miss Lindsay, what is this here in this marvelous little vessel?"

"It's medicine, Sam. My mother thought you might be coming down with something, so I have brought you the remedy."

"You are a physician?" he said in disbelief.

"I am of sorts."

"What is it I got?"

"It's the start of influenza."

Sam's eyes hardened. He froze for several moments until he took a step, backing away from me. I thought he might refuse me and my medicine.

"You'll be fine, if you let those pellets dissolve under your tongue."

Pressing his lips closed, ensuring nothing would escape, he abided by my instructions. After a moment, his shoulders relaxed a bit, as did mine.

"To say I'm much obliged is quite short of the bottom of my heart."

"Your headache should clear, along with the backache. I mean unless it was from hunching over your desk. I'll leave a few more of the pellets to take tomorrow. But not with food or drink."

"Understood, Miss Lindsay."

George's footsteps thudded in the downstairs foyer. Sam and I waited and listened. Several seconds of quiet passed. The only sound between us was Sam's breath as he blew a couple of smoke rings into the air. They floated toward his desk.

"Did my mother ever share anything with you about her other journeys?"

Sam wrinkled his mouth to one side before puffing on his pipe, sending whitish smoke up above his head like a thought bubble.

"She said she'd been with her ancestors."

"Did she say which ones? Did she name a country?"

I could see visiting either our Korean lineage or our McDonnell clan being equally enticing to my mother.

"She mentioned a queen. At first, I thought she'd meant getting herself to England to see Miss Queen Vicky, but she said no, not her. I asked her why bother with any of that imperialism nonsense? She said that it was exactly the point—the crowned heads held all the power."

My brain flip-flopped with thoughts—my mother bowing to Queen Seondeok in an ancient Korean court. Then I remembered the outfit I tried on.

"Can you recall any western queens in the 1500s?"

Running his hands through his hair, inadvertently dropping ash on the floor, Sam pondered for several seconds.

"Well, there's Mary Queen of Scots who was related to the Tudors—bushels of English queens there." Sam straightened his shoulders, asserting confidence in his contribution. "The one I'd be most concerned with is Queen Elizabeth. They say our first colony was Virginia, named after the Virgin Queen, herself."

A cold electric current ran through me, standing the hair on the back of my neck at attention.

"Got your mind going with that suggestion," he said.

"Yes, but what does she have to do with our ancestors? We're Scottish and Irish," I puzzled aloud.

"Elizabeth was a cunning one. She went after colonies everywhere. I reckon you'd be best served to look up your Irish and Scottish history."

That suggestion gave me goosebumps. Sam blew out a long curl of smoke and leaned forward, as if telling me a secret.

"If I had your gift, I'd go find me King Arthur."

I paused.

"Now that would be a story to tell, Sam," I said.

His slight smile shifted to a contemplative gaze.

"Miss Lindsay, I pray you can see yourself back to call on me in the future. I've grown accustomed to Sara's summer visits and I hope you'll continue the tradition in your momma's place."

The familiar wave of heavy emotion rose up into my throat. I nodded, if nothing else but to show him my gratitude. He nodded as well, before pointing to a chair in the corner.

"Your mother always sat there for her journeying to the future."

I complied and took the seat. He stopped at the door, turned to me, and waved. Closing the door behind him, he paused before starting down the stairs.

I pulled out my iPhone and took in the juxtaposition of having it in 1878. I couldn't help myself, taking a quick selfie against the backdrop of Sam's desk, before meditating. I envisioned sitting in the abbey with Dorje and whispered the Amitabha chant. A deep chill and loss of breath came, followed by a flipping feeling, worse than any rollercoaster. Nausea was moving in until I landed in a hard stop. Upon opening my eyes, Dorje was standing in front of me, beaming.

"Yes, you do have to reacclimate. Your mother said it was more intense on the trip back to our present moment," Dorje said.

Now, sitting in the twenty-first century, having just spent a moment with Mark Twain in the nineteenth, joy spread through me, like a small sun taking up residence in my core and shooting its energy across the whole spectrum of my being.

"That was the most astounding, the most blessed thing ever. He was phenomenal." I managed to get the words out of my mouth after a moment of speechlessness. "I can see why she loves him."

I caught myself but left it alone. I didn't need to correct myself and put her into past tense. I mean, the man I just met is dead too, and so is George, his servant, as well as the woman who emerged from the carriage. Seems they have a second life, somehow.

"And how did he take to the remedy?"

"Almost obedient. He took the pellets right away. But he did ask about my mother, and I had to tell him."

Dorje nodded and we sat in silence for a moment.

"Lindsay, you are now initiated."

"What happened to me while I was gone?"

"You looked like you never left physically."

"But I really did, right? It wasn't a hallucination."

"Yes, you have experienced slipping into the past, without it occupying any time in the here and now. It is perhaps an indication of the next progression of human consciousness, to live without the chains of the past replaying," Dorje said.

"That would be amazing, to not be defined by your past. I'd love to not have to wear any labels anymore based on what I did or didn't do or who I loved."

"The dharma teaches us to consider that we are no one thing," Dorje offered.

I sighed. I understood this from a whole different vantage point now.

Upon arriving home, I struggled to keep the joy that filled me from draining out onto the floor of the dark and empty house. Running up the stairs to my mother's office, I found her Mark Twain collection expanded once again, and I did a little dance in place. I pulled down

The Adventures of Huckleberry Finn and opened it up, smelling the aged paper. Flipping through the chapters, The Trouble with Royalty, The Funeral, I closed the book on Family Grief. Moving down the spines, I paused at *The Prince and the Pauper*—I remembered watching the movie; this was about the Tudors. Mark Twain was writing about the Tudors. How and why? I took the book into my hands while scanning the shelf for what I most needed to see: *A Connecticut Yankee in King Arthur's Court*. I turned the pages, thinking about Sam's desire to meet Arthur and that this very book my mother read to me when I was little might owe its existence to her real-life time travels.

Tucked into the end of the book was a pamphlet, bound in salmon-colored cardstock and bearing a library bar code from Idaho Falls, entitled *Mark Twain's 1601: Conversation as it was... by the Social Fireside in the Time of The Tudors*. My thoughts whirled and flipped over, wondering if an alternative reality was taking hold, at least in my consciousness. Published in 1889, I wondered if my mother was responsible for this too.

Written inside the back cover was a historical timeline of Queen Elizabeth I's reign. Sam was right, this was the queen my mother was seeking! Also there, clipped to the back cover, was our McDonnell family tree. Highlighted in pink were the names of a set of great-grandparents from many generations ago, Mary O'Neill and Sorley Boy McDonnell who lived in the northeast corner of Ireland during the Tudor dynasty. This set off hours of research with a need to understand the complex connection between our McDonnell ancestors and my mother's quest to travel to Elizabeth Tudor. I googled Sorley Boy in hopes he existed somewhere on the web. He had a Wikipedia entry but instead of a portrait of him, there was only one of Elizabeth I.

I rustled through pages of Sam's novel as it was clearly a file for my mother's most secret work. There were a few pages of what seemed like therapy session notes, obviously misfiled, and on the last page written under 'the end,' also in my mother's hand, was information on a future bus tour of Northern Ireland and a note that it had been paid for by a check, with the phone number. "Are you kidding me—are you fucking kidding me?" I said aloud, feeling like I'd found the Holy Grail.

I cycloned down the stairs to grab my phone. Swearing loud and frequent, I could not find it in any of the usual spots. With hands on the top of my head, I looked in all directions, finally recalling throwing it on the couch.

My fingers shook as I swiped and tapped in the long phone number, mistyping several times. Finally, I was listening to the sound of quick ringing.

"Dalriada Tours, you're speaking with Declan, how can I help?" The voice coming through was young and cheerful, perhaps belonging to an angel speaking to me in that moment.

I strained to sound calm as I explained the situation.

"I'm so sorry for your loss. Please accept our condolences. Would you be wanting a refund then?"

"Can I come in her place?"

There was a slight pause. "I can't see why ever not," Declan chirped. "Sounds like you would be honoring your mother to do so."

"Thanks for saying that, Declan, it means more than I can say."

After finishing the arrangements, I sat, giving myself a chance to digest. Then, with a burst of profound purpose, I made my plane reservations. Even my packing was guided with no ambivalence in thought, only world traveling wisdom. That same awareness told me to get a self-charging battery for my phone and to bring a well-stocked homeopathic kit. Although, I pretty much have that with me always.

No doubt both my parents would have told me I was being irresponsible to pick up and go, but my heart told me that my mother needed me to try and intersect with her centuries ago. Please God, let it be so.

CHAPTER THREE

After a night of little sleep, I awoke with little pleasure left from meeting Mark Twain the day before. Everything was shifting, and too fast. Requiring some sense of normalcy, I washed my face, slipped on a pair of jeans, and stepped out our front door into the dewy morning to go for a walk around the neighborhood. I inhaled the perfume of the creeping phlox, a mix of pink candy and blue moon petals striping each side of the walkway. From the street, it looked like my mother might be inside having a cup of tea with her morning *Boston Globe*. But if she had, our ruby red front door would have been left slightly ajar. Today, it was closed and locked. Her intention of painting the door red after going through a feng shui period was in hopes of improving the flow of life energy around our home. Now, its absurd brightness accentuated the newly borne hollowness that lay within.

Pausing at the mailbox, I couldn't remember the last time I checked it. The once stark white letters on the side that read McDonnell were graying from when I'd applied them as an act of solidarity. I did this after my father left us and I changed my last name from his to my mother's maiden name. I thought it would cleanse us both while deepening our bond, but she was so pissed. Saying it was like a proclamation that our family had broken up for the whole neighborhood to see.

Inside was a padded envelope from the ever-helpful Joanne, who I should further explain was my closest friend and intended business partner as she was a massage therapist that I planned to share office space with downtown. The smiley face on the package sparked my guilt as I deposited my letter to her explaining the discovery of my mother's planned trip, which would delay launching my homeopathic practice. I enclosed a rent check, hoping she wouldn't lose her patience with me. It was a relief to realize my feet would be planted on Northern Ireland soil by the time the letter reached her. I opened her package to find a T-shirt of the elephant-headed Indian God, Ganesh. As far as I understood, he was both the remover and creator of obstacles. But did he have any experience in reversals, like finding my mother alive in a long dead century?

Searching for a note, I found a flyer bearing a drawing of, yes, a raven, on a rock, pecking into the surface of a stream. Across the top it read, *Shamanic Journey to the Sacred Ancestral Garden*. Underneath, Joanne had written some of the most loving words I had seen in a while:

I thought you might be able to make contact with your mom.

The gathering was that night, a ten-minute walk, downtown. Shamanic journeying was something my mother and I would do on our yearly retreat together. Energy rose in me knowing she was probably trying to communicate. God knows she has a lot of explaining to do.

The woman ticking off names had gray hair with a stripe of purple streaming through her long braid. She wore a shirt emblazoned in sharp clean letters, 'No Farms No Food.' Her face was kind, even in its businesslike role as she took time to make eye contact and bade me welcome. This helped me forget my desolation, for the moment. I walked into the meditation room lit by candles placed within the center of a circle of wooden chairs. The group consisted mostly of baby boomers, clad in natural fibers and speaking in muted tones, respectful of the sacredness of the space.

Just then a loud-mouthed bell rang out. This set off a ritual of taking seats, silencing phones, and turning one's attention to the front of the circle. There, a gruff, bearded man stood.

He struck the bell again, this time without as much assertion. I observed the faces of those in the circle, most sporting various versions of grins, happy to be where we were.

"I'm Hank, glad to see you all here tonight. In most spiritual circles we often introduce ourselves and talk about what brought us here. But for this, the only thing that's important is, as you make your journeys, you remember there are fellow beings traveling beside you. I find getting into everybody's identities only muddles where your focus needs to be as you prepare to connect with an ancestor."

An elderly woman dressed in a well-ironed button-down shirt and creased khakis raised her hand. "Do we have to pinpoint the exact ancestor we want to meet?"

Hank scanned the circle. A few people shifted in their chairs. I hoped he knew the answer to this one. Hank smiled and said at last, "No, you really don't, but I'll explain as we go."

He proceeded to tell us the story of how through his anthropological studies he met shamanism and fell under its spell for all it can do for people on the soul level. "All humans have a need to build a channel to the invisible. We can each find greater alignment moving beyond our three-dimensional world, to other spiritual realities."

I wondered if my mother discovered the doorway into one of these spiritual realities, and if now that she was no longer on this earth, was she in the ultimate one. It was the first time I intuited a twinge of 'things might be okay.' Maybe the time travel prepared her well for death, even in its suddenness.

"How many of you have journeyed before?"

About half the room raised their hands, including myself. A couple of years ago, my mother took me to a giant holistic fair at the community college. We sang with the radio on the whole way over; she was so pleased I was up for trying it out. The journeying entailed lying on the floor, while drums beat over us in a constant rhythm, as we ventured into the Lower World. Afterward, when we debriefed in the group, I was the second to raise my hand to share how I met my first power animal—a raven so black it shined luminescent in green, blue and a blaze of purple. My mother later told me that, in the Bible, the raven was one of the birds Noah sent out after the floods, but it never came back. She also said that in other traditions, ravens are shapeshifters and bring magic to a person's will and intention.

"You surrendered to the process so much more than I did my first time. I worried that you'd either be thinking the Lower World was like hell or that the whole thing was bullshit," she said.

"This practice resonates body and soul for me," I told her, which made her smile wide.

In my hope of connecting with her here and now, I already sensed a pervading healing coming my way as if I had thrown open all the doors to our house, inviting the life back in.

"As you proceed along your journey to your ancestral garden, you'll be led by guides. Most will show up as animals or insects, possibly a tree. Communicate with them, ask them questions—they won't think you rude."

Laughter rose throughout the group as a sense of anticipation grew in me. Hank resumed his instruction.

"Once you all find your way to lie down, I will start to beat the drum. The rhythm will shift you into a state that allows for spiritual contact."

As we collectively made our ways to the floor, entrusting our psyche-souls to Hank, I found my space on the edge of the circle. Once the drumming started, my mind and spirit went right into the journey. Entering first a downward passage to the Lower World, I slid down on my belly and landed on my feet at the side of a stream which shimmered as if it had been made of melted emeralds. Surfacing from below were solid, smooth rocks that allowed for an easy crossing to the other side. With a summer forest unfurling around me, I walked a barely discernible path emerging from the sandy bank of the water.

Out from an oak tree, a bee of bright lemon and shiny black stripes buzzed next to me.

"Can you guide me to the garden?" I asked.

The bee flew a short distance before me, and I followed him up a hill paved with circular stones that glimmered of mother-of-pearl. As soon as I reached the top, elation pulsed through me as the stones led out to a labyrinth, reminiscent of my mother's backyard garden.

The bee's antennae swayed as it delivered me to the entrance of the labyrinth's outer spiral. Small evergreen bushes lined the way but also made it difficult to see what lay in the oncoming path. I wasn't sure if I was walking this alone. As I reached the innermost curl, I found myself in a grassy clearing across from a stalwart, stone bench.

Perched there was a honey-gold owl, the largest I had ever seen. It turned to acknowledge my presence, and stepped back as it bowed its head. I reciprocated. Its large indigo eyes became iridescent as it smiled at me, which pulled me to approach. The owl extended its wing to offer me a place to sit on the bench. I felt the cool, hard stone that was now to be my spiritual seat.

"I have lost my mother. Can you tell me where I can find her?"

"She is inside of you, as am I," he said, his voice humanlike and masculine.

"Who are you?"

Bringing the tips of his wings together where a feather from one and two from the other became interwoven, he spoke, "I have been the oak and you the acorn. But it is you, Lindsay McDonnell, whose trunk grows strong with branches of the utmost reach."

A soft, quiet rain began to sprinkle over us as a blessing, and my owl's feathers became a dark ginger color.

"I do not feel my strength," I whispered, surrendering my truth to him.

"Because you think yourself alone, but as your ancestral grandfather, I have been alongside you, your entire life."

Warmth filled the space between us. His words set me ablaze with longing—an ancestral grandfather of my own.

"I have a profound challenge ahead. Will you stay with me?" I asked.

"Your challenge will lead you to your divine power. From nurturing its source, it is you who can come to us, your kin, at a time when we are in most need."

"But I don't possess this power. It was my mother's—"

"Take your training and I pray you come to us."

"How would I find you?"

"Bonamargy Friary, by the sea," he said slowly.

"Bona Mar-gay Friary?" I repeated.

He bowed again and ascended to an almost suspended flight.

By repeating 'Bonamargy Friary,' I made sure to keep my link to his words. While I ran underneath him, his round eyes closed and his face morphed into that of a serene Buddha. The air warmed, enveloping me as he lengthened his wings and lifted upward.

The sound of the drum slowing in tempo and then speeding up intruded into my awareness. In that moment, my heart wrenched open once my ancestral owl dissolved from view.

The change in drum is a signal to return from the journey. Now it was time to run back through the labyrinth garden and down the stone path. A snake slithered on beside me, as a guide. She was green with a thin white stripe resembling a slice of moon glow. In shamanic journeys, the snake is a symbol for mother connection. Fresh elation rushed through me as she led me back to the emerald stream. She followed me up the original passage until I reached the sunny flat land from which the journey originated. I bent down to thank her, but she melted from sight as the last slow strikes of the drum sounded. Soon, Hank's crackling voice directed us to open our eyes when we were ready.

I wiggled my toes and my fingers before fully emerging from my altered state. I had never experienced such an otherworldly connection on a journey. I was there with my ancestor as if he'd been waiting for me to show up.

Rolling to one side, I gently hoisted my body up to a seated position. My eyes now open, I saw my fellow travelers in various states of messed hair and clothing adjustment. Some were reaching into colorful bags to retrieve journals; others sat and stared, processing where they had been. Soon the room filled with collective scribbling and an occasional scrape of a chair leg against the wooden floor.

I took out a small Moleskine notebook and black pen but could not write fast enough, afraid I would lose the essence of what had transpired. A flash of relief came to me as soon as I wrote 'Bonamargy Friary' above the margin of a clean page. Once I did, I stared at the strange words. Panic started to bite inside my gut. Then more words landed, like a wish granted, *Come to us, your kin*. Having kin was a foreign concept to me. What are kin? Who counts as kin? My mom was my kin and I guess those cousins I never see in Virginia are kin. Whenever friends, clients, people on TV talked about their family life, I often felt like a puzzle piece lying under a dusty couch, never making it back into the box. But now, I was being claimed by the spirit of a grandfather who wanted me. Bigger yet, I understood what he said to mean that my mother was present. That surely had to be the best sign.

After looking over everything I jotted down, I rewrote more clearly where my handwriting was a mess because I needed to preserve this. I needed to be with this experience for a while. It had more to unfold, and I sensed my mother all over it.

Hank rang the bell and asked us all to come back into the circle. The elderly woman in khakis raised her hand and shared she'd spent her journey sewing with a great-grandmother in the nineteenth century.

A tall man in a Boston Celtics sweatshirt asked, "What if you couldn't tell what time period the ancestor was from?"

I said "Yes" aloud, as I was at a loss of knowing from when my owl arrived. Hank said to ask yourself what made that information so important to you and wait for what answer would arise.

Making my way home, I wondered what it meant to be chosen twice from within the past. My ancestral owl—my great-grandfather —has called me to heal a bloodline backward in time. Now, more than a moral emergency, I viewed saving Mark Twain as the first step toward something bigger than Dorje knew and maybe my mother realized.

Pressing the button above my visor, the garage door made its usual rude grind as I pulled the car inside. I hauled my body out and through the door of the dark house. Despite me wearing fresh coats of awe and obligation, the house felt like it would always teem with emotional residue, laden with loneliness. Grabbing for the light switch, I cursed myself for not yet getting things on a timer. This house hadn't needed it before—it didn't feel like that when there were two of us living here, well, three with our kitty, Merlin, and my mom was almost always home at night.

My keys thudded as they hit the counter. Almost without thinking, I put on the kettle to warm the water for tea. I didn't want it boiling. As I leaned against the counter, waiting for the din inside the kettle to raise in volume, I remembered my Tonglen meditation practice, which I'd neglected the last couple of days despite it helping so much with my grief. I began it by breathing in the heavy void and breathing out compassion to all the other sentient beings who were also burdened and by themselves. I thought about all the other creatures in the world who had lost a mother—those who lost months ago, those who lost today and those who would be thrust into grieving tomorrow. I called to mind my ancestors and all the losing of mothers that happened to them.

I wondered if there was anyone else who might be charged with taking up time travel and it took my breath away. I turned the kettle off and sank to the floor, leaning against the cabinet. Staring up at the kitchen appliances, listening to the hum of the mighty fridge, it all struck me as impermanent because it would never be enough to live in only this time.

CHAPTER FOUR

2018, BONAMARGY FRIARY, BALLYCASTLE, NORTHERN IRELAND

After negotiating a roundabout, our bus pulled over to the side of the road where we disembarked at the outer edge of an expansive golf course. Andrew, our seasoned guide, motioned for us to follow him. He shared his experience as an extra in the *Game of Thrones*, as it was filmed in the area.

"I played one of the townspeople in one scene and a priest in another—no lines of course but I had a good ten seconds onscreen when I was the priest." The group clamored around him wanting to hear more.

We all took pause when a golf ball streamed through the air, then smacked the turf a dozen yards from where we stood. It only frustrated me. All I wanted to do was to be in the friary. Moving on, our feet collectively shuffled over the gravel path between the wire fencing of the golf greens and a wall of lichen-stained stones enclosing the burial ground of the friary. The group quieted as we passed under a grove of low-branched trees and through the friary's black iron gate that offered us a squeaky greeting before the latch caught behind us.

Framed in foliage, the path took a left turn into the ruins. Once through a crumbling arch, we were now upon the gravestones, jutting out at all angles. My breath quickened, and my intuitive senses set my neurons buzzing. A soft wind blew the verdant blades of grass, which seemed to stand guard around the archaic stone chapel, roofless but still steady in its faithful form.

I made a strong connection to the peace infusing the space that had once been the inside of the chapel. Open to the elements, it was now three walls around a bed of lush grass, freshly mowed. A few steps in was a cut stone circle marking the grave of Julia McQuillan, known locally as the 'Black Nun.' Andrew recalled the local legend that says to summon her ghost you walk around her grave seven times in each direction and then place your hand through the hole in its inner circle.

I asked why her grave was near the entrance to the chapel.

"She wanted to show her humility, being trodden over by the worshippers."

A couple of the tour goers nodded.

"How can a nun be a ghost?" asked a lanky boy from Sweden.

"Someone murdered her—pushed her down the steps leading up to the friary," Andrew said motioning behind him. "There have been a number of sightings of her over the decades since she died in the 1600s."

"Who pushed her?" asked the boy.

Andrew shrugged. "Maybe a McDonnell," he said laughing. "They're the other famous buried here."

A hot and icy streak went up my back.

"It's a wee bit funny they being so close, because the McQuillans and the McDonnells were often at each other's throats," he said.

"Which McDonnells—where are they buried?" I asked.

"Several of the Earls of Antrim and Sorley Boy, from who they all descended are right there behind that wee green door to their family vault."

"Sorley Boy," I said aloud and hightailed over to the spot Andrew noted. My heart thumped until I stood before the weathered green door. Then it pounded.

"Oh my God," I said, under my breath, stepping into a small puddle before the door, looking for markings. The energy was swirling and heavy. The others followed and assembled around the vault.

"Sorley McDonnell was the youngest son of the Lord of the Isles in Scotland. He was born a bit yonder and was very rooted to Ireland. He even took an Irish princess as his wife."

"Was she Mary O'Neill?" I asked.

"Yes, Mary O'Neill, daughter of Conn O'Neill, King of Ulster. Throughout Sorley's life he took up the cause against the English, who were trying to colonize the land, taking it away from the Irish and the Scots that settled here."

"He wanted independence," I said.

"He absolutely did, for Ireland," Andrew said.

"Did he ever get it?"

Andrew cocked his head. "Yes and no."

"Those darn English, always wanting to rule the world," said a blonde woman wearing a South Carolina T-shirt and a large, oblivious smile.

"You Yanks would know," said a tall man, in a good-natured, clear London accent. Andrew took that to be an opportunity to direct the group to explore the grounds. I remained fixed to the spot.

"Got you thinking about our McDonnell clan?" Andrew said as he stepped up to my left.

"You don't really think the McDonnells killed the nun, do you?"

"No one can say for certain what caused her to tumble down the steps. She was a prophet, so you'd think if she was to be murdered, she'd have known about it. I can tell you she was pretty accurate about a few other deaths."

"Whose?" I asked.

"She predicted a red-headed priest would drown, soon after giving a sermon."

"And it happened?"

"It did."

"She said Ireland would become an independent country and that someday there would be horseless carriages and boats made of iron. She must have had God's eye for the future."

The green door to the vault beckoned me to place my hand there, and so I did.

"Andrew, I think I'll stay here and not finish the tour."

He stepped back looking a bit hurt. "But there are still so many of the filming sites to see. There's Giant's Causeway and—"

"It's okay, being right here is everything."

His eyes searched for something else to convince me. Some of the others stared at me with surprise.

"How will you get back?"

"I'm only a ten-minute walk from where I'm staying up the road."

"Well, I can't say I've ever had anyone leave after the first site."

"It's all good. I came to do some research and this place is key."

He paused and then nodded while looking around.

"Yeah, this place is a wee bit special."

With that, he walked toward the chapel entrance, calling to the group to follow him back to the bus. Once they'd all filed past, he waved to me and took his leave around the corner.

Remaining at the McDonnell vault, I listened. At first, I only perceived the honeyed song of the nearby birds. A moment later, the tour bus started up, its engine surging in a roar as it pulled away. I replaced my hands on the green door, as its hum came to life with the vibration of the place. From my pocket, I retrieved my black obsidian as well as my moss green rhyolite stone my mother gave me last year. As an offering to my ancestors, I placed the rhyolite in a crevice near the vault's latch. "I wish you peace."

I tried to perceive the essence of my mother. Had she ever stood here?

"May you all know freedom from suffering, past and present."

As I said it aloud, my heart expanded, as if my wish for my mother and my ancestors was being poured back into me. Welling up with happy tears for once, gratitude filled me for being recognized from beyond. Letting the tears stream, I let them fall to the ground as a part of me mixed into the soil. After a few moments, a deepened peace rolled in, or maybe it was always there, and I had now been invited in. With that awareness, I treaded back over to Julia McQuillan's resting place. Taking a seat on a cushion of greenery, I studied the speckles of lichen taking up residence on her gravestone.

Someone's gaze was upon me, but they remained unseen. My slow breathing told me it was a good thing. Boldness permeated my attuned consciousness and then the power of the place infused into me, telling me to try the ritual. *Julia has something to say to me.*

As I prepared, my eye caught a shimmer of movement through the hole in the circle of Julia's grave. Inside was a tiny, eight-legged inhabitant, creating its silken snare.

I sighed. On Irish land you don't mess with the spiders. In my American family, you never disturbed the spiders. Today would not be the day to perform the ritual by sending my hand through the hole. But I didn't want to leave. Instead, I shed my fleece and bundled it up to place under my tailbone. Moving into a cross-legged position, I once again closed my eyes and took in the feel of the place.

After several inhalations, I wanted to open my eyes, but with each out breath, I heard a distinct message to trust. A warm breeze met the skin of my face and hands followed by a much cooler burst of wind. Still I kept my eyes closed, reminding myself that this was like swimming in a lake, where passing through cool and then sun-warmed swaths of water was a natural occurrence. You didn't think about what was in the water with you.

In my mind's eye, I visualized performing the ritual, walking around the grave, over and over again. Soon, I saw my hand moving through the circle. The thumping in my chest returned but I could not initiate breath. I tried to move, but instead gravity poured down on me as if the moon was pinning me to the ground. A frost whooshed around me and I comprehended, I was in the neural wormhole.

When I opened my eyes, the force released me, and I sat up. The gravestone was gone. I was on the earthen floor of the chapel, roof intact, roughly hewn benches set up in rows facing the altar. Sunbeams streaming down through the high windows muted as they landed, providing a gentle light across the space. I startled to see a woman peering at me across the rows of benches. As she rose and glided over to me, I knew it had to be Julia herself. Her nun's habit was darker than the blackest ink, as was the cloak she wore. The cross around her neck slung still and dull. Her eyes were soft with compassion and outlined with a glow of another time, yet in the here and now.

"You have answered your beckoning and your intention has been received," she said.

The ridiculousness of the moment made me reach out to touch her. She let me, and I felt her solidity.

"You're not a ghost," I heard myself say.

"No, I've traveled like you."

She led me out the door and several yards away from the chapel. From the outside, it now possessed a luster as an enlivening air folded around it. Within seconds a robed monk emerged to sweep the steps to the entrance. He stopped and regarded me and Julia, bowed his head, and continued his cleaning before returning inside.

My head ached as if my brain wasn't sitting right in my skull.

"When is this?" I asked.

"You've arrived in the year 1560."

"Oh my God!"

Julia dropped eye contact and crossed herself. It was undeniable I had transported. A hilly meadow of high grasses outlined with thickets of trees replaced the golf course. There was no continual din of tires on pavement—there was no road! And behind me, all the gravestones were gone.

As I had not said the mantra, my mind searched for a way to connect my new reality with this accident of fate.

"But I only performed the ritual in my mind to summon your ghost."

"And you came overseas to follow your ancestry," she said.

"Yes."

"And that is who summoned you. Your intentions were joined with that of your kin. The sum of those intents land you here."

My eyes hurt as I stared at her. Finally, I managed an expression of a coherent thought.

"I did come here to see where one of my sixteenth-century great-grandfathers lived, Sorley Boy McDonnell."

She smiled as if to shine her knowing into my confused brain.

"He's waiting to see you, over yonder."

"He's waiting for me?"

"Do you understand, your truest intentions joined with his call to you."

This was a collaborative effort.

I looked to the hill where she pointed. I was sure an abyss of nothingness lay past its height and my body instinctually tried to remain rooted to the earth. Julia undid the clasp of the cloak at her neck and placed it around my shoulders.

"Propriety," she said.

I nodded, making sure the cloak covered my form fitting T-shirt and jeans.

"Would you come with me?" I asked.

"McQuillans never did mix well with the McDonnells."

A trembling rose up from my core, and still I stood, unmoving.

Julia glided her face toward my ear and spoke. "This was your intention."

"I didn't think to be here like this, I'm not prepared," I said.

"Search your heart."

With that, she walked back and around the chapel, leaving me with my fear. And there he appeared, at the top of the hill, empowered in stance.

He was a tall, magnetizing figure. His saffron-colored tunic billowed under a cloak fringed around the neck, draping down his chest. The sleeves opened at the elbows and from there hung to the knees of his bare, well-muscled legs. I stopped when I spotted the scabbard at his hip. I never saw anyone wearing a knife in real life. Quite sure my heart was exposing my vulnerability, beating so strongly as if it might escape from my chest, I thought about running away. But my legs walked toward him.

Sorley McDonnell extended his hands, beckoning me, as he studied me up and down. He appeared more mesmerized than aggressive. His hair was thick and flaxen with bands of white at his temples and his eyes were a dark, deep blue. A mix of recognition and jubilant disbelief shadowed across his face. Was this who I visited in the shamanic garden?

He greeted me in thick Gaelic, which I mimicked, no doubt, in an American accent. Taking my hands, he welcomed me, dubbing me his 'Anam Cara,' his soul friend.

CHAPTER FIVE

Sorley walked with me to a looming stone structure, on its own promontory perched above the sea. Crossing the drawbridge, our footfalls echoed down toward the water flowing below. A young man, working the gears within the gatehouse, bowed his head as we passed into the courtyard, specked with men feeding horses and a trio of women singing as they transported baskets of dirt-ridden carrots stacked above the rim. Rushing toward us was who I hoped was Mary O'Neill. The evergreen hue of her dress set off the mass of auburn hair pulled up into a bun. Her wide eyes relayed a dumbstruck welcome. As she came closer, her mouth formed a perpetual o-shape as she alternated taking me in and looking to her husband. Sorley was all grins which seemed to prompt Mary to embrace me, praising the Divine in Gaelic. Her shoulders were strong and her frame graceful yet sturdy. She kept an arm around me, walking us toward the castle keep.

I tried to fathom this being with Mary O' Neill and Sorley Boy McDonnell, my fifteenth grade, great-grandparents as we stepped inside and down a torch-lit passageway. Mary maintained her arm around me, clasping my opposite hand in hers. Between her long, layered skirts and Sorley's bare legs I was confused about the century I'd landed in. It seemed a mishmash, or maybe it was that Hollywood had yet to touch this time in Irish history.

We soon entered a long room with a few high windows. The purr of the turf and wood fire offered a soothing warmth through Julia's cloak. Substantial russet and clay-colored rocks framed with smaller stones comprised the walls that climbed up to the wood-beamed ceiling. Stretching above the hearth hung something familiar from my mother's notes: the McDonnell crest. Carved and painted in four panels was a roaring lion, a jumping fish, a formidable ship, and an arm with muscles tensed, the hand holding a cross. Empowerment, nourishment, expansiveness, and faith was what it meant to me, but what it really stood for was sovereignty over land and sea, as God's will.

Mary pulled out a chair for me. I paused, confronted by the large band of leather slung across its frame. Both she and Sorley took seats across the planked table of heavy wood.

"Coner ta tu?" she said, and to my joy, I thought I understood her to be asking me how I was.

"Taim go maih," I said, telling them I was well. Mary's eyes crinkled as she threw a glance over to her husband. She poured me a milky drink I'd describe as watered-down sour cream gone a bit funky. As soon as it hit my tongue, I swallowed it down, if only to get it to vacate my mouth. She gazed at me with kind but amused eyes. Speaking in Gaelic that I did not understand at all, she pointed to my cup and left the room.

Sorley pushed the wooden cup farther away as if to protect me from the offending beverage but then pulled the handle toward himself and took a sizable gulp. He placed it down on the table with a thud, landing wood on wood.

Reading me, he leaned forward onto the table and extended his large hand. I recognized the invitation and placed my palm on his. He completed the connection resting his other hand on top.

His touch was gentle. He spoke to me, and I recognized his again calling me Anam Cara. I repeated the phrase back to him, letting him know I understood.

It was then that I managed to ask him if he spoke English. He frowned and spoke in an accent as thick as bog mud. "Aye, and I'd rather not." It took me a moment to decipher the syllables. He sat back as he withdrew his hands, while eyeing me with concern.

"Chan eil mòran bruidhinn—agam," I uttered with poor pronunciation, which revealed the little Gaelic, albeit modern, that was at my disposal. I wished I'd learned more from my grandfather, my mother's dad, when I had the chance.

He seemed to understand me well enough and asked me in English, "From where do ye belong?"

I hadn't realized he was actually asking my name; instead I heard the words through my twenty-first-century filter. He laughed when I shrugged, but then demonstrated what he was asking by uttering his own name in his preferred language. "Somhairle Bhuide MacDomhnaill." Once leaving his mouth, his name resounded about the castle walls, despite him speaking in an even-pitched volume. I tried to say his name in the same way but from my mouth it sounded inadequate. I tried my own name.

"Lindsay McDonnell. I mean MacDomhnaill."

He nodded with pursed lips.

Leaning forward, he looked me right in the eye. While concentrating all my ability to comprehend him, his message was clear.

"It does me sadness that you, my kin, speak like that of the Tudor English. This does not bode well for our cause."

"But I am not from this Ireland. I am from the New World, westward across the sea."

"And that is where England aimed her eyes in conquest?"

I needed him to repeat the question.

"She did, but we have been independent from England for centuries."

A gleam sparked in his eyes. He raised his mug and exclaimed, "Praise Independence! And how many years?"

I spoke slowly. "Since 1776 and I am from 2018."

Joy flooded his face as he jumped to his feet. Slapping one hand on his thigh, he offered me the other to dance as he sung a Celtic tune. I tried to follow his stomping and hopping until he twirled me about the room. I had never thought to dance in gratitude for our American freedom.

"Your new world, it be a blessed land?" he asked, stopping.

"Yes!" I said, widening my arms to describe how blessed.

"It is said St. Brendan sailed west from Ireland to find paradise, the Garden of Eden. Could it be the same land?"

"Oh… maybe… perhaps."

Sorley frowned but soon recovered his enthusiasm.

"What other news do ye bring to my home?"

The question flooded the inside of my brain. It went to gather all kinds of things to tell him and then I realized, some of what was coming up for me was really bad. And there was the really good but my ability to discern the two faltered. Maybe having cell phones wasn't such a tremendous thing. And the bigger overarching thought arising like a leviathan out of a deep cold ocean was, maybe, I should inform him of none of it. I tried to remember the specific precepts Dorje told me.

I pulled my bag over to my side. As I unzipped the front pouch, the sound made Sorley sit up, fascination playing across his face. I yanked the toggle back and forth a few times and told him what it's called. He repeated the word, 'zipper,' which only made me chuckle.

From the front compartment, I drew out a Hershey Kiss and placed the tiny silver package in front of him.

"That's for you to eat."

"Eat?" he asked, picking up the kiss by the white-and-blue printed banner that sprouted at the pinnacle.

"You unwrap it," I said, leaning over to show him. He examined it closer as I revealed the deep brown chocolate under the silver. At first, he took the foil in his fingertips and studied it, marveling at its pliability. Then he looked at the white banner, running his finger across the wording.

"More English?"

"It says Kisses—this is called a chocolate kiss," I said as I motioned for him to place it on his tongue, causing his forehead to wrinkle up and his lips to disappear under his mustache.

"What is this choc-o-late?"

"One of the most blessed substances I have ever known," I said.

He sniffed the bottom of the kiss and placed it against his lips. Once it was on his tongue, his head jerked, as if the morsel came alive in his mouth.

"It will melt like butter or you can bite down."

Sorley swirled it around from cheek to cheek and within seconds his eyes were wide and shiny.

"Is this God's nectar?"

I laughed down to my belly at his discovery.

"That's exactly what it is."

"Is it the angels or faeries who deliver you such a substance?" he said teasing.

"It is a gift from the New World."

"Shall we share this with my Mary?"

I plunged my hand into the pouch of my bag, but it was my last one. I felt bad as I shook my head. Mary came through the doorway, mugs in hand. Sorley went to her and planted quite a kiss on Mary's lips, surprising both of us.

"Taste that? It's a kiss of chocolate," Sorley said in English.

Mary drew back, astonished at what she'd heard and tasted. She licked her lips.

"Pray God, have ye become bewitched?"

"Chocolate is one of the best things I can share from my time," I said.

Mary reddened. I thought you'd put a love spell on him for me."

"Aw, I've kissed ya like that before," he said.

"But not with such sweetness on yer lips, husband."

Sorley slapped one hand against the other, and did a little dance around his wife, giving her another kiss on the cheek.

Chocolate puts me in a good mood. I wondered if this was like crack to the uninitiated.

"You honor us well with such a gift," Mary said. I wanted to ask them if I was the only one to ever bring them something of a future time. They made me feel like I was the most glorious and bliss-bringing being that had ever incarnated in their presence. I decided to spring my inquiry in the morning, ready to lose my specialness to hear them tell me about meeting my mother.

CHAPTER SIX

I have an understanding now that traveling through time is not a twenty-first-century discovery. It used to happen in a manner of ways, like being carried back and forth in the arms of angels, when human perception aligned with the deep powers of nature and the channels to the Divine were clear and unimpeded. The society that shapes us now, the one we all unconsciously agree to, decided the role of all that is magical falls firmly away from what is godly or what is of science—and with that agreement, the veil between the realms descended and thickened. The mind is trained to not sense the full continuum of what is. But centuries before I was born there were forces my Celtic ancestors accessed. That is how one battle, four hundred and fifty years ago, set my future tumbling backward, into this moment.

During my first night in the north of Ireland, Sorley shared the sickening details with me by the fire. I was traumatized imagining the man before me partaking in such brutality and surviving it, not only physically, but on a soul level. The battle happened the year prior, in 1559. The opposition came in, riding with fury, sinking into the bog, thigh high in mud and screaming in desperation. Sorley's men waited until most of the McQuillans, a rival clan, ran into the trap before bounding into action and finishing them off.

Swords clanged, but the McQuillans made contact only out of clumsy defense. Some tried to free themselves of the mud that was swallowing them up, only to be struck down, heavy blades cracking down onto skulls and scapulas, red sputtering down a flurry of necks and backs. After a time, their battle cries died off as Sorley Boy McDonnell was victorious, winning back the coastal swath of ancestral land where his clan was bulwarking themselves against being ousted by English colonization and English rules.

Sorley Boy raised an exultant voice above the growing clamor of his troops. "Heaven smiles upon us this day, delivering unto us a victory for Clan McDonnell—and for Eire!" Cheers thundered upward into the air.

Sorley surveyed his people with well-set eyes that mirrored the color of the sea. His beard in shades of blond, striped with white-gray, set off a strong nose and complexion which hinted of rosy hues. All that was placed above broad shoulders on a six-foot frame made for weathering. After riding through the late afternoon, Sorley returned to Dunanynie, his castle perched hundreds of feet atop the North Channel. He dismounted from his steed, leading the animal over the drawbridge which crossed the wind-whipped moat, to relieve his wife, Mary O'Neill, of her burden of worry.

Finding her kneeling in prayer encircled by her herb garden, Sorley crouched down next to her and reached over to stroke her hair. Mary startled and fell into him, her eyes wet with gratitude. Sorley wrapped his arms around her shoulders with little a word exchanged between them. Her eyes turned upward to the God who'd brought her husband home.

"We McDonnells have won possession of the Route—and it is one more day we evade the grasp of the English and those clans who would side with them," he said, releasing her. With her auburn hair coming loose, Sorley could still see her as a young lass, her eyes gleaming with pride. A pride that bloomed over their many years together.

"Perhaps we Irish have earned Heaven's favor with this victory as my brother Shane has also seized his rightful title of The O'Neill once again," Mary said.

Sorley sat back on his heels.

"This is not good news to you, husband?"

"I fear this will set the English much more savagely upon him as he is making bold disregard of the agreement between King Henry and your father."

"Och, you accept that the title of The O'Neill shall remain lost to us?" Mary asked.

"Mary, Shane also now incites the wrath of his Irish brethren when he killed off your relations in line for the O'Neill title."

"Shane's cause is for Ireland," Mary said jutting her hands into the air.

"I pray it be true, and that he has a plan," Sorley said. "Preventing the new English queen from seizing what is ours will require discipline in our diplomacy. I am not sure Shane will agree."

"Perhaps he has already won the battle of wills with the English."

"Or the queen will be so enraged she orders the full might of her army to destroy us," Sorley said shaking his head. He reached out and took both his wife's hands and they rose, she helping him, more than the intended other way around.

"You need a meal, a rest, and a wash," she said, shifting the subject.

"And a visit with my secretary. There is much for him to write."

"But now, you shall eat," Mary said, looking her husband straight in the eye.

By the next morning, Sorley was sitting by the fire with his secretary, a young man named Finlay McNaughton, educated in Edinburgh and sent over by Sorley's older brother, James, who was the family's patriarch in the Scottish Isles. Finlay read aloud the letter Sorley had just dictated to the new Queen of England, Elizabeth Tudor.

"She shall understand our intentions to defend the Route," Sorley said.

"The English should already realize your influence," Finlay said. He moved over to do the customary pausing for Sorley to touch the quill he would use to sign his master's name, as Sorley was not a man of the written word.

"I fear like Henry Eight, another of his lion cubs will be bent to make Ireland an English colony," Sorley said.

Finlay stopped and nodded. "She is indeed one of his lion cubs."

"We will now see what the queen writes and what the queen does," Sorley said.

At that, he dismissed Finlay and added a slim, long stick of wood to the peat fire. Once alone, Sorley shifted the branches and bricks of burning turf creating a wave of sparks. He stood back from his work, watching the flames sprout from their source. Satisfied, he half-paced, half-wandered about the room, thoughts awash with expectancy and strategy. Looking down at his hands, bruised from the battle of the day before, he dropped down into a chair by the now crackling blaze at the hearth. He put his booted feet toward the fire, playing with what little distance it was between finding warmth and risking a burn.

Will God stay on our side or will he favor the English taking it all away? he contemplated. Finding no clarity, Sorley scraped the chair back along the floor and stood up. He wrapped his fur cloak around his shoulders and made his way out of the castle.

While Sorley walked, he inhaled the cool and cleansing sea air. Holding his breath in his lungs, he allowed it to warm and exhaled as its nourishment was spent. More attuned, he sensed the sun's rays upon his exposed skin as he moved to his knees, next to a deliberate formation of rocks. From the pouch on his hip, he brought out a small bronze cross followed by a reflective black stone and, with reverence, laid them down on the grassy earth.

At a hypnotic pace, he brought one hand through a flowing genuflection and commenced his hands into a prayer position, fingertips resting on his lips. He lowered his eyes and then shut them.

He acknowledged the manifestation of the Sacred around him, sharing his gratitude for the sun, the landscape, the water bodies, and the spirits embodied within them. He thanked God for his recent victory.

"Shall I never be too proud to ask for your mercy. May you hear my prayer for my kin to survive and our descendants to flourish from what transpires here in Ireland in my lifetime."

A small whisper of a wind blew across his face as the sun's balm relayed a blessing from the Divine. Sorley opened his eyes, as if instructed, and he looked down upon the reflective stone. In it, he saw a fluttering of dark wings and then an indelible image of a woman's face. He welcomed the accompanying mist of peace and breathed it in.

"Come sit," he said to Mary as she entered the circle.

As she joined him down on the earth, he handed her the reflective black stone.

"And, did the Holy Spirits provide you any instrument of wisdom?"

Sorley ran his fingers down his beard.

"I believe their instrument is on its way."

QUEEN ELIZABETH I, 1559, LONDON

At the same moment, that very enemy to my ancestors, the freshly crowned Queen Elizabeth, sat at the head of her privy council's table with one of her most faithful men, Dr. John Dee. For his thirty-two years on the earth, he was now a leading academic who studied the continuum of science, mathematics, and magic, any of which might have cost him his head in the prior reign of Queen Mary I.

William Cecil, the queen's Secretary of State, appeared at the threshold to the chamber and waited for her to wave him in.

"Well, Cecil, tell me the thick of it."

"Your Majesty, the McDonnells have ousted the McQuillans, taking over the entirety of the Route."

"God's teeth! And so the council miscalculated the advantage that would now be England's had we sent our own soldiers."

"The McDonnells have more men willing to fight for them from Scotland than we knew," Cecil said in a grim voice.

The queen huffed, as she pushed her palms down on the table as if to steady herself for another challenge.

"They can come from Scotland and settle the Irish land, but I, their rightful queen, have to fight for every inch? I shall continue with Dr. Dee and confer with you and the council on this later."

Cecil gave a quick bow while throwing a glance at Dee as he took his leave.

Alone again, the queen leaned toward Dee. "You see how the power of these clans in Ulster grows unchecked. And still worse, it is from within my kingdom."

Dee collected his words. "Then it is with greater urgency I ask Your Majesty to consider this gift that shall serve your kingdom and the whole of England."

"Do you come again with promises of magic to help me keep my crown?"

"All I possess is in your service, like my father to your father, the king."

Elizabeth sat back waiting for Dee to speak. He explained receiving a second visitation from the wise-woman Sara.

"Pray acquit me of this ridiculous fable of likely illusion. I did not enjoy it the first time," Elizabeth said, slapping the table with the flat of her hand.

"Your Majesty, I acknowledge this remains beyond all imagination."

The queen stared at Dee for several seconds. Rising from her chair, she clasped her hands tightly in front of her bodice. "I never had a reason to doubt your word, but this seems like dark sorcery."

"If it be sorcery, then it is at your disposal, Your Grace."

She balled her hand into a fist and ran her knuckles against her lips as she deliberated. "Tell me of this visitation."

"I learned the secret of Sara's fortune telling as she took me forward, through more than five centuries from this present day."

Elizabeth's eyes widened as her hands covered her head, as if to protect herself. "You, sir, are requiring much trust. Never in the life of any prince has there been the expectation to entertain such impossibility!"

Dee lowered his eyes, using the silence to reframe his explanation. Once ready, he looked directly into the queen's eyes. His steadiness unnerved her.

"To what did you bear witness?" she asked in a subdued voice.

"Near to me as I arrived, I saw a carriage that shone as if painted in crushed jewels. Its wheels were thick and made out of a black, grooved substance. I did not spy any horses or oxen or a way the animals would be harnessed to carry the craft forward."

"What did the woman—the sorceress then show you?"

"Sara walked me past a labyrinth garden guarded by what I thought was a trained owl, but instead it was a true likeness perched upon a stake. She took me inside her dwelling. There on a table was a closed cylindrical vessel, very colorful and reflective of the sun. It bore the words, Pepsi Cola."

"That is not a language I recognize."

"Nor did I, Your Majesty, but apparently it is the language of this future people."

"What else?" the queen quickly asked.

Dee placed his hand on his heart and gave a slight bow of his head.

"A flag depicting a man's head wearing a star with the words, New England Patriots, painted on the bottom."

The queen's mouth opened. For several seconds, she appeared as if she had been frozen.

"A new, England? Did she tell you that the realm grows?"

"Madame, it was quite clear—Sara not only knew of my navigational studies but foretold they would be the key to England's success across the globe."

"Yet England does not possess money enough to send any one of our scant ships into waters that may swallow them whole. Such a venture leaves us vulnerable to those who would push onto our shores."

Dee contemplated how best to deliver his proposal. He then reached into his satchel and pulled out the object that had become most sacred to him. He placed it in front of Elizabeth. She stared at the glittering Pepsi Cola can, and after several seconds, laid a fingertip upon it. Shooting a wide-eyed look at Dee, Elizabeth took it up in both her hands. She ran her fingers over its smooth sides.

"Is this a talisman?" she asked under her breath.

"It is evidence of a future time," Dee said. "Sara said it is a common vessel, but I saw it contained an elixir that bubbled and sparkled, as she poured me some to take to my lips."

"It could have been poison, my dear Dee."

"My Queen, I found it to be restorative. All that I experienced there was thus, and to that end I declare utmost faith in the wise-woman Sara when she tells me her intent is to counter the prophecies of Nostradamus, foretelling your short reign."

The queen shuddered.

"She has said as much?"

"Sara told me it was her aim to see you, Elizabeth Tudor, prosper among men—unhindered. She said you command the fortitude, compassion, and intelligence to serve the world through your reign, so much so that it would touch her future time."

Elizabeth brought both her hands to her chest, one clutching at the jewels hanging from her neck. Hope entered the pictures in her head but it was replaced just as quickly with her deep-held anxiety. Could she ever outrun her vulnerability as a lone queen whose kingdom was less than two islands?

Elizabeth took hold of the Pepsi can again and spoke in a low voice.

"The black ravens at the Tower ensure the continuity of the monarchy. Yet I spy them soaring high here with the sun as their company, only to drop themselves near to the ground, as if portraying a fall from grace—and I think they are a dark omen of what Nostradamus has prophesized."

"Ravens portend the gift of magic, Your Grace."

"And death, do they not?"

"Do the ravens remain at the Tower, whilst you receive winged visitation here at Whitehall?"

Elizabeth nodded.

"Perhaps your reign is twice protected," Dee said.

Elizabeth returned her gaze to the Pepsi can still in her hands.

"What would Sara give us in her century that shall save us?"

"Knowledge."

"Of our enemies?"

"Of what will strengthen your soul and get you closer to God. Of what will heal you of your fears."

The queen sat back in her chair. "How is she privy to my fears?"

"Your Grace, Sara can only be a direct messenger from God, who is all-knowing, and she is His angel sent to you for protection."

Elizabeth tilted her head, her face breaking from the tension it wore, pleased at the idea of Heaven smiling on her.

"Madame, I also believe it would anger God to not partake in this divine gift that he bestows upon you, the mother of England."

"Then pray tell me what plans you have conceived."

"Your Grace, the sojourn forward in time would have to occur in the strictest of secrecy. Dee swallowed hard and pushed himself on. "It would have to be taken by you and—"

"Good God! All my family has died before me. As I am the last, I will not hasten my end with an untested force. Perhaps Sara fools us as she is sent from the Devil."

"Yet has any woman been so verily blessed to become sovereign as Your Grace? That is surely God's work."

"Dr. Dee, I cannot disappear, the realm needs their monarch."

"Your Majesty, that remains as no concern. When I took my journey, no discernible time had passed here, and I estimate I'd been away half a day."

The queen raised her eyebrows to this bit of news. She motioned for Dee to come closer. Once he was near enough, she patted his chest and shoulders, then inspected his hands.

"You deem yourself intact, despite traveling what must be a treacherous road to future days," she said.

Dee explained that Sara had held his hands in hers as he followed her instructions to close his eyes and fill his lungs with breath. A flash of deep cold surrounded him, no longer than it took to perceive, and then he was delivered to the year 2016.

"My heart did beat wildly, and I lost my breath, but would not anyone in my position?" he said.

Elizabeth sat down on the edge of the closest chair.

"I require time to take my own counsel, and that of God's before I decide," she said with a catch in her voice.

Dee nodded and bowed. "Your Majesty, while you ponder, perhaps the interim is best served by my hand calculating the most opportune time to endeavor such a journey by consulting the stars."

The queen's breath quickened. "And if there is none?" she asked. "Perhaps Sara is a siren, calling us to the rocks."

Dee stepped back a half step. "God's eyes are upon this, and the stars will confirm His bidding."

The queen clasped one hand in the other, tight enough that the skin over her knuckles remained white, which showed in contrast once she placed both hands on her flushed face. "I suspect this is a test laid at my feet by the Almighty."

CHAPTER SEVEN

The story Sorley told me of battling the McQuillans caused my stomach to tighten. The closest I had ever been to war was still a state away when the planes hit the towers on 9/11. I told Sorley the thought of being assaulted on land where I lived my twenty-first-century life was almost beyond my comprehension. Sorley assured me of the security around the castle, but his words were overcome by a cacophony of masculine yells from outside which had him over and investigating out the window. A servant came to the door and announced the arrival of Mary's brother, Shane O'Neill.

Sorley shot a look at his wife. She curtsied, almost sarcastically.

"Not a bother husband, he wrote me to say he'd be making a sojourn to see his kin."

Sorley scowled.

"What kept him from sending word to me?"

"He did—I read you his letter. Did you forget?" she said.

"It wouldn't leave my mind if I knew Shane the Scoundrel was coming to see us. This isn't a visit of good tidings, Mary, I can tell you that."

Mary bit her lip, probably to hold her tongue. Sorley looked at me with apprehension and then to his wife.

"Granddaughter, stay here, I do not want you seen."

With that he lumbered out of the room. Mary pulled me back so we could observe from the corner of the window. I remained behind her, desperate to not reveal myself, or anger this man—my many times over, great-grandfather.

I saw Sorley step outside the entrance taking his stead in full height and breadth. He greeted "Shane the Scoundrel" from a place of power. Shane opened his hand wide before offering it to Sorley. He was also a man of height and confidence, with a broad face set upon an equally thick neck. He wore a woolen cloak of the darkest earthen brown echoing the color of his large, round eyes. They spoke in Gaelic and Mary relayed to me what was being said.

"From where have ye traveled?" Sorley said.

"The south," Shane said.

My mouth went dry watching the exchange as both men placed their hands on their swords. Sorley must have put a sword around his waist as he made his way outside.

"We have much on which to decide," Shane said.

Sorley regarded him. "I suspect we always will."

The two men walked out of view and into the castle. We heard the heavy door shut and a brief flurry of sound that faded as they moved to a more distant chamber. Mary patted my arm and told me to stay put. I searched her face for any worry and wondered if she was just a good actress. Before she left, I asked her how she'd learned English. She explained her father, trying to maintain some sense of a title and lands as King of Ulster, was more than willing to comply with King Henry VIII's decree that English be spoken in his Kingdom of Ireland. Mary said, from then on, her father would only speak English to her. It was his way of keeping her protected. For that I was grateful, as she was easier to understand than Sorley.

Now alone, I automatically reached for my phone. As I laid fingers on it in my jeans pocket, I realized what I was doing but decided to pull it out anyway. There were no circles lit up at the top, but the phone was still on. Somewhere in my brain, I thought, if I really went back this far in time, this instrument could not exist. But I realized by that logic, my jeans would not exist, and I would not exist. I put the phone back into my pocket.

I caught sight of a portrait of a man above the hearth. Studying his strong features, I surmised his cheekbones and chin were like those of Sorley, so this must be a relation.

Moving to the farthest window, I watched the ocean hurling itself at the rocks far below. Down in the harbor there was no parking lot, no commercial ferry ships, and not one bright colored rain slicker worn by any of the people at the water's edge. Maybe I missed those unnatural colors, leaving my heart to come to terms with my unfolding reality. The words of the Buddha came to mind, *with our thoughts we shape the world.* My thoughts were certainly shaping my world. What had I manifested?

I took a few minutes to calm myself, sitting down in Sorley's chair. I tuned into the feel of solidity, as it has been carved from an ancient tree trunk. Through the rubber tread of my hiking boots, the firm pressure of the earth moved up through my legs. To enhance the connection, I shed my boots and socks, placing skin to stone, and letting the coolness refresh my soles. My mindful awareness only quickened my pulse, more from excitement than fear.

Like a high wave splashing down, Mary rolled back into the room, squinting at me. "We need to get you up to a bedchamber. I don't want my brother seeing you," she said as she ushered me from the chair.

I followed her out and up a set of well-worn stone steps. We arrived at a room with a thick wooden door which she threw her weight against to push open. I hurried in first, at her gesture. She struggled to close the door behind us and turned to face me. I felt like I was in trouble as my father's mother used to do the same thing when she was unhappy with me.

The room had but one window, but several candles had been lit and set around the existing furniture, including a table of oaken planks that had a half-sewn shirt lying on top. The fireplace was aglow with warming flames. Its color matched the ocher tones in the woven rug underneath our feet.

"Is there a dress I can wear?" I asked.

She went to the window and peeked out.

"Aye, we will soon remedy that," she said.

"Then I can move about?" I asked.

"On that I am not certain. Your grandfather and Shane might end each other."

A cold shudder ran along my spine.

"Why do you say that?"

"Their men have come to blows, defending the edges of their lands," she said in a pointed whisper.

"They have battled?" I asked, my stomach tightening.

Joining her at the window, I did not see anyone.

"Where is Grandfather, is he—are we in danger? And doesn't it matter you are a sister to one and a wife to the other?"

Mary stared upward and crossed herself. Did she hear me?

"The men talk in another part of the castle. Methinks my brother comes with a demand to unite against the English."

"Are the English invading?"

"They try to colonize Ireland for their own gain. Your grandfather won't have it. The English run like fire and ice, they promise peace on one hill but then strike on another."

"Does Shane think they will strike here?" I asked.

"I pray not, but Shane must suspect something is afoot."

Shit, Shit, Shit. I wanted to leave, back to 2018.

She read the fear on my face and embraced me full on. It only took a few seconds for me to melt into her body; these past several weeks were the longest stretch I had ever gone without a hug from a maternal figure. When we parted, her eyes shone with tears.

"I didn't think God's Spirit would send us a lass," she said.

"But has he ever sent you a lass before, maybe someone older, a sage woman?" I asked, hopeful to find some trail to my mother.

Mary shook her head and frowned at the floor.

"We should never squander our miracles. Did God only send but one of his children for all of us?"

Her words fell heavy, like boulders tumbling down a cliff and across the road I was traveling. After a few moments of silent angst, I rallied myself.

"Perhaps I should meet my uncle then."

"It will be up to the wisdom of your grandfather."

"Well, I'd like to look Shane in the eye and see what's up for myself," I said.

Her eyes clouded over.

"I mean, I should like to look him in the eye to see what is in his heart."

"There has been trouble in the past, but I do not believe there is malice against us now."

"But you just said—"

"We share a common foe."

A knock came at the door. Mary rushed over and opened it slightly to see who was there. Some conversation passed in Gaelic between her and another woman and the door closed again.

"No matter, you will need a proper gown. She contemplated my appearance, running her fingers across my jeans around the calf.

"Soft," she said.

"Yeah, I guess they are."

Another knock came, and Mary took pieces of a gown from a servant's arms and then dismissed her. She closed the door with her foot before bringing the ensemble over. A grass green weave dominated the top and indigo lacing kept the sleeves and bodice together. The colors were similar to the ones my great-grandmother wore herself, as was the skirting. Placing them against my body, Mary tilted her head and glanced down.

"This may not fall to your feet as you stand taller than most men."

"Well, we can try," I said, not wanting to miss my chance to sit at the family table.

She guided me to undress. I hesitated—wanting to ask for privacy. But she wasn't going anywhere.

I pulled my shirt over my head and peeled off my jeans, careful to keep my phone pushed down deep into a back pocket. While I stood in my underwear, Mary came closer to inspect my bra. She pulled on the straps and tested the clasps.

"What is this called?"

"It's a bra."

She nodded. "You won't need it here."

I swallowed and put my hands on the straps.

"Let me try keeping the bra, and I'm definitely keeping my panties," I said.

"Panties—such a small garment," she noted.

"They do the job," I said.

Her eyebrows came together for a second, until she got my meaning. She gestured for me to put my hands above my head as she placed a wheat-colored shift over my body. The linen flowed against my hands as it dropped over my body.

"There's no fleas," she said.

"I would think not," I said, thinking her comment was strange.

Mary stooped and attempted to pull the shift to the floor, but it was several inches above my ankles.

"No matter," she said.

She had me step into a skirt, which required her spinning me around to cinch the waist. Next, she wrapped a V-necked bodice, stiff with contrasting braiding, around my torso. Each sleeve involved the pulling of laces, to get all the fabric into place. Mary spoke under her breath while she yanked and smoothed. Still, the tugging and enclosing brought back memories of being bundled up before going out to make snowmen and snow forts.

"You're a wee bit of a giant, my dear," she said, urging me to try moving my arms about. The lacing between the sleeves and bodice had to be loosened to accommodate the length of my limbs. Mary rushed to the door and called for the servant. Giving her an instruction, the maid left and returned with a band of fabric. Within seconds, both she and Mary were down on their knees, sewing a bottom tier onto my skirt. To help them, I remained still, like a stone.

After a time, Mary got to her feet and circled around me, inspecting the fit. I contemplated my transformation. This was so much better than what I had done back in Mother's study.

"This getting dressed is a lot of work," I said to express my appreciation.

"Is it then?" she said without taking her eye off my neckline. She again dismissed the maid, who I learned was named Siobhan.

"I think you're safe, wearing your bra—I do not see it," she said in a low voice.

As I looked down my own front, I could see it, but there was no way in hell I was going to offer that information.

Mary then eyed my hair, pulled back into a clear plastic clip. She pointed to it, and as I took it out, she clasped my wrist to inspect the spring mechanism. I handed it to her.

"Clever," she said, sliding it into her pocket.

Next, she sat me down next to a table and proceeded to handle my tresses with deft skill. I closed my eyes. Other than running her fingers through a few tangles, her hands in my hair lulled me into another blissful reminiscence. I had no idea what she was using to make my hair stay up. My brain didn't care. If I did remain, maybe she'd be the one to arrange my hair each day. On that alone, I would have stayed forever.

Mary's face appeared in front of mine. She wet her thumbs and proceeded to rub underneath my eyes. "These smudges have given me bother, nearly since you arrived."

Crap, I hated to lose my eyeliner.

"That's from my century," I offered with cheer. She frowned.

"Looks like dirt."

Placing her hands on my shoulders, she used them to push herself to a full stand. She walked over to another table and opened a carved, wooden box. After arranging a few things, she took hold of a smaller box, and in opening its lid, she lit up. She was quick to place the treasure of a necklace hung with three small gems across my décolletage. I dared not touch it while she tied the chain with a ribbon at the back of my neck. Coming around, Mary took one of my hands and lifted it, urging me to stand. She appraised her work before pulling me to the other side of the room where there was a mirror of sorts.

"This is what you look like this day," she said beaming.

Her joy helped me appreciate my reflection as I gazed into the glass.

"Wow, wow... wow," I said. "I mean it's really good," I translated.

Mary stopped smiling. Instead, she set her jaw.

"Lass, best to speak little."

Now afraid to open my mouth, I nodded.

"Particularly when you are in the presence of my brother or anyone other than your grandfather."

"Do we need a story? Whose daughter am I? I mean, what shall we tell Shane and his men?"

"How many years have you been walking the earth, 15... 16?"

"I am 26."

Mary took a step back, hand over her mouth.

"I'm too young to have a granddaughter so old, so let's say you are as you appear. And Shane remains unacquainted with any of Alastair's children as they have been in Scotland. He's one of our eldest. You are to be Alastair's daughter."

I smiled. "I think, I am descended from him."

Hands on hips, Mary winked at me.

I jumped at the sharp knock on the door. Mary swooped across the room and opened it a sliver. I heard Sorley's voice. Mary stood aside and let his gaze fall on me. I got a kick out of watching his eyebrows shoot up his forehead. To enhance the impact, I curtsied as I held my long skirts.

"Mary, our lass is a butterfly," Sorley said, clapping one hand against the other in delight.

She laughed. "Husband, I thought the very same."

I think they were proud of me.

"Yet, is she ready to be exposed to Shane's sensibilities?" Mary said, again placing her hands back on her hips.

"Shane is asking for our clans to unify."

"Against the English crown?" I asked.

Both my great-grandparents turned their faces toward me.

"Aye, as a way of showing force, but the McDonnells will maintain neutrality. As we speak, English soldiers unite with our brethren in Scotland to battle against the French," Sorley said.

My heart wanted to ease the strain on both my ancestors' faces.

"How can I help?"

"We shall all pray on it," Sorley said.

Mary lowered her eyes and crossed herself. Both she and Sorley placed their hands together in prayer.

"Oh, okay, we're doing this now?" I said, having left all Christian rituals behind in sixth grade after my mother took me away from my life in Catholic school to bring me toward Buddhism.

I made the split-second decision to sit and meditate, one hand underneath the other in my lap with thumb tips touching. After several minutes of silence, Mary said, "Dear girl, you need to put your hands together in proper prayer."

"This is how I pray," I said.

"You need to pray the way Jesus did."

"This is another way."

Mary guided my hands into Christian form, but I naturally moved them to my heart center. She pulled them up to rest at my chin. My face flushed with heat brought on by a bolt of anger—the urge to place my hands into mudra flashed across my mind. I turned toward Sorley for reprieve.

"You will need to pray as the church teaches," he said.

"Lindsay, your ways will be looked on with critical eyes," Mary said.

I inhaled into my belly.

"The church no longer has a coming together of hands?" Sorley asked.

"It does, but… there are other ways to be with oneself and the Divine," I said.

Sorley laughed.

"We understand that, dear Lindsay. Church is church and then there are all the other guides beyond the veil, the ones that are part of the *land, this land*. They all meld together, in our hearts."

"Do you believe in more than one God?" I asked.

"I believe in one almighty God, and I know there are other sacred forces the church won't name."

"It's how he summoned you to attend to us," Mary said.

"Wow," I said.

Mary turned to her husband. "Wow means that, in her eyes, it is good." Sorley nodded.

"Do you—" I started.

Mary put up her hand.

"When we are in the presence of others, and when we are alone, you should always address us by Grandfather or Grandmother and in a gathering like supping tonight, you should not speak unless spoken to," Mary said.

"Speak only a wee bit, my lass, as you would not pass as a Gael and your English does not sound like us," Sorley said.

I nodded quickly to give my anger an outlet. They exchanged looks of doubt.

"Are our ways unheard of to your ears?" Sorley asked.

I searched his face, trying to decide what should be said or left inside, for now.

"Women speak often louder than men, in my century, or at least my part of the world."

"'Tis the same here," Sorley said.

Mary bobbed her head.

"You are young and should never speak ahead of your elders," Mary said, realizing my disconnect.

"Oh, it's not because I am a woman?"

"It is because you are just a girl," Mary said.

"It sounds like the same thing," I said, regretting it immediately.

Mary's face flushed and Sorley set his jaw.

"Pray tell, what does your century say about us lasses?" Mary asked.

"That they are equal to men," I said.

"Do they rule in your time, in your New World?" Sorley asked.

I swallowed and shook my head. "But I think women should rule. They would do a far better job of it."

Sorley moved closer.

"A woman does now rule over Ireland. And she does not show herself to be making better of it. She aims to take Ireland and make it a colony for the English—if she triumphs, what is to become of us?"

He studied my face.

"Be warned you might be taken as traitor to your own kin," he said.

I panicked. I was just hoping for a spirited debate—get the feminist wheels turning a bit early in my family.

A choking silence descended into the room, only the sound of the fire spitting and cracking took up space, leaving the rest of it to land like damaged air and energy. I stood up to talk but my grandmother put her hand out to stop me.

"My lass, you do not seem ready to be met with our other family," Sorley said.

That triggered me. I'd only been here a short while and I was already failing, already agitating the ancestors who'd summoned me here.

"I will not speak, even if spoken to," I said.

"Then it will seem like your tongue has been cut from your mouth," Mary said.

"Then how? How do I speak?"

"If I've got it in me to speak in a gathering, I clear my throat and then wait for the invitation," she said.

Oh my God, this struck me as ridiculous.

"Ahem," I uttered as delicately as possible.

"You might need to be louder than a mouse scrounging about," Sorley said.

"Ah hum," I said with greater volume.

"Good, so let that be how you speak to me, only me. I'll fetch you when we are to gather at the table," Mary said, making for the door.

"Shouldn't I help with the food preparation?"

"No, you are of nobility. You should be spending your time in pursuits of your station and in spiritual communion," Sorley said.

"For now, can you remain with your own entertainments?" Mary asked.

I nodded. The two left the room, and with a sizable exhalation, I went to the door to lock it. But there was no lock, no latch. Listening, I waited until it all went quiet. Reaching into my bag, my hand landed first on my mother's copy of *A Connecticut Yankee*. I also ensured I still had my self-charging battery. While finding a number of tampons in the bottom, I searched wildly but my homeopathic kit was gone! "Fuck, I left it on the bed at the Airbnb," I hissed, throwing my hands up in the air.

Feeling inside the pocket of my folded jeans, it was a relief I had my phone. Holding the device in my hand helped me feel grounded and a little more soothed. Swiping it, the set of displays lit up. Back at home, to deal with stress, I'd blast some tunes. I wondered if I could get away with unleashing a Beyoncé song, at lowest of volumes of course, into the sixteenth century. Watching the door, I turned off the phone and slipped it back into hiding instead. Could I really pull off being a sixteenth-century Scot to an Irish native?

Remembering when I was ten years old, before things got bad between my parents, my father was attempting a climb up the pegs of tenure as a professor of economics while also courting success as a C-suite consultant in a major condom company, of all things. On any given Saturday night, it was not unusual for my parents to throw a party and for me to whirl around the clusters of adults holding wineglasses and munching on hors d'oeuvres. I found that if I spoke like them, either with a cerebral flare or with great animation, depending on the crowd, I would evade my parents exiling me to my bedroom. The place where muffled laughter escaped through the floor only to amplify how much I was alone in the dark. I grasped that the financial crowd liked my questions about what they were drinking, while I entertained the university bunch by expounding upon random psychological concepts. By speaking their lingo, I also won myself non-stop attention and praise. I'd ask questions like, "What's a bull market?" or "What does self-fulfilling prophecy mean?" Once I had the whole neuropsychology department applauding when I recited all the lobes of the brain and their corresponding locations.

On Sunday mornings at breakfast, amid the mess of near empty bottles and stacks of small plates encrusted with remnants of hardened dips and shrimp tails, my mother would commend my maturity. Before I registered the warmth of her praise, my father began prepping me for my next performance.

Now about to face another crowd, I shook out my hands to release the nerves. This has to go well, I thought.

CHAPTER EIGHT

I pressed my palms into each other to get them to stop shaking while descending the steps behind Mary. As we approached the great room of the castle, notes of a harp accompanied by a mandolin met me first. A crack of laughter over the conversation and an intermittent banging on the table rang out my senses. My eyes met the glow from the grand fireplace throwing light toward the middle of the room. Gathered there were a dozen unknown faces and two male servants laying out metal plates and cutlery. Taking sight of the McDonnell coat of arms, it inspired my honor to walk with grace. Mary made a small gesture to the seat next to hers, to my great relief. Keeping my head slightly bowed, I managed to scan the room until my eyes found the familiar face of Sorley, seated at the head. The slight upturn of his mouth was a reassurance. *My Lindsay, you can do this.*

While the men were fully engaged in their conversations, most in Gaelic, and some words in English about horses, lands, and planting, it was clear there would be scarce notice thrown my way. I breathed a bit easier, sipping the wine from a weighty chalice made of bronze.

"What do you make of these fine vessels?" Mary said.

"They are weighty, Grandmother," I said as I leaned toward her ear.

Without turning to look at me, she smiled and nodded. I hoped I was meeting her standards.

Pushing his chair from the table, Shane stood and offered a toast, but in English.

"To alliances and the blessings they offer for those brave enough. Lest we be left with only this wretched language."

"My brother tries to goad your grandfather, speaking in English," Mary whispered to me.

His companions grunted out their agreements. I watched Sorley. He raised his chalice but said nothing. Shane slapped the table and threw back his shoulders before he sat back down. His confidence reminded me of a Hollywood actor, bigger than life. I probably stared at him too long as his gaze now fell on me.

"Dear Brother, you've met Alastair's eldest daughter, Lindsay, have you not?" Mary said with a lilt to her voice, speaking in measured English.

He narrowed his eyes and shook his head.

Mary put her hand on my shoulder.

"She's come to stay with us for Beltane," she said.

I managed a quick bow of the head in deference to his glare. The bottom line was that Shane was a severe force. His demeanor was forthright and capable of damage.

"How fares your father in Scotland?" Shane asked.

I started to answer only to find my voice weak. I cleared my throat and replied, "He is well, Uncle."

Shane nodded as satisfaction spread across his face. It must have appeared that I was joining with him in taking up the Sassenach tongue at Sorley McDonnell's table.

"And on what side of the sea does he place his eye?"

"Where he feels it is wisest," I said after a pause.

"And where it is best for his kin," Mary said, holding steady eye contact with her brother.

Mary patted my hip with her closest hand.

The meal was then served. The truth was I was quite hungry and grateful to partake in the thick bread, fish, and pie which I welcomed onto my plate.

"My grand-niece eats like a man going off to war," said Shane, over the din of the room.

A line of sweat started down my back.

"Uncle, I arrived just today and have not eaten since early this morning," I said.

Mary leaned in close. "You should only take wee amounts. If you are still hungry, you can always go to the larder later."

"Shall I put it back?"

Mary shook her head and focused on her own plate. Heat rushed into my face. I tried to recover by telling myself large amounts of food do not reveal a time traveler. At worst, they'd think me gluttonous.

Using a three-pronged forklike utensil, I sunk it into the pie and lifted it to my mouth. I immediately smelled animal flesh and put it down with a clink. Shit, I stupidly thought this was going to be made of berries not animals.

I tried to cut around it, but the crust was brimming with an intermingling of feathered and hooved creatures. Mary nudged me.

"You took it, lass, now eat it," she said. One of the few other women at the table laughed at her jibe.

"You do not care for the fruits of the hunt?" Shane asked.

Dick move.

I forced a smile and looked to Sorley.

"Is it not spiced to your expectation?" Sorley asked.

I nodded. "Aye, Grandfather, I thought it would be sweet not savory."

God, I sounded like an airhead, but my grandmother patted my hip again.

As the meal progressed, the men kept up the conversation. I slowly ate my food, working around the meat, as my tongue and brain searched for tastes that were somewhat familiar. After taking a bite of a very salted fish, I struggled to chew. Hitting a bone with my teeth did not help.

Shane glanced at me for only a moment and continued his discussion with Sorley. With as much composure as I could muster, I grabbed my chalice and took several sips of the wine. A serving boy stepped in to replace what I had just imbibed, and I could not help but flash him a grin of appreciation.

As I ate what food seemed safe, I realized my big portions were no longer obvious, now they had been consumed. Getting through this meal, I wondered how the hell I was going to eat here.

"Grandmother, what is next?" I asked.

"We will wait to hear what the men will do, they may stay here, and we may retire elsewhere, or they may take to another chamber of the castle."

"So, it's up to them where we may spend our time?" I said.

"Take heart, the world is not ending," she said, with a hand on my back.

I sensed Shane observing me, like a cat watching a fish in a shallow pond. Sorley realized the game and pounded his hand on the table demanding a toast to some place I never heard of.

"I refuse to celebrate that battle!" Shane said, standing.

Sorley found his legs as well.

"You never could be happy in the McDonnells' victories, could you O'Neill?"

Suspended in an agitated silence, the two stared at each other until Shane shifted his eyes to his men.

"We'll take our leave in the new light," Shane said.

"Can't take a crack of wit neither, can you, Shane?" Sorley said.

The room remained hushed, some gazing down, others looking to each other.

"My family, we are all kin here, I should like to plan on future meals within your collective presence," I said, standing up to my full height.

All turned to me, including the serving boy. I was midway through a jump across a chasm where I might not make the landing.

"Our lass remembers what is vital," Sorley said, offering Shane his hand.

Shane did not move.

"It was a mere joke," Sorley said.

"You ought to check the devil that urges you to agitate me as I come to you with earnest intent," Shane said.

I had to give Shane credit. Macho bullshit aside, he named his feelings and asked for respect.

Sorley nodded and dropped his eyes, for a second.

"I'll watch THAT devil—but just that one," Sorley said.

The room broke out in laughter. While the comment didn't strike me as funny, it was a massive reprieve to feel the energy shift in the room. My grandmother left my side to embrace her brother and her husband, looking back at me with gratitude.

CHAPTER NINE

The next morning, I awoke before the sun rose. It took my brain a few minutes to realize I truly was in 1560, receiving the hospitality of family fifteen generations removed. The quiet here sounded different. I could hear the air move and the oceanic churn far beneath the castle's edge. My full bladder was urging me to seek out the chamber pot in the corner. Pushing back the blanket, my feet met the cool but not cold wooden floor. Lifting my shift, I squatted and almost lost my balance. Secure I was in dead aim within the pot, I let the warm stream go, pinging down to the bottom. But there was no toilet paper or anything that might serve as such. I stayed in my crouch, hoping I would dry speedily. After several moments, my muscles registered fatigue and I stood up.

"Ugh."

Returning to bed, I lay back, listening to the sounds in and about the castle again. Pushing through was a horse whinny followed by a distant rhythmic clopping. Was Shane leaving anyway? I went to the farthest window, seeing nothing but the last shimmer of moonlight falling against the trees.

The sound of a horse's hooves was coming closer. I leaned out the window watching. What is happening? The thought occurred to me that we were about to be ambushed, and I shirked back into my chamber. Finding my petticoats, I tried to secure them in a makeshift way. Raising the top of the chest at the foot of my bed, I felt around in the low light for my cloak. Running in the back of my mind was the thought of going back to my century. It would be easy: whisper the mantra while imagining tracing my finger around the placemats at my kitchen table.

Compelled to peer out the window again, I jumped upon seeing a face staring right up at me from the ground below. It was Shane, next to his horse. I pulled back, caught. After a few moments, he coughed, waiting. I tried to slow my breathing as I returned to the window. He offered a tight smile and motioned for me to come down. I shook my head. He raised his hands and showed me his palms. I didn't understand what it meant.

"Uncle, do you take your leave?" I whispered.

"When I do not find sleep, I spend time walking in quiet contemplation," he whispered back.

"I hope you find your peace," I said.

"Peace must be tended."

"Uncle, you are wise."

"For what reason do you choose to speak in English? You know it raises the ire of your grandfather," he asked, testing me yet again.

"It pleases Grandmother."

"Does it now?"

I nodded. "She said it reminds her of your departed father."

Shane gave a slight sneer and shook his head.

"Niece, you should help my cause."

I said nothing.

"Your grandfather should align with us against the English crown."

I stared down at him, which gave him a chance to read my face. He then placed one hand over a fist and raised it up over his head. He unfurled his fist into an open hand as if offering it to me. Unable to decipher this gesture, I stayed motionless. Shane lowered his hands and tapped his temple with his index finger and returned to his horse, taking up its bridle and leading it away.

I stepped away from the window and sat down on the bed. Acting out the gesture to see what it felt like, I assured myself it wasn't aggressive toward me, despite it evoking an assertion of power. As the sun's early rays were beginning to light up the dawn, I wondered what Shane would do.

There was a shuffling at the door. It swung open and there was Mary. She entered the room and took up with both her hands on her hips.

"Are you planning on an early morning journey, or have you now returned?"

"I heard a horse outside. I thought it meant danger," I said.

Mary took a seat next to me. "We are most safe here, Granddaughter."

"I am new to all of this and trying to understand."

Her face softened as she put her arm around me and pulled me to lean against her. Her faint scent of lemon balm and salt was becoming familiar.

After some time, she asked, "Did you take any sleep?"

"Oh yes, I was spent. I woke up only a while ago."

"Do you desire to return to your rest?" she asked.

"I don't think I can. Has Uncle Shane taken his leave?"

"Pray tell what makes you wonder so?"

"It seems he and Grandfather remain at an impasse, they still cannot agree," I said.

Mary took this in. "How do you know this?"

I told her about my exchange with Shane. She became peeved as I filled in the details, setting her jaw as I continued.

"We shall soon find out where the negotiations lay," she said finally.

"Please let me know how I can help," I said, unsure if I had the courage to back up my offer.

Mary looked me deeply in the eyes. She shook her head and kissed my forehead.

"God may have sent you just to give us joy and hope of a far-reaching future."

My chest was heavy as her love swirled around me, so freely given. I leaned back into her, letting myself take strength from her warmth.

Mary soon led me down to meet Katherine, a young cook recently graduated from her apprenticeship. To 'break my fast,' she served me porridge and a thick slab of brown bread made hot from the griddle, laden with the creamiest melted white butter. I ventured to ask for a second piece. Amused, Mary and Katherine granted me my request. The meal buoyed me to seek out Sorley.

I entered the chamber where Sorley and Mary first brought me on my arrival to find my grandfather sitting at the planked table, his bare feet extended, and a parchment laid out in front of him. It was a rough map of the area. Clearing my throat to gain his attention, I offered a curtsy.

"Time to speak?"

"Aye, my lass. You are a wonderful sight to behold, this morn. How did you find your rest?" he said, pulling a chair out for me.

"Quite well," I said in truth, realizing I normally didn't sleep well the first night of any trip.

"Where is Shane?"

"In the livery, with his men."

"Did you come to any agreement?"

Sorley shook his head.

"But, Lindsay, we could be farther apart, save for your courage. You have a gift for speaking in a manner that unites and you prevailed right at the moment when we were sure to come to blows."

A glimmer of true purpose surged through my heart.

"You are a peacemaker, which be a more precious skill than possessing all the might in the world."

I bowed my head as I checked my soul for a fit. Did I deserve such a pronouncement?

"I believe I have been training in peacemaking and healing much of my life."

Sorley nodded, laughed, and looked skyward.

"Let's take joy in our common hours together. I should like to know ye, my acorn."

I reveled in him calling me that; I recognized it from our shamanic visit. Basking in our family connection, I pointed to the portrait above the hearth and asked who it was. It was his older brother, James McDonnell, the sixth Laird of Dunnyveg in Scotland. As I stared at the image, Sorley told me about James and his love for kin and skill for diplomacy. I did not express it, but I hoped to meet him as Sorley's admiration transferred to my own heart.

"Grandfather, shall we talk outside? I am yearning for outside air."

He sat back in his chair, rolling up the parchment.

"I shall prefer you to call me in Irish," he said.

A memory came alive in my brain from when I was little.

"May I call you by the name I had for my Irish grandfather?"

He tilted his head forward, waiting.

"Daideó," I offered.

He broke out into a full-out grin and drummed his fingers on the table.

"And I'd like to call Grandmother, Maimeó."

I treasured the name Maimeó, as it sounded like a word we'd use to begin our sangha meditation in front of the Buddha.

"I too like to think outside. Let's talk by the stream."

Jubilance coursed through me, and it was a challenge not to rush out. As we left the room, my newly minted Daideó stopped and took his sword, placing it back around his waist.

"Do you always put on your sword, when leaving the castle?"

He regarded me as if it was the most bizarre question he had heard in a decade.

"Lindsay, I may have need to defend us."

I noticed he was not making an effort to put anything on his feet.

"Where are your boots kept?"

He waved his hand to dismiss the idea. I fell in line behind him, biting my tongue to ask more questions; my anxiety was rising watching the backs of his bare heels. We emerged into the sunshine, and I fell in step with him down the path leading to the farthest side of the castle.

"It is good to have the sun warm us, this day," he said.

As we walked, I took in the air, fresh with the scents of the blooming wildflowers and sprouted trees. One bright blue bird chased another through the brush and up into the branches of a lone evergreen tree. Daideó steered us down a steeper path which veered increasingly away from the castle walls. We found our way to the edge of a forest that ran parallel to the sea. There the path was smaller and less worn. He held back branches of sapling juniper trees, obstructing the path.

After a couple of minutes, the forest floor turned from dirt to massive, rounded rocks which extended out over the foam and bubble of the stream.

"Here?" I asked.

"Aye."

I did not wait for a further invitation but instead sat, my skirts acting as a padding upon the rock. Sorley situated himself, watching both behind me and toward the path we traveled on, as I turned full on to look out on the water. He tapped me, indicating he wanted me to face him.

"My lass, you will need to tell me if you see any movement behind me," he said.

"What kind of movement?"

"There are men and there are animals, any of which could be unfriendly."

I took this information in. Oddly, I found the inclusion of animals to make our need for vigilance not so bad. But still, I comprehended the need to stay alert. Using his chin, Sorley pointed to my feet. I hoped he wasn't going to tell me to take off my boots.

"Those are some bonny boots you wear. Is that a clan emblem?" He pointed to the Timberland logo.

"It's an emblem of a merchant who makes boots in New England."

He spit through a scowl. "Pray tell me there is a New Ireland."

"It's called Boston," I said happily.

"And is it far from new, England?"

"It is *in* New England."

He cursed in Gaelic.

"But there is a new Scotland, called Novia Scotia and it is *not* in New England, how about that?"

"Good, that much fills my heart."

"We also do not celebrate any English holidays, but we do mark St. Patrick's Day in honor of the Irish."

"In New England, you celebrate the Irish, eh?"

I didn't tell him that last St. Pat's Day had me vomiting up beer and green pretzels on a back street near Fenway.

"Tell me more about what is transpiring with the English," I asked.

"We are at a tenuous peace with the English crown, but I fear it will be short-lived."

"Can you offer a marriage to make an alliance?" I asked, thinking I was on to something for sure.

"It is not only the McDonnells and the O'Neills. The English look to colonize the whole of the region." He leaned toward me. "No English should ever rule Irish land." His voice was cutting and bitter. "Do you understand?"

I swallowed hard and nodded. "Needing to be independent of English rule is what the New World was built upon by those who ventured there."

"And when those venturers arrived in the New World, there were no others who had already tended to the land? It was without clan and kin?" he asked.

"Those venturers—my past and your future generations, and yes very much the English, took the land from the clans. Those clans call their kin tribes and they lived in the New World for centuries before our generations arrived."

He uttered some Gaelic words that bubbled up from his gut as he glanced above. I think it was an invocation to God by its tone. I was grateful; we would need the help.

"Daideó, please tell me more about Shane's quest."

"He is looking for the English to recognize his title as The O'Neill.

He wants the McDonnell clan to support his claim and prepare to defend it in battle."

"And what do the McDonnells get for such loyalty?"

Sorley looked at me with a small cock to his head.

"That is always my first question with Shane. While we are family, he is not to be trusted."

"No?"

Sorley threw a stone into the stream with some force.

"More than one of his brothers have been killed in his name."

A loud crack of branches sounded through the woods. Sorley sprang to his feet. Out from behind a tree across the stream a great buck emerged, antlers stemming out high and curved inward as if holding an invisible orb of sovereignty above its head. With black eyes that shone like obsidian, it aimed its gaze at us.

"This is a blessed sign, to have *Damh* show us his reserve of mighty power. He tells us we are to seek our independence with his protection," Sorley said.

I, too, recognized a missive from the universe.

"It is a message to go forward in peace," I said.

With its meaning transmitted, we watched the buck leap back into the forest. Sorley and I caught each other's eyes, and after a second passed, we both laughed out loud. He gestured as if toasting the animal and the heavens. I leaned over and put my hand up, palm facing him.

"In my century, you would clap my hand with yours, like this." I proceeded to demonstrate a high five with my own palms and fingers. I raised my hand toward him, but he put his up to mine and clasped it, giving it a shake instead.

"Aye, we join hands too in celebration," he said.

Now more attuned to the natural phenomenon unfolding around us, I observed as small sticks and pointed leaves journeyed through the bubbling water of the stream. As I inhaled, the earthiness of the forest took up my full awareness for several breaths.

"Lass, I wonder what have ye left behind to be here?"

I searched my mind.

"A husband? Your wee ones?"

"I have none."

"Well, you are young yet," he said after a few seconds. "What about your kin?"

I braced myself and pushed out the words I'd had to say so many times.

"None, my mother died last month—in my time."

"My Lindsay, for this I'm most sorry to hear, that her light is extinguished." Sorley reached his hand to me. "What was said about her, when she laid her feet on the land?"

The invitation opened my heart and I began to extol my mother's finer qualities.

"You admire her wisdom," Sorley reflected back to me.

I nodded, needing a moment to gather myself.

"She shared her wisdom and took me to places where I could find my own," I said. "After I grew into womanhood, she made me feel like raising me was one of her biggest joys."

But it didn't feel that way through my adolescent years. I was in college when my father left, and it wasn't until the last few years that we became best friends. I was lucky to know my best friend loved me, my entire life.

The moment arrived for me to ask the question.

"Daideó, has she ever come to you, in secret?"

"From the Otherworld?"

"Aye—or maybe it did not seem so. She may have arrived as any other woman might."

Sorley's face warmed with a compassionate softness.

"We would not be twice blessed," he said.

"And you would not keep that from me, if she had visited?"

He offered his hand. I placed my fingers in his palm and listened to the gurgling water over the constant, steady current, while allowing my pain to recede. It was not as tender as I'd come to expect. A solace was now present in sharing 'common hours' with Daideó.

"Is there anything you want to ask me about my time?" I asked.

"The McDonnell line continues. That is enough."

It blew my mind he didn't need more.

"Perhaps there is something that would put you at an advantage," I said, testing fate.

Sorley widened his eyes in recognition of an opportunity he shouldn't let slip by.

"What about warfare?" he said as I swallowed the danger laced within the question. "We have ways we plan and carry out battle. An army can barrage a castle with arrows or attack at night while the foes sleep," he said.

"Yes, that changes with time, but I know very little of this."

"Aye, being a woman," he said.

All the muscles in my face and neck tensed and I blew out an audible breath.

"No, that's not it." I faltered, annoyed at his comment and myself, as he was the last person I wanted to be irritated with right now.

"Then what can ye tell me?" he said.

"We are tough and do things much like men, including going into battle," I said with pride.

He paused. "In your century there is still no peace, men still need to wage war and now so goes women."

I was dumbfounded.

"I would have thought under God, men and women would someday understand the way to live in peace," he said.

I shuddered to hear it said so plainly. The sounds of nature around us only echoing the meaning.

"Your someday is my someday too," I said.

He gave me an acquiescent nod before picking up a stone under his toe and skimming it across the water.

"Daideó, why do you walk in bare feet?"

Sorley laid his hands against the rock beneath us and closed his eyes.

"With my hands and feet on the earth I listen to the rhythms. At times, they are a quick flow and at others they are nearly still. It tells me how to understand a circumstance. A slow rhythm tells me to be patient with the situation—wait and more will be revealed."

I realized what he was telling me. Taking off my boots, I set my bare feet against the steady stone. To find more connection to the rock, I also placed my hands on its porous, white surface, warmed by the sun.

"How do I serve?" I asked out loud and then listened.

The pour of the stream dropped away to a sound farther removed, a roar from over the hill.

"I hear the sea—the waves coming and going back out," I said.

Dropping into deeper perceiving, I sensed the rush of a breeze over my skin.

"I sense the wind. What direction is it blowing?"

"Southeast."

I opened my eyes.

"What is southeast of here?"

"England."

I already knew it would be England. It was in alignment for both finding my mother and in somehow serving this new family of my ancestors. Sorley shut his own eyes and placed his hand on his heart. He soon bid us to return and we both stood, him offering to hold my boots. Guiding us onto another path, he led the way. Navigating my skirts, I steered through the branches and the stinging nettles while avoiding sharp stones under my bare feet.

Serenaded by birdsong and breezes singing through the trees, we journeyed back to the castle wordless, but thinking. When it was time for me to go, it would be another break in my heart.

Shane's voice boomed from the great room, where we'd gathered the night prior for dinner. Despite Sorley holding me behind him, I still saw the tension drawn across Mary's face. Shane stood, hands on hips. He and Sorley exchanged what I believe was sarcasm in Gaelic and then my grandmother joined in. Shane stopped and studied me. He spoke in Gaelic, with eyes fierce and fixed. He invoked Queen Elizabeth's name, and they were right back to their disagreement.

Mary rescued me, speaking back to Shane in English as a way of translating for me. Shane accused me of being a lover of the Sassenach. The argument only escalated between Shane and Sorley, and then something effervesced within me. I had not yet run it by the rest of my brain, but my soul spoke.

"Daideó, Maimeó, what if I, as one of your kin, was offered to serve in the English court, as an envoy of peace?"

The question struck Shane speechless. Sorley stepped back astonished as pain shaded over Mary's features.

"We would not give you to that Tudor devil," exclaimed my grandmother. She rushed to my side as if to protect me then and there. In contrast, Sorley's wheels were turning, trying on the idea.

"Mary, the queen might look kindly on us if she had one of our kinswomen at her side," Sorley said.

"Lindsay, think on what you suggest. You would be with an enemy," Mary said.

"What if it does deem her more friendly toward us? I am seen as serving her and a representation of the peace between Ireland and England?" I offered.

My grandmother put her hands on my shoulders and searched my eyes, worry residing in hers. She turned her gaze to Sorley.

"You would dispatch your own flesh and blood, and a wee lass no less, to go off alone to be among the enemy. And you McDonnells claim neutrality," Shane said.

"This is not a swipe to your position, Shane. It could put the queen in a better mind to allow your claim," Sorley said.

"It's the Devil's shite! England will surely see us as divided."

The two remained locked in eye contact.

"They see we are not savages. They see Ireland should not be taken by sword and fire. They see it is better to be with us, than against us," Sorley said, his voice rising.

"You are a Scot by blood, Sorley McDonnell, you forsake—"

"I am a Scot by blood but an Irishman by heart and soul."

"By God and by Hell I will not let the Sassenach take what is ours," Shane roared.

"We are agreed, brother! But the battles have raged for years. We require a new way and Lindsay serving at the English queen's court is a sanctified act."

Shane scoffed.

"Your diplomacy is foolishly placed," he said pointing to me.

"As it is our collective clans' destiny to lead Ireland, it is Lindsay's to make a lasting peace—woman to woman."

With that, Shane threw his hands in the air and kicked a chair as he barreled out of the room. Mary followed him leaving Sorley to simmer. Brother and sister exchanged fire as Shane thundered out from the castle.

Sorley called to Mary. She appeared at the entrance of the room, tense and red.

"Husband, he is all wrath. What do you think he will do?"

Sorley shook his head. "I pray not an act of consequence where all will collapse on top of us."

CHAPTER TEN

Later in the evening, I lay in my bedchamber and thought about the Bodhisattva, Green Tara, for the first time since I'd arrived in Ireland, in either century. In my heart's eye, I conjured her image, focusing on her right leg, always poised to step out to help us mortals move across the water of suffering, until there is no suffering. I admired her surety in knowing her mission. I said her mantra in my mind, *Om Tare Tuttare, Ture Soha*, asking for her help. A flutter of wings and loud squawks thrust me out of my inner focus. Perched at my window were two ravens, black as a lake at midnight and reflective so I could almost see myself within the feathers. How were they fighting a second ago but can stand calm beside each other now?

"Do you have a message for me?" I asked, knowing their visitation was not random.

They cocked their heads but remained silent. Did I think animals were going to talk to me now?

I took care rising slowly from my bed. The birds remained. One turned and faced outward, but still it remained. As I stepped closer, the other bird thrust its beak at me until a gust of wind blew, and in a mass of wings, they both took to the air. Leaning out from the stone-cased window, I trusted an undeniable urge to go for an early morning walk to see what nature had to tell me. Eyeing Julia's dark cape in the corner of my room, I also thought to seek out her counsel.

This was only the second time I'd attempted to dress myself here. It was easier to don a simple 'everyday' gown and a relief to leave the usual twenty-first-century maintenance undone. I tied my hair back with a wide black ribbon and took my own shaggy cape.

I moved through the castle without encountering anyone but the boy who attends the fires in the kitchen. A few of Sorley's servants congregating around a fire by Dunanynie's outermost gate expressed trepidation for me to pass over the drawbridge unaccompanied. Telling them I was out to pick flowers over the hill, they let me leave on my own as one ascended the top of the tower to keep watch. On my way, Bonamargy Friary, my threshold into this sixteenth-century world, strengthened its call to me, once again.

The ocean's rumble accompanied my trek as I passed through the long grasses parallel to the shore. Once reaching the friary path, I pictured the ravens, knowing them to be creatures of transformation that moved between worlds. Maybe I was becoming a raven.

After descending the same hill on which Sorley had stood waiting for me, I came upon two monks, kneeling and praying next to the chapel. I stopped. Was I supposed to be here? One of the monks began to chant. He was loud and earnest. The energy coming from him was formidable. Another pair emerged from the building. These joined the others and got to their knees. As I shirked back to avoid being seen, I sensed someone was behind me. I spun around to find Julia. She was magical in her black habit and veil while I was nowhere near as magnificent in my plaid and linen ensemble. Her blue eyes shone as I came closer and handed back her cloak.

"Have you accomplished your time here?"

"I've barely started."

Another loud chant arose from the monks. I peered around the corner of the chapel to see at least a dozen now kneeling, chanting straight from the passion released from their souls.

I turned to Julia.

"I never saw such a ceremony in real life."

"What other life is there to see but what is real?" she said.

She took my hand with some force. "Come, we must not be a distraction to them in their devotion." I let her lead us away, as the sun shining white, beat down on our backs. The intensity of the chanting fell into the background as we arrived at the edge of the friary's lands. There were several large rocks that called us to sit down and take a rest.

"You will be best served by becoming learned of the customs, history, and expectations of this time. Soak up what your kin have to teach."

"They have been teaching me," I said.

"Are you allowing the learning in?" Julia asked.

I nodded. "I believe so. I definitely speak differently than before."

"And you understand what is being said to you?"

"Some—I am learning more Gaelic, but they have been kind to speak to me in English."

"They honor you. To honor them, you shall test your newly acquired knowledge, otherwise you may default to your original way."

"Well, I have the advantage of coming from future centuries, I'm not just an outsider."

"Yet you must live in this time as an embodied inhabitant."

The chanting ceased, leaving us with the rumble of the waves from the other direction.

"Julia, may I ask where you have traveled?"

"I went back to hear the teachings of John, the disciple, to understand how God is in the mundane as much as He resides in the exalted."

"What did that give you?"

"It bestowed within me a heart to perceive how God is everywhere. It would be sacred perfection to see God in the visible and invisible, and to have reverence for it all."

"Is that your mission?"

"It resounds in my prayers."

"And what do you see in this time traveling?"

"It is best to be clear on what has been put askew and requires correction, but touch nothing else," Julia said.

From afar we saw a train of monks walking uphill.

"Do they see us?"

"They do, but they comprehend that we are now in sacred process."

"Did you know I was coming?"

She smiled.

"Your mother knew."

My leg slipped off the rock and I became faint for a couple of seconds. Julia put her arms out to take both my hands. I sank to the earth to get my grounding as my heart and brain surpassed their capacity to process any more. Someone in the sixteenth century knew my mother, and I was in her wake.

Julia kneeled down next to me.

"When did you see her?"

"She said she was from the year 2016. What is your year?"

"2018—what did she do here?"

My right hand squeezed my left to quell my impatience to find out more.

"Lindsay, your mother met your grandmother, Mary."

Would she keep this from me? I contemplated the countryside, the undulating lines of the land and blue-gray canopy of the Irish sky: the signature of a place that only welcomed me in. Why was it withholding that which I most needed to know?

"Sorley and Mary told me separately I was the only one."

"She thought your mother was a seer come to tell her of the future. Sara bid her to use her influence for making peace with the English, for an acquiescent Ireland could be a shining jewel of Elizabeth's queendom and well regarded in the time to come."

"But my mother could not be certain Elizabeth taking full possession of Ireland would create such an outcome." I sat with my heart freefalling into the pit of my stomach.

As I spoke, a bee flew around my head. Julia and I maintained eye contact as I tried not to move.

"You call creatures to your cause."

The bee hovered around the crown of my head as if deciding what to do with me. I committed to not swat it away.

Julia intuited my struggle. "It will pass its message and then depart."

A few seconds later, the bee took its leave, flying southeast.

"That is where you mother took her sojourn," Julia said.

"To England, yes?"

"Yes, to meet a pious wizard at the court of Elizabeth."

The direction was further validation, but the rest made no sense. Time traveling is science; wizards are fiction.

"Who is the pious wizard?" I asked.

Julia had compassion in her eyes. She'd tell me if she knew.

I lay back, letting all this new information assimilate into my brain. I closed my eyes and tried to feel the cushion of the grass underneath me along with the hard and constant support of the earth itself, but the confusion won out.

"Julia, what can I do? Maybe it's a new kind of sin, but I yearn to be with her. Maybe I could help her to help our ancestors, but she's not here and perhaps I'm never to lay eyes on her again."

"We shall pray and trust God's good counsel gives us clarity."

Shit, that still wasn't working for me, unsure how I could connect with a paternal God. I hoped Julia, being more tapped in, would emerge with some guidance. As soon as I instinctually shifted into my meditation posture, Julia chided me for not taking to my knees.

"Lindsay, you must be careful about your practices. Any journey is considered only after solemn contemplation with Divine counsel."

I let her assumption about my practices go. Especially as she lit my path with hope. After some time with us on our knees, I waited for Julia to come out of her prayer.

"What would you and God have me know?"

"You shall limit your leaps in time, as it takes a toll on the feminine organs as well as the heart."

I gasped, my hand to my chest. "Would it make the heart stop beating?"

"This gift has claimed most travelers in that manner," she said, crossing herself.

"My mother—her heart stopped a month ago. Julia, do you believe it was her time traveling?"

"Perhaps she took only her own counsel and pushed the limits too far."

Julia told me the body needs a great deal of time to heal between journeys, but she could not tell me how long to wait, as it's connected to God's will.

"My dearest girl, if you invoke your mind's ability to move your body in time, you can never venture back to reside in the hours you have already lived."

"After you leave it, you can never come back?"

"That is why I remain here as long as I have," she said.

"It's like you are a prisoner."

"Nay, this is sacred work in service of God."

"How do you always trust that to be true?"

Julia's blue eyes appeared rounder but sweeter.

"I am that I am and I am here." It was all she said.

That truth swum inside my head as I let it sink down and take its place as a new anchor of reality. I was here too.

"But you are close to your kin's enemy. Even I, being a McDonnell, am your enemy," I said.

"Do not define yourself as anyone's enemy, only as ally to all. Jesus was an ally to all. Mother Mary was an ally to all."

And the Buddhas and Bodhisattvas are allies to all, yet I had a sick feeling my mother had set herself on a path which could hurt our ancestors—our family.

CHAPTER ELEVEN

After I took my leave from Julia, I trekked back to the castle. Hearing of my mother only made me long for her—but I was pissed. She didn't have to die in 2018. As I made my way across the drawbridge back into the confines of Dunanynie, I waved to the gate minder, and wondered if he had ever seen my mother. I pondered my approach with Mary, and if it would be wise to tell her who Sara is to us.

Once inside Dunanynie, I climbed the stairs and heard Sorley and Mary in one of the upper chambers. They were in mid-argument about me.

"Mary, she has been summoned for a sacred reason. Lindsay is God's instrument for the care of Ireland. Her arrival tells us now is the time."

I knocked and let them know it was me. Mary opened the door. Stationed in front of the hearth, Sorley stood and waved me in.

Mary eyed me.

"Lindsay, do you believe in this God you are serving?" she asked.

"I want nothing more than to help create peace," I said.

Reddening in the face, Mary shook her head.

"Are you of the old religion?"

I decided to be honest. "I am no longer of the old religion despite being brought up in its teachings—and I am uncertain if I still believe in the Christian God as I practice Buddhism from the east."

Mary grabbed my hand to pull me closer to my grandfather.

"She is not of the reformed religion! She is not even Christian. How can we send her off to the center of Elizabeth's church? They'll cut her to pieces."

"Mary!" Sorley said.

Did she think they'd torture me? My stomach began to roll and tumble.

"Your brave proclamation at dinner got us all to reflect on what is common between us," Sorley said, encouraging me. "That is the heart of any Christian teaching I can recollect. Yet my Anam Cara, you cannot let on you are anything but in agreement with Elizabeth's expression of faith. You must show yourself eager to worship as she does."

"She's not as bad as all that. She is not her bloody sister," I said from my pre-trip research and twenty-first-century perspective.

"You cannot predict what she will do," Mary said.

"I know from history she is less interested in 'making windows of men's souls.'"

"Husband, the queen is not the only force here. Anyone at her court could throw aspersions at our lass—anyone!" Mary flung her arms toward me. "And history is already changed because you are here. It would be dangerous to rely on your knowledge because it might no longer be true." Tears leaped down her face in a continuous stream while her words slammed into me and filled me with a churning dread. What shifts have I put into play simply by being here?

"Maimeó, has a wise woman, a seer, who spoke like me, ever seek your audience?"

My grandmother thought for several agonizing seconds.

"Aye, she spoke in a strange way, but in our own Gaelic tongue. She said it was the future of our language."

My mother seemed so close in that moment.

"And she bade you to see England with eyes of assent?" I asked.

"Of submission, of surrender! I sent her away and told her to never again undertake to have my ear."

"Did she tell you from where she came?"

"Lass, what do you know about this woman?" Sorley said.

I had to tell them.

"Our own kin… against us," Sorley said. Gone was his kind regard for my mother he had shown me at the stream.

"She didn't realize—she was trying to help," I said.

Mary threw her hands up, but I was watching my grandfather.

"And will you follow your mother?" Mary asked.

"I must do something—I am fearful for all of us," I said.

Sorley peered into my eyes.

"We can wait to petition the queen. You can think on it and still prepare."

"I will take spiritual counsel," I said. Mary embraced me, holding me so close, her heart beating against mine.

I excused myself to my bedchamber to find my grounding. As I trod down the passage, I heard Sorley say, "She is on her toures d'anam (journey of the soul) and she takes our fate with her."

CHAPTER TWELVE

For the next few days, I pushed the decision aside. Mary's words of violence prowled around my consciousness like a dark, toxic mist. I had to overcome the fear it brought and follow my mother's trail. I was here for a reason and committed to my intent—expanding to find my mother and help our McDonnells. I had to accomplish both. My head and heart throbbed as my thoughts spiraled down a pit of unforgiving doubt. I recognized I should not venture here. This is not where warriors dwell before their service.

To stay centered, I roamed through the castle, sometimes several times a day, exploring and absorbing its vibration. Nothing here was built for convenience. Getting dressed was an event; so were most meals, and meeting with nature integrated into almost all activities. Even in the innermost chambers, I could touch the naked wood under my feet and smell the natural air.

Dunanynie's long halls summoned me to move through them, and to be a part of the human occupancy of this time in its history. Many of these passages were clear of decoration, bearing only the white and gray speckled stone that reflected the weather. On occasions where the sun held the clouds behind her, the passageways wore a brighter light and the warmer air tasted purely of the salt risen up from the sea below.

There was a turreted room on one of the uppermost floors. It was the sunniest and to me the most supportive to self-train. There I engaged a yoga practice rich with warrior one and two poses that flowed into the stillness of meditation. At the start of a sit, I would not place my hands in a high prayer position but one holding the other, palms up. I felt like a spiritual bandit, but at worst, a servant walking in would beg my pardon for the intrusion. I also began to murmur my Tara mantra, but never loud enough to be heard by anyone. I was calling on the power of all the Taras to infuse me with wisdom and clear seeing.

Deep in meditation, I remained with this new here and now. This day in 1560 being the present moment. I also explored the quality of the quiet. There was no buzzing of cell phones left on tables or tucked in purses. There was no tension of constant electricity running through the walls. No vroom of car engines, no thunder of jets overhead. Any conversation heard was coming from live people in actual interactions, never a staged production of television dialogue. All sound was from natural and living sources, with one exception.

I snuck my phone into the privy a few times, where I was alone. With my precious earbuds, I would listen to a song on my iTunes. That music was my inspiration and reality check. Those chords and lyrics buoyed my perspective. I was the warrior, the rock star, and a version of the Walrus that Lennon could not have conceived. I was a Girl on Fire, Eye of the Tiger and someone was going to hear me roar. In my walks by the ocean, I'd sing those same songs to myself. This was all part of my preparation for whatever would manifest next.

Other times I treasured spending in the company of one or both of my great-grandparents. It was especially healing when Maimeó would invite me to pick herbs or wildflowers.

"Ye have a fine eye for nurturing the plants," Maimeó said.

"It's been passed down," I said, inspecting what I hoped was a fennel plant.

"Glad this stays in the lineage."

I taught Maimeó how to make a tincture to lessen a headache. She was glad to have that to add to her own catalog of healing agents and concoctions. I informed her that, on some level, that was my profession back in my century.

Mary grabbed my arm and held me close to her.

"Be careful how you dispense with that knowledge, you are too young to be known as a wise woman, and in England, you may be taken as performing witchcraft."

I told her that anything which heals in accordance with the body's natural tendencies was good.

"If they do not recognize your medicine, the English may suspect it has evil to bestow," she said, still holding me.

"Then I should say nothing," I said.

Mary released me but remained in my personal space. I found it hard to make eye contact, mostly because of her intensity. To break the mood, I kissed her cheek and whispered a blessing in her ear. Something she had done to me almost every night and, occasionally, some mornings. Right from her belly, she laughed at the change in roles. I think I also messed up the blessing.

On rainy days, my grandparents and I drank mead by the fire after our midday meal. Often, Daideó and I would inhabit our spot at the stream where he would tell me stories of far-flung neighbors and of our family. My favorite was how he first met Maimeó. The marriage was brokered but they met years before, at a wedding celebration. He said he spied his Mary across the gathering.

"She was trying not to laugh at some tomfoolery taking place on her side of the great room. But, in her mirth, I caught her eye and kept it. Right then, not a thing would stop me from exchanging a word or two with this twinkling lass."

I stopped him there. "And Maimeó is still that twinkling lass?"

He broke into a full on, appreciative smile that took years off his face.

"During a dance, a rather spritely one, I took up and presented myself in the line. We whirled and turned, and I heard her laugh again. Afterward, she spoke to me."

"What did she say?"

"Those are fine boots but ya feets in them are still a wee bit clumsy."

"No!"

"Aye, and then she left me there with my tongue tied in knots," Sorley said.

The moment hung between us as we laughed together. With that same full grin, he nodded, picked up a small stone, and chucked it into the stream.

"Now you watch. I could go ahead and tell her that story and she'd deny every bit."

The worst story he told me, as it left me unable to sleep, was of his grandfather who had been executed in Edinburgh for high treason against the Scottish crown. That one he shared by the firelight on a dark and rain-drenched day. The chill in the air made me almost feel like I was there with our shared ancestor. The next day at our spot by the stream, I told him how the story haunted me.

"I'm sorry, my lass, it's a story which rattles my bones as well."

I wanted to ask all the new questions hatching in my mind, but I stayed silent.

"Out with it, you've got something spinning in ye throat."

"Daideó, does that not scare you about the Scottish monarchy?"

"From the Scots, nay. Mary the queen is an ally to McDonnells. The English crown is the truest threat."

"So, *they* scare you then?"

His eyes narrowed while he kept his gaze on me.

"Ye can't be afeard of the English," he said finally.

I gazed out at the stream, envious of its easy flow. The fact was, I was becoming afraid. I picked up a stone and tried to skip it across the water, but it plunked down, falling under the froth and flow of the rushing water. Sorley was studying my face.

Standing up, he surveyed the area, a near 360 degrees. I rose to my feet too.

He clutched my hand and led me back down the path to go home. His silence and tight grasp told me he was worried as well.

Late the next afternoon, my grandfather called me out to the stables. He told me, "A ceasefire and amity has been struck in Edinburgh. With the help of the English, Scotland will be free from the invading French. As a Scotch Irish, I shall press our gratitude to England with the offer of your service. There could be no more opportune time."

His words blasted into my brain, breaking into shards of excitement tinged with fear, pushing me further into my destiny.

"I shall dispatch a letter to London," he said, anticipation in his eyes.

"And if they say yes, I am given to go?" I asked.

"If the queen and her counsel agree, you will need to prepare yourself like a soldier. They will test your loyalty and subject you to inquiry on the McDonnells and perhaps on Shane, as well."

"I will plead ignorance—after all, I am just a lass."

Sorley seemed to be sizing me up all over again. I pulled my shoulders back and lifted my chin.

"My sex is our advantage, is it not?"

He nodded slowly but with a spark of growing confidence in his deep blue eyes.

"What shall Maimeó say?"

"Your grandmother will still not agree," he said.

"But you believe it is a good plan?"

"It will go against what Shane wants us to do, he will see it as disloyalty to Ulster, and perhaps all of Ireland."

"But it truly is the McDonnells creating a path to peace," I said, trying to convince myself.

He put out his hand. My family and my mother all circled around my mind. I wondered what would become of my relationship with my Daideó if I retreated. Would I lose his love? I had to reconnect to my mother. How else, other than following in her path, could that happen? I laid my fingers on his palm, then took his hand in both of mine.

CHAPTER THIRTEEN

I now know the reaction our proposal set off at Elizabeth's court: The queen rustled the folds of her gown as she took her seat. Sir William Cecil, watchful and pensive, steadied his gaze on the queen's expression as she read the letter. Her brows came together and she smiled bemusedly before looking at her most senior advisor.

"These McDonnells will not take a side, yet they bid for one of their own kinswomen to attend my court."

Elizabeth opened both her hands into the air, her dark eyes open wide.

"What say you, Sir William?"

The candles flickered in the room as the wind outside blew through a sky now losing its sun, as it descended into dusk.

"Madame, I am in a quandary over the matter. There are advantages and risks."

"It does seem that Sorley McDonnell can take our side, without having to declare it so," the queen said.

"Yes, Madame, and we shall influence this girl. Perhaps marry her to an English nobleman, smoothing an alliance. But this girl may be a fox in lamb's fleece."

Elizabeth stood and walked around the stout wooden table, in thought. She clapped her hands and turned back to Cecil.

"We can invite her in and instill her with confidence that the English do care for the fate of their clan. They will sit well and high, as we still colonize past the Pale. And that, she can report to Sorley and James McDonnell," she said.

"Yes, perhaps the McDonnells are looking to be won," Cecil said.

"Shane O'Neill is Sorley's brother-in-law, yes? Yet the McDonnells still do not pledge their support to his cause against us," Elizabeth said.

A knock at the door signaled a servant arriving with a flagon of mead. Elizabeth and Cecil ceased their discussion until the servant had poured both cups and closed the door on his exit.

Elizabeth took several sips and placed her cup firmly on the table, as if the refreshment bubbled up an idea.

"Yes, my Spirit, methinks they seek to be wooed with such an offer—after all, it is Sorley's eldest granddaughter who he sends… and out of gratitude for us sending our army to Scotland's aid."

"Madame, we must consider the McDonnells are likely in league with the Scottish crown."

"Let them!" Elizabeth challenged. "Perhaps once we have her, we needn't give her back—what is her name?" The queen grabbed the letter among her pile of papers and read through quickly.

"Lindsay," she said, appearing a bit like an eagle spotting a salmon jumping upriver.

Elizabeth tossed the letter down toward him. "My Spirit, you are not yet convinced."

"You read me well, Your Majesty. If we are to receive this girl, it warrants our vigilance. Lindsay McDonnell will need to earn our faith and the trust of your ladies. They should be instructed to provide only simple direction to her on attending the English court, nothing else."

Elizabeth's eyes sparkled. With a flourish, she found a fresh piece of parchment and dunked a quill into the inkwell.

"We are pleased to heaven we see eye to eye on the matter. My heart tells me this may prove a better inroad into Ireland—and that it can be done peaceably."

"Madame, you shall then grant the request for us to receive this McDonnell to court?"

She looked up from her response. "We look forward to the time when she can be delivered to us."

꩜

Returning from another one of our walks, as Daideó and I came into the clearing by the castle keep, a young serving boy came running toward us. He said that the mistress had him on the watch for our return. Sorley and I quickened our step to find Mary by the entrance, folded parchment in hand.

"It's come," she said.

Sorley ushered us both down the hall passage leading to the room where we had our first meeting.

"Read it to me," he said in a low voice.

Mary unfolded the letter. The message was brief and proud, yet respectful in tone.

We agree that in trusting your goodwill toward our conjoined kingdom, we would be served well by taking your granddaughter into our royal house. Thy offer is taken as an act of conciliation to please God and this queen, for which so, you will be smiled upon in future days.

"How is it signed?" Sorley asked.

"By the queen, Elizabeth R."

"She wrote it herself?"

"That she did, husband."

A pause full of collective thoughts hung busy in the room.

"She thinks the McDonnells have taken a side," Mary said.

"The McDonnells make good on our neutrality. If we entertain Shane under a peaceful roof, then we shall also build a bridge through our kin to meet a benevolent English crown," Sorley said.

Mary bit her lip.

"What say you now, my lass, now that the queen's words have registered?"

I swallowed, and my heart's beating was making itself known.

"Ye does not have to do this bidding," Maimeó said, her eyes filling.

Sorley kept his eye contact with me.

"Of course I'm going to go," I said.

"Our lass is becoming a warrior," Sorley said.

Mary threw up her hands, turned on her heel, and left the room. She wept loudly as she left us. Sorley dropped his head, closed his eyes for a breath, and set his jaw.

"Come with me. Finlay will write our answer to Elizabeth," Sorley said, all business. I wanted to ask about Maimeó; should I go to her? But like one of his troops, I followed him in line.

"My lass, upon your arrival you would do well to spend your time watching and listening."

"Like a spy?"

Sorley considered my question and tilted his head, fingers to his beard.

"Perhaps it would be more in the service of understanding whose interests are being forwarded at Elizabeth's court and how they have won her over."

"Then I am to be a diplomat?"

He slapped one hand on the other while sparking a full grin, a Sorleyism I had come to love as it always inspired courage in me.

"Aye, my lass. That is the spirit of your post. In my years, I find you get much further with a foe when you know the taste of wine they favor."

Now, my training began on how to 'win friends and influence people' at the English court. Though unhappy, Mary agreed to teach me the etiquette. But she founded her knowledge on stories from kin who had spent time at the Scottish court, and I suspected the English customs might be different. The fashions certainly were, but I based that on my TV knowledge. It did seem that the Scotch and Irish were more practical, as this McDonnell household liked its dark sea tones in tartans accented by a little red. I had no idea how Elizabeth's royal palaces might receive my Gaelic styles.

Nevertheless, two new gowns were made for me in haste.

"I think I shall wear this one upon meeting the queen for the first time, as it shows off all our colors," I said as Siobhan helped me dress in the wool gown made of our ancient McDonnell tartan.

Maimeó and Siobhan looked at each other, doubt passing through their gazes.

"Granddaughter, a plainer gown might do for your arrival."

I asked her why. She told me it was best if I did not outshine the queen.

I stifled a laugh, but both women caught it.

"Ye disrespect your elder?" Maimeó said.

I shook my head with fervor.

"It is just new for me to talk about gowns I am to wear to meet a head of state—a queen no less!"

Maimeó wasn't really buying it, but she let it pass.

"Methinks you will find humor in what the English wear, with all their fluff and puff. Seems like a wasteful lot. How much cloth does one need for a sleeve?"

"Or a man's breeches?" Siobhan added as she used her hands to gesture a ballooning out about the bum.

We all laughed hard, from both the stress and Siobhan pointing out the truth. Oh God, please let me keep my composure once all that costume is in my sight. What if the court is ridiculous?

Siobhan helped me undress. With care, she laid the pieces over her arm and took it to another room.

"Who will help me get dressed once I'm there?"

"The queen's other ladies," Maimeó said.

"I hope they are kind."

"Your English will help. They will soon forget where you come from."

"Maimeó, I fear I will not speak just like them," I said, thinking about my American accent.

"You sound like a Sassenach more than you think, and ya won't resort to Gaelic, when you can't think of the word you need in English."

"No, I am far from mastering the Irish language," I said.

Maimeó crinkled her nose.

"You can learn yourself better of it when you come back to us."

A warm glow hatched in my tummy and moved through my heart. She kissed me and hugged me close to her chest. We stayed in the embrace for several seconds until Siobhan returned.

As we parted, Maimeó wiped away a tear. To counter, she placed her hands on her hips, surveyed the room, and mentioned the rest of the day's itinerary of activities.

"The trunks have been airing out for two days," Siobhan said.

"I think we should wrap the sweetest smelling herbs and place them at the bottom of the trunks before any packing takes place," Maimeó said.

"Yes, please include the herbs."

Siobhan took her leave from the room. Maimeó busied herself with inspecting the inside of the trunks—a task she had already done. I wanted to distract her.

"Maimeó, why have I not met any of our family?"

She stopped.

"Only Shane," I said, frowning.

She sighed. "Your grandfather keeps them away. How would we explain you?"

That made sense.

"Yet, he dispatched word to our eldest son to come to Dunanynie. As our story to the crown is that you are his daughter, your grandfather thought he should be aware of his role."

"So, I will meet him."

"Alastair will arrive the day before you are to leave. He and your grandfather will ride out with your carriage."

"It will be a goodbye in stages," I said, trying to keep my voice steady.

CHAPTER FOURTEEN

Sitting on a rock ensconced within the summery spread of the castle garden, I rose from my meditation full of fresh air and a calm, steady joy. This is how I want to feel, as I leave for the English court. If only I could remain in the thin transparent orb of peace which encircled me.

Continuing my slow and full breaths, I swallowed all serenity when Maimeó thundered down the path, red in the face.

"Lindsay, from where you come, does a boiling pot know when to cease its bubbling?"

I jumped at remembering I had set a pot of leaves and water on the fire to make Maimeó a special tea to ease her joints.

"The burnt herbs leave an unholy stench, and the pot shall never be the same."

"I am so sorry."

She pulled me toward the kitchen where, once over the threshold, the skunky odor became sickening. Katherine, the cook, pointed to the pot now blackened on the inside with stuck vegetation.

"What do you want me to say, I am very sorry."

Katherine's brow furrowed as she took a place next to Maimeó.

"Apologies only matter if you work to remedy the offense," Maimeó said, locking arms with Katherine in solidarity.

"This won't happen again," I offered, thinking there were plenty of pots about the kitchen.

She unhooked herself from Katherine and pointed to a shelf where there was a small wooden casket. Maimeó told me to wet my finger and stick it inside.

"What is this?" I said, wondering if this was my punishment.

With a jabbed thrust of her finger, she told me to stick it in my mouth.

"'Tis salt, yes," I said slightly relieved.

"You scrub this forsaken pot with that salt and realize how fortunate you are to have no nicks and scrapes upon your hands. Although it would serve you well to feel the burn in your wounds."

Holy Christ—I wanted to run.

"Where shall I—"

"Outside by the well."

Maimeó handed me a swath of linen and marched me outside the kitchen door. Kneeling at the well, I spread the salt along the inside, wet the cloth, and began to scrub. I wished I could magically produce a Brillo pad or just let the damn thing soak in hot water somewhere.

Standing over me, Maimeó bent down, face to face, sweat dampening her skin.

"You need to understand how deeds left unfinished bestow an awful toil on others."

Her words stung as I rubbed the coarse salt against the unyielding residue. I could not even glance at her as she straightened up, but I registered her wincing in my periphery, as she walked away.

I had let her down.

After a few moments, I ventured to peer around me in hopes of pinpointing where she was, but she was nowhere to be seen. I also checked for Daideó, hoping he wouldn't find me like this. As I scrubbed, I remembered pieces of my past shame, like getting yelled at by my mother in front of my friends for bringing home a shitty report card. *Lindsay often cites excuses for not handing in homework. Lindsay continues to not apply herself.* I remember my father stopped talking to me when I forgot to go to a college interview. His silence was like being pushed out into a winter night, sopping wet.

My tears now added to the scouring mix but I didn't dare bring my salt-covered hands to my eyes. Seeing so little progress on the pot, my heart spilled over with angst wondering, "What the hell am I doing here?"

Up came a mouthful of stomach acid that, together with my fingers becoming raw, propelled me to take the damn thing right back to the kitchen. I paused midstride once spotting Maimeó inside, but continued, telling Katherine I needed boiling water to make further progress.

"That's what sent you to penance to begin with," Maimeó said, approaching me.

"It makes no sense to scrub my hands to flames right before I am to take my leave for court."

"Should have given thought to that before—"

"What's this?" Daideó said in a booming voice, standing at the other entrance.

"This McDonnell can scarce brew tea without mishap. How can you let her go off to be on her own?" Maimeó said, her voice the loudest I had ever heard it.

His face darkened and tensed but he said nothing right away.

"I am making my amends. To do it properly, I need to have boiling water."

Daideó told Katherine to heat up the water. He took Maimeó by the hand, clearly intending to usher her into another part of the castle. They exchanged sharp words in Gaelic as they left the kitchen.

I leaned against the large wooden worktable as I tried to hold myself together, relieved to see Katherine pour water into a large kettle and place it on the heat. The cracks and hisses of her stoking the fire made the silence less awkward between us. Once it had finally boiled, I transferred the rumbling water into my poor pot and took it back outside, where I watched the swirls of steam rise, wishing I could follow them up to the atmosphere.

The swish of footfalls on the long grass preceded my grandfather's arrival—him now looking calmer.

"Aye, your grandmother is none too pleased with either of us."

I wanted to ask what had crawled up her ass but chose something tamer to say.

"She needn't assassinate my character while I am trying to build my confidence," I said curtly.

Daideó was surprised. "Is that how your century speaks about your elders?"

"I'm just telling the truth."

"She wants you to stay here with us, 'tis all it is, my lass."

He took a seat on the ground next to me. The quiet between us created space for my fear to kick up. I couldn't swallow down the knot in my throat. Tears were the only expression I could manage, despite myself.

"You are of a changed mind?" he asked.

"What if I become the cause of more suffering? What if I anger the queen?"

Even the chieftain, Sorley McDonnell, appeared overtaken by the prospect, but he found his footing.

"Other than this pitiful pot, you have made matters here much better."

"How?"

"A prayer answered gives hope and faith. I called for help and, Lindsay, you are the one who took heed. Were you not born but centuries from now? And yet you are here, and after many a day, you are still here."

I nodded. I heard the truth in what he was conveying.

"It took great love to use the magic to find your place with us."

"It was your love which called me here when I needed it the most. I have treasured my time here with you and Maimeó."

"My lass, always remember where you come from—and remember our common hours together."

New tears sprang up, but they were from gratitude, liberated from my inner bullshit.

"I'll remember," I said, marking the moment. "And Maimeó?"
"She will pray for your return."
"Do you command it?"
"No, it is freely offered," he said.
I reflected back his smile.
"Daideó, I need to finish my scouring," I said, noting the release of the herbs off the sides.

He rose, gave me a pat on my arm, and left me to finish my task. This experience was the jewel of my training, finding fortitude and deepening my commitment to following through and figuring it out. That was the moment when I was sure I had chosen the right path.

On the day before my departure, I wondered if I would ever return to Dunanynie Castle. I processed what it meant to be leaving my refuge made from the air rising off the sea, the sight of my beloveds and the countryside that expanded my soul.

I entered the kitchen, and Katherine, who had softened toward me, served me porridge without me having to say a word. While savoring the rounded barley on my tongue sweetened by the creamy milk, fresh from the cow, Katherine placed a hunk of bread smeared with one of her amazing berry jams on a plate next to my bowl. I'd miss her too.

Later in the afternoon, I embarked on a solitary walk beyond the castle's walls, to commune with the ocean. I was preparing for separation from my new-old family. It helped that the sparkles on the water were the same in any century and place, as was the sun.

Breathing in the brine of the cool ocean air, I appreciated there were no chemicals here and all I was eating was naturally organic and sustaining. Would England be the same? I mused about the everyday of being at a royal court. An idea flitted through me. This might actually be fun.

"Yeah," I said, immediately, "fun is probably not even close."

CHAPTER FIFTEEN

By that evening, Alastair, 'my father,' arrived. Resembling Mary with his dark copper hair, he had an easy way about him, more like Sorley. As I am not sure how much of the true story was told to him, I trusted him to his role. His bright face stoked my faith.

In contrast, Maimeó wore a drawn and sad face, as she readied me for my departure. In our final moments together the next morning, she examined my hands. She then kissed them which led us into a massive bear hug. We both had trouble letting go.

Once I'd climbed into the carriage and taken my seat, Maimeó handed me a quilted cushion through the door. "Lindsay, you will need this," she said.

The padding of my layers of skirts was enough, but the pillow meant an infusion of comfort and soothing from Dunanynie. With my final expression of thanks, I didn't try to hold back my tears. She smiled at me through her own, as the horses, starting their slow pace, jerked the carriage into motion. Daideó and Alastair flanked each side.

As we traveled along the road, my grandfather peered in at me.

"How do you find your time, my lass?"

"Better, now that we are on the journey."

The trip was brief down to the port. At the dock, there was a small galley-type ship with porridge-colored sails, not yet fully bleached by the sun. The crew seemed like mere boys, but the captain had a few decades on them. Daideó assured me he was well weathered and well trusted. He then kissed me on the forehead and held my face, transmitting his pride.

"Remember where ye come from," he said.

I ascended the gangplank, my heels knocking loudly the whole way, announcing my presence. The captain extended his hand to steady me as I stepped onto the ship. His full cheeks played up his round and amiable eyes. He bowed his head and called down, "It's an honor to serve ye McDonnells."

Daideó nodded. "We trust ye will tend our lass well."

The captain tipped his hat and directed me to the best vantage point to wave goodbye. As I acclimated, I was grateful there were a few other women onboard and one had children in tow.

Working my way to the side, I found a foothold to hoist myself above the ship's banister. Daideó stood tall on the dock, next to Alastair and their horses. The first time I waved, neither saw me. But I spotted a hooded creature behind them, cloaked in black. A pale hand gave a wave and then took down the hood. It was Julia. I gestured back and placed my hand over my heart. Her seeing me off reminded me I was leaving yet another friend. One that shared one of my most secret of intimacies as a fellow time traveler. And then there was my admiration for her willingness to stay put, unnoticed, for her cause.

In another attempt to catch the attention of my McDonnells, Daideó saw me, but his smile was tense. My instinct was to blow him a kiss—to him and Alastair—and so I did. Daideó laughed and Alastair took a half step back, after which he blew a kiss back to me, albeit a bit awkwardly.

Soon the ship separated from the dock, its movement steady over the lapping water in the harbor. I beheld the bustle at the shoreline as my family got smaller and smaller. It surprised me they stayed. In fact,

I never saw them leave. They might still have been standing there next to their horses for all I knew.

As the sails caught the wind to propel us south and east, the late afternoon sky promised to keep the sun for us. While the ship cut through the dark green waves, an older boy found his place next to me, taking delight in seeing how the vessel sliced through the water.

When the wind became too much for my ears, I climbed down. With feet on deck, the cutting movement across the chop left me woozy. A shipmate read my face. His accent was the most English I had yet heard.

"Keep looking at the horizon," he said. "And if you feel sick, aim it over the side."

I nodded a thanks.

A young woman, her face framed in blonde curls, caught my eye. She spoke as she sidled up to me, but it sounded French. I wasn't sure how to say that I didn't comprehend in 1560s French. I gestured to my mouth and ears. I finally said it in English.

She touched her head and opened her eyes wide. I think that meant she got it. Pulling on my hand, she wanted me to follow her down into the ship. Trying to negotiate the steep ladder in long skirts made me almost want to give up and stay on deck. But her words had an encouraging tone to them. We then found a bench, among most of the other twenty or so passengers.

"Aller en Angleterre?" she asked.

I shrugged and tried to apologize with my eyes.

"Do you speak any English?" I asked, feeling every bit like the ugly American.

"English?" she said and pointed both her hands back to herself and nodded. "Je vais en Angleterre." I think she understood what we were talking about better than I did.

"London?" I asked.

"Oui, London, toi?"

"Oui." I nodded and pointed back to myself.

"Toi France?" I asked.

Her small eyebrows came together. She must have thought me a bit soft in the head.

"Non—London," she said.

"I know, I was asking where you come from."

She eyed me as her wheels were turning. I used my hands to move forward saying London and then pushed them off to the other side as I said "France." She laughed and clapped her hands—good, we understood each other. Wanting to continue our connection, I foolishly rubbed my stomach while frowning. My French companion nodded as she lost her smile. Great, now we're both thinking about it.

"Don't make me swab yer sick down here. Up on deck and off the sides for that," barked a young but hardened shipmate.

"Shit," I said to the floor.

"None of that right where you sit neither," he said loudly in my ear. He stood over me, waiting for me to acknowledge him. I looked in the other direction. Instead of moving on, he yelled the original warning again to the galley. In my peripheral sight, I saw my companion avert her eyes and slump her shoulders. Gambling that I was going to be taller than this obnoxious dick, I stared straight ahead and stood up slowly, rising above him. He wasn't having any of this and moved on, scowling as he made his rounds.

My French friend gawked at me for several seconds, mouth slightly open. Then through a snarl, she flicked her thumb along the top of her teeth and threw her eyes in his direction. I nodded and sat down, wondering what chapter she was starting in England.

After some time, I was unable to sit any longer in the dark underbelly. Specters of ships splintering apart played across my consciousness, leaving me wondering if it was possible to manage even one swim stroke in all these layers of wool and linen. I pointed to the steps as an attempt to ask my new friend if she wanted to go. She shook her head.

Back up on deck, I walked over to the spot from where I had last seen Daideó and Alastair. Finding the horizon made it more bearable. In this time to myself, my new reality struck me: I was on my way to become part of Queen Elizabeth I's court.

Captain McCallister made well on his promise to Daideó, inviting me to dine with him each evening along with a couple of other notable travelers. Marie, my French friend, was one of them. She was but a month into her marriage to Francis Kirkpatrick, a broad-shouldered merchant, who appeared at dinner bedecked in a multicolored silk jerkin and fine gauge hose, which seemed a bit much for this ship's voyage.

"Master Kirkpatrick, I'd mistake you for an Englishman," the captain said, on more than one occasion.

Kirkpatrick translated for Marie. Each time, she'd turn her eyes to me, to check my reaction. At her prompting, Kirkpatrick asked me about my purpose for traveling to England.

"We have family business in and around London," I responded.

Both the captain and Kirkpatrick scrutinized me with matching frowns and pinched brows.

"Forgive the query, but why has the chieftain not sent one of his sons?" Kirkpatrick asked.

Marie looked at the two of them and then to me.

"The business is delicate in manner—a woman's work," I said.

Neither of the men appeared satisfied but the captain relented.

"So be it. England is again ruled by another of Henry VIII's daughters, and Scotland has her queen regent."

"Captain, you speak in jest, this cannot be the way of the world henceforth," Kirkpatrick said.

"I agree with your sentiment. But perhaps the chieftain comprehends matters in a way we do not."

Both men returned to their meals. Without making eye contact, the captain threw a glance over to me, checking in. But Kirkpatrick was not done. His eyes lit up and he leaned forward.

"I have heard it said, Elizabeth Tudor will not remain Queen of England."

"Master Kirkpatrick, how do you mean?" I asked.

"She is weak, perhaps illegitimate, and in France, Nostradamus prophesized she will not live far into her realm."

"Kirkpatrick, you should take care not to speak of any regent's end," McCallister said in a low, forbidding voice.

"What is to be her end?" I asked.

Captain McCallister slammed his open hand on the table.

"This conversation must cease."

Marie eyeballed me, as if I was responsible for the captain's actions.

Kirkpatrick stared at the captain dead on but acquiesced as he continued eating. I struggled with needing an answer.

I hoped to get Kirkpatrick alone. On the last day, I found him on deck, but he kept himself locked in a conversation with another gentleman of trade. With only a bow of the head, he opted out of making a mere introduction.

"Sir, I entreat you to speak with me."

"I dare not, but I wish you Godspeed," he said turning away.

Thoughts of being delivered to a queen with a death sentence took up residence in both my waking and dreaming hours. It clung to me with a cold chill as the ship anchored at the royal dockyard. It amplified in my mind as two of the ship's crew lowered me down into a rowboat, manned by another duo of crew hands. I thought about what Maimeó said, that I should not trust my knowledge as history was no doubt altered by my mother and I coming here. Would this new trajectory hurt Ireland? What about the myriad of issues for humanity. Did we have any power to weaken the hold of slavery, to prevent an iota of damage from the mistreatment of indigenous people? Instead, by being here, could we be intensifying the factors that put the planet into climate crisis? Oh God.

Marie waved to me from the ship's deck. I must have worn my distress as, at last, with pity in his eyes, Kirkpatrick lifted his arm to bid me farewell and good luck.

It was a few minutes before we reached the dock, and I was helped out over the edge of the boat and onto land. There, I was met by a footman and a finely attired lady.

"Mistress Lindsay McDonnell?"

I sized up the lady and the footman and affirmed my identity.

"In service to her queen's Majesty, I, Lady Skew, am to accompany you to court," she said with authority.

I nodded while checking the tendency to thrust my hand out to shake.

"My trunks," I said.

Lady Skew pointed to the carriage behind us.

"Your trunks will be collected and delivered to your room at the palace. Despite your origins, the queen's ladies are most anxious to meet you."

I liken this to her patting me on the head with her hand while crushing my toes with her heel.

"Making their acquaintance will be my pleasure," I said.

"You will find yourself more like bedfellows, remaining constantly in their company as your standing is to be a lady of the queen's privy chamber."

"Lady Skew, pray tell is that a well-placed rank?"

She sighed while making a show of pulling the hem of her gloves past each respective wrist.

"I do not foresee you becoming a lady of the bedchamber, if that is to what you aspire."

Once inside, Lady Skew sat across from me, her skirts taking up far more room than mine. With my own dignity, I arranged my gown as best I could.

"Mistress McDonnell, how did you find your journey?" She spoke as if we were starting anew.

"I am happy to be on land," I quipped.

A hint of a smile.

"How long is the ride to the palace?"

"Less than a half hour hence," she said as if I should have known.

I nodded, realizing it was harder to communicate with Skew than it was with Marie.

After a few minutes of silence, I gathered that Lady Skew was by no means uncomfortable maintaining the trip in quiet. Maybe not every space had to be filled with conversation. Instead, I focused on the spoked wheels vibrating across the ground. It was a welcome contrast to rocking over the sea, until the road became bumpy, hurling us to and fro, returning me to the familiar nausea.

Fortunately, that did not last long, and I began to feel twinges of hunger. From my bag, I fished out a hunk of bread.

"Would you care for some?" I asked, bare-faced brazen.

Lady Skew tsked. I am not sure I had ever been tsked at before. It made me feel like I was the Cookie Monster, so I ate delicately, in small pieces, chewing thoroughly. From time to time, I would cast a quick glance to try and read her face. It was emotionless, solidly disinterested. Good, so maybe I wasn't already mucking things up, looking like an Irish savage. I mean people gotta eat.

After I'd finished, I took in the dwellings and close-set buildings of London, discerning how it was different from the open hills and hollows of Ballycastle. There were so many more people here. And they were quite friendly, waving and cheering as we passed by. I couldn't help but gesture back.

"They see Her Majesty's crest on the side," Lady Skew said, pushing out a sigh after the third incident.

"Is it proper to wave back to them?"

"They see you are not the queen," she said.

"Maybe they are left to think you are the queen."

"Mistress McDonnell, I am most certainly not pretending to be the queen," she said, her eyes glowering.

"My apologies, I intend only friendly conversation, Lady Skew."

She lowered her shoulders but kept her gaze looking out the window. I hated not knowing where I stood.

"Lady Skew, do you accept my apology?"

She glared at me for a moment.

"The queen's ladies need to make much work of you," she said.

Bitch, I thought.

CHAPTER SIXTEEN

As the carriage rode through the gates into the inner courtyard, the sounds of the horses' steps ricocheted about the palace walls. Guards outfitted in breastplates of armor and standing at attention held axe blades mounted on sturdy wooden poles. I wondered how sharp they were and if they ever had to use them.

I was grateful to arrive at Hampton Court since it was familiar to me, having been here when I was fifteen, when the bricks weren't so red. Now it was vastly more daunting, knowing a breathing Tudor resided here and was in charge of it all.

The carriage stopped near a line of well-appointed women led by Kat Ashley, a firm maternal figure in stance, with features carved from kindness. Through the carriage window, she sent me a genuine smile. My breath came and went a little easier within her friendlier air. I hoped Lady Skew would take her leave as I worried she'd report my inadequacies and that one grin coming my way would disappear.

"Mistress Ashley, it buoys me to see you in such good health," Lady Skew said as if she had never held a negative thought in her life.

Kat bowed her head and welcomed Lady Skew to Hampton Court. Within the carriage I rose to a deep hunch and took my first step outside, my height being a hindrance now. The footman assisted me with both hands as I uncurled myself.

Lady Skew gestured as she showed me off, like I was a piece of art she'd crafted herself.

"I present you, Mistress Lindsay McDonnell of Ballycastle in Ulster," she said.

The other ladies began eyeing me up, unsure what to make of me. Kat extended a welcome and introduced herself as the First Lady of the Queen's Bedchamber.

"We trust that Lady Skew kept you in good company."

"Yes, she kept me well," I said, telling my first lie at court.

"Was your journey eventful?" Kat asked.

"No, just long in duration," I said.

Kat laughed. "Down from the northwest lands of the kingdom, the queen will be glad that her realm extends in a 'long journey.'"

I surveyed the other ladies to read Kat's intent. But they all wore versions of the same wan smile. Kat and one of the youngest of the ladies guided me into the palace, up the wide stone stairs, and through a set of adjoining rooms. As Kat closed the heavy wooden door with great care, I noticed the walls of the chamber wore russet-colored wood panels. Upon them hung brightly threaded tapestries of woodland scenes depicting a deer hunt.

How cool, the story of a hunted and tormented animal, exactly what I want to look at every day, I thought.

"These will be your lodgings with Mistress Bexley," she said, and Bexley gave me a small grin. Kat then took a gander at my gown.

"Mistress McDonnell, may we inquire about the contents of your trunks?"

"I have two gowns made for the occasion of serving at court."

Kat placed her hand around her chin, and Bexley took that as her cue to pull my dresses out for inspection.

"Is this the style in Ireland?" Bexley said, a hint of ribbing in her tone.

"It is, but pray tell, will this not suit me here?"

"Not when you attend unto the queen," Kat said.

"Kat, perhaps Mistress McDonnell shall meet the queen in her native Irish dress, to remind Her Majesty whence she comes," Bexley said, her smile wide. "The queen may like to see the transformation of the mistress from a far edge of her kingdom to here in its heart."

"Your guidance on such matters would be most helpful," I said.

Kat tilted her head, chin still in hand.

"Mistress McDonnell, the queen will inquire about your speech. Your English is plain spoken yet it is out of the ordinary and not matched to that coming from Gaelic lands."

"Mistress Ashley, I owe that to my Scottish nobility."

Bexley gawked at me and then at Kat. This comment I came to learn was a magic bullet. They now knew I was from an Irish chieftain whose family also ranked high in Scotland.

Just then, the chamber door was thrown open and a guard made a terse announcement.

"The Queen."

The three of us waited as the icon herself strode into the chamber. I was slow to curtsy as the other ladies had done immediately. Elizabeth wore a simple silk gown, un-bejeweled, save for the two strands of pearls hanging down to her solar plexus. She wore a tiny tiara of pearls that emerged through the top of her reddish gold locks. To my surprise, her eyes were not blue, like in the movies, but dark umber orbs charged with unapologetic intelligence. Fortunately, while she was taller than all her ladies, she wasn't as tall as me.

"Kat, is this the arrival from our Irish kingdom?"

"Yes, Your Majesty, allow me to present Mistress Lindsay McDonnell."

I bowed my head and stood with my hands folded before me. The queen met my gaze, looking amused. Not able to help myself, I smiled. The queen cocked her head while extending her slender, ringed hand. I took it in my fingers and gave it a small peck, hoping I was following protocol.

"What news from your grandfather, Sorley McDonnell?"

"He sends blessings and peaceful tidings to Your Majesty."

"And he sends you," she said, beaming with a good dose of triumph mixed in.

"That he does," I said.

She then leaned forward to inspect my skirts. "Mistress McDonnell, I see you wear your kin's plaid."

Kat opened her mouth. Elizabeth raised her hand, signaling for Kat to hold.

"It is only to show Your Majesty from whence I have been sent. A reminder of the harmonious intent of the McDonnells."

"That intent is understood. But now you are at the English court and as one of my ladies, you shall wear gowns more befitting to your service. I trust the McDonnells sent monies for such gowns to be made."

Kat took a step and opened her hands. I stopped breathing.

"Sorley McDonnell sent a purse for such purposes, Your Grace."

"As requested, and we are happy to know of his obedience."

"As am I," I said relieved.

"You would doubt your grandfather in his bid to secure you here at court?" the queen asked.

"I could never doubt him. I am just glad the purse arrived safely."

The queen pressed her lips and took her leave while commenting, "It is reassuring to have those on which to depend." Her remark seemed kind, but I wasn't sure.

The queen stopped at the threshold and whispered a quick word into Kat's ear.

"I look forward to seeing you in attendance at church," the queen called back, leaving us to sort out the energy kicked up by her presence.

Kat forced a smile. "And now that's done," she said as she bobbed her chin.

"How did the queen find me?" I asked.

"I do not think you irritated Her Majesty," she said.

Mistress Bexley took up my Irish gowns and proceeded to place them back into the trunks. A lump of guilt rose in my throat; Maimeó took such pride sending me off with those gowns I would never wear.

Kat looked at me and signaled Bexley to stop.

"Methinks that until a new wardrobe is supplied, Mistress McDonnell would be better suited in the blue gown for church." Bexley nodded blank-faced and laid it onto the bed.

The tension in the room remained. The initial light-heartedness of Kat and Bexley was replaced by silence, heavy with conditioned reticence.

"Church will be within the hour. I shall help you re-dress," Kat said, dismissing Bexley.

Once the door closed, Kat began busying herself in undoing my ensemble. The long seconds of quiet inspired me to speak up.

"Mistress Kat, I wanted to express my appreciation for the kindness you have shown," I said from my heart.

Kat's eyes creased into a smile.

"My wish is to be marvelous in my role as one of the queen's ladies," I continued.

"You do speak so forthrightly, my girl, but no matter, I will help you to find your way."

I tried to make eye contact with her as she unsheathed my arms from their sleeves, but she remained focused on her work. I choked up and tried gazing upward to quell my giant tears.

"Mistress, is this your first time away from your homeland?" she asked.

"Aye, and I am sorry. It's not what a queen's lady should show the world," I said.

"It is not the world in here, just us."

I pushed out a long, quiet exhale, taking refuge in her words as she pulled my skirts away from my waist.

Kat gave my linen shift a rub and her approval. She then wrapped a too small corset she referred to as a *body* around my torso, and with deft hands began tightening. As it flattened my breasts, I wanted to stop her—Maimeó never bound me up like this at Dunanynie. I tried to take in a full, deep inhalation, but my encaged ribs could not expand out. To stave off anxiety of not being able to breathe with ease,

I placed my hand a few inches below my collarbone, taking comfort that the tops of my lungs were still free.

"I am of a new thought about a proper gown for you," Kat said, disappearing into the room adjacent. I immediately tried to jam my hands under the corset to pull it out, but I only managed to slide the tips of my fingers underneath.

I sat on the bed while I tried to get used to the constriction. The bed itself was firm and stuffed with wool; its coverings were a muted crimson hue. Pulling it all back, I ran my hand over the linen sheets and imagined the immediate future, starting with tonight when I would be lying here in the dark, sensing this time and place.

Kat returned with a deep green gown in her arms. My heart jumped, banishing the thought of asking to have the corset let out.

"Mistress, we shall try this one. If it fits you well enough, methinks it will be most pleasing to the queen."

With several layers of skirting on me, Kat frowned as she ascertained the outer gown was not hanging as it should, given my height. She reached under the layers and adjusted my farthingale down lower on my hips. Last, she added the sleeves which billowed out from my arm but came up short no matter how much she tugged.

"Mistress, do not permit this to draw across your plate," Kat said. "If it is not within small reach, take care in asking to be served."

"Do we serve anything to the queen?"

"You surely jest. The servants of the hall serve all of us, the queen being first in all matters. Through the meal, we perform the duty of providing Her Royal Majesty with court news and feminine accompaniment. As we sup, she will on occasion ask for a recounting of a tale, so you shall set yourself up well to have a collection."

"Of stories?" I asked.

"Yes, the more fanciful, the better," Kat said and winked.

"Pray tell what Her Majesty has already heard?"

Kat widened her eyes. "There are too many to count."

I'm not sure what I was worried about—I had the benefit of the last five centuries of stories to share.

Kat stood back, fiddling with the locket hanging from her own neck as she focused on my throat.

"I have a pendant," I offered and went toward my trunks to find my jewel bag. But as I searched, it was nowhere to be found.

"'Tis taken from your trunks by a ship scoundrel no doubt," she said. It panged in my heart to think of already losing my McDonnell accessories.

Grasping a wooden box sitting atop a small narrow table against the wall, Kat drew out a necklace of three dropped pearls. As she fastened the ribbon at the back of my neck, she said, "I shall inform Mistress Bexley that you don these pearls with my permission."

I swallowed—what could possibly go wrong here?

She then gave my hair a once over and smoothed a few pieces.

"You'll look a fine addition to the queen's table," she said, leading me to the looking glass. Surprising, it was not as clear as the one back in Dunanynie Castle, but it was good enough for me to see myself through another outward transformation. Here I stood, resembling a stately sixteenth-century noblewoman, as the light played off the shine of the damask fabric of my sleeves. And can I just say—I freakin' loved that dress. I met Kat's eyes in the mirror.

"Methinks you like the English style best," she said.

Looking at the tartan skirts now in a pile on the bed, I felt like a turd, but turning back to see myself, I could not stifle my enthusiasm.

"This gown is beautiful, and I am grateful. Is this someone else's as well?"

"It was made for the tall-statured Lady Humpford, before she became with child and needed to retire to her husband's Devonshire estate."

"Will she be back for this loveliness?" I said, pulling out the folds of the full skirt.

"Nay, I think not."

My growing giddiness surprised me, but it seemed to please Kat and made an instant bond between us. Checking herself, Kat set her lips into a serious countenance.

"Mistress, be well warned that some courtiers shall scrutinize your arrival at church."

"Do you have words of guidance for me?"

"Do not bask in their attention and do not take any disdain to heart."

"Then I shall not become an entertainment to the men and not be upset by the judgment of the ladies."

Kat paused, her intelligence recognizing mine. She then gave it to me between the eyes.

"It's the queen's estimation of you that shall be your only concern. All will turn away from you if Her Majesty finds you displeasing."

CHAPTER SEVENTEEN

I followed the other ladies into the chapel where I was a magnet for bemused looks. I attempted friendly eye contact, but with very little reciprocation. Rousing hope, I scanned the assembly for my mother. Adrenaline spiked through me once my eyes caught sight of a woman with a frame like hers. I waited for her to turn around, but she stared straight ahead for an interminable amount of time. Her eventual side glance and unfamiliar profile hurt my heart.

Once nestled in our pews of hard wood, I appreciated my large skirts. As I spread the layers of fabric across the bench, I found if I bowed my legs and sat toward the front of the bench, a close approximation to my usual meditation posture, no one would know. A little grounding mindfulness was the best antidote to my rising anxiety.

Taking in this moment of heavy and sacred silence, my eyes migrated upward to the royal blue of the vaulted ceiling, glinting with six-pointed stars of gold. My gaze rested on the stained-glass window that, instead of having depictions of a dying Christ, exhibited a massive figure of King Henry VIII assembled in reds and greens, lit up by the sun.

All heads turned to look up behind us. We bowed as the queen entered her own pews which sat fifteen feet above, looking down and out on the whole chapel. She appeared to match the gilded medallions and trimmings of the chapel's structure with her own gold-threaded and cobalt gown, accentuated by ropes of pearls intermixed with jewels that sparkled in attunement to the stained glass at the other end.

She released us with a gesture of her hand and all our necks slowly swiveled to face the bishop as he started the service at the front of the chapel. Having started life out as Catholic, I had never been to a Protestant service before. At best, I remember breaking into the Methodist church when my friend, who was in charge of watering the plants while her minister was on vacation, locked the keys inside the building.

Coming out of that memory, I saw my reality spreading all around in sober, dark shades of religion framed as eternal life or damnation. I tuned into the sermon, checking my hands were properly in my lap, like the other ladies. Practicing an inward smile at my secret leg position, I soon thought this might be discovered from the queen's perch —so that put an end to that. Following the example of my fellow ladies, I clasped my hands in the appropriate prayer position. The recitation of the Lord's Prayer was one I could manage, albeit within the decibels of a mouse.

After the service, the queen addressed us from her perch in a proud voice twinned by the gratification warming her features. "Take the guidance that has been offered today for it is the soul's language and keep it close to thy heart."

We all bowed in unison to Her Majesty. She seemed both softened yet emboldened by being the other object of worship, after the Trinity, of course. She maintained her smile as she beheld her court. As I contemplated the assemblage of her people, my breath caught in the back of my throat as it appeared that several of the men were sporting noticeable erections—clad in silk and brocade, to match their outfits! I realized these were codpieces, designed to impress. To me they were obscene, especially in church. I hoped none of these men would try to talk to me—ever—I don't think I could keep a straight face.

In contrast, the queen's eyes brightened as she locked gaze with one of those well-decorated male courtiers. In his hand was a hat plumed with a particularly large feather which curled around itself. He bowed his dark head to Elizabeth but maintained confident eye contact with her throughout.

Damn, I thought. What is this all about?

As the sun receded from the horizon, the dusk filled in all the space with its purple sky. Soon, Kat dismissed both me and Bexley to retire to our shared bedchamber. It was like being sent to bed early, while also being a respite from having to be on, for the whole of the group.

Bexley led us into our chamber, stout candle in hand, which did little to chase off the gloom of the creeping blackness waiting in the corners. Seeking the brightest part of the room, I stood square in front of the low burning fire and slipped off my shoes, where the warmth played across my toes.

At Dunanynie, I had little need to seek refuge in watching a screen, as I loved sitting in the genial upstairs rooms with my grandparents— my ancestors. But here, there was a greater tension about this English castle. Craving a way to unwind, the old habit of ending a long day with a good show on TV was asking to be fed.

"Mistress, I must inquire, do you sleep in fits?"

"What do you mean, Mistress Bexley?"

"I slumber lightly and do not take well to being tossed by another's turning or noisome breathing," she said looking at the floor.

"I have never heard I do so, but you are welcome to wake me if my breathing does offend."

"Oh, it is with appreciation that I receive your offer. And you will not strike me if I shake thee awake?"

"Of course not, my dear. Has that happened to you before?"

She averted her eyes again as she shook her head.

"And will you ensure I do not oversleep? I would not want to vex Kat."

"That is my duty. To help you learn your way as one of the queen's ladies."

"Is it a hardship for you, Mistress Bexley?"

"I am glad of the honor. For you represent the vastness of the queen's realm. My wish is for you to be welcomed here. And for you to know your place."

I forced a smile, as her tone sounded rehearsed.

"Now we shall ready ourselves for bed," she said, gesturing for me to turn so she could unlace me from my gown. It was a relief to loosen all the pieces that bound my torso, including the English *body*.

"Forgive this extra labor for you," I said after some time of her tugging at the fabric down my back."

"In Ireland, are all the women of such height as you, Mistress?"

"No, I am the tallest I have ever seen there, or here."

"Well, you will have to marry a taller man," she said.

Bexley handed me a shawl to place around my shoulders once I got down to my shift. It was already warm as she pulled it from a chair close to the fire. She started to smile as if suppressing a laugh.

"Forgive me, Mistress, I had the thought that you and your taller husband may have a house full of giants running about, instead of mere children."

"Don't wish that for me, lest it come true," I said, appreciative of her playfulness.

"Shall I free you as well?" I asked.

She twirled a half circle and backed up, placing her arms out to the sides. I did my best to unfasten her layered sleeves. It was easy to ask her for direction, and she obliged, her enjoyment clear in teaching the Irish one about how English fashion works.

Taking down her hair, Bexley snatched a wooden brush from a nearby table and began running it through her mane, which fell to her waist. She gestured she'd brush mine. I let my hair tumble down from my French hood, exposing that it only grazed my shoulders.

"Mistress, is this an Irish custom to keep your locks shorn to such a length?"

"It is, we cut our hair on certain birthdays. It is like picking the harvest, allowing all things that grow to lessen their burden and progress unencumbered."

Bexley took what I said with a sober nod as I offered her the back of my head, smiling to myself. With gentleness, starting at the crown, she pulled the brush down to my ends.

"Did you have to cut it all off?" she finally asked.

"My birthday was just before the spring," I said.

She laughed, relieved.

"You thought I cut it all off from the top of my head?"

"I did, Mistress. Methinks I would not know what to do if I lived in Ireland. Maybe I should have to run away on my birthdays."

We giggled imagining her running through the countryside, taking cover in barns under haystacks and inside horses' stalls.

"What is next?" I asked.

"We take prayer and lay our heads down to sleep."

No Netflix then.

Once in bed, with the canopy curtains drawn around us like a cocoon, my standing here at court was niggling at me.

"Mistress Bexley, how long have you been serving the queen."

"Since Michaelmas last."

"And how did you know if your service pleased the queen?"

"She spoke kindly to me and often."

"Then if she does not speak kindly to me and often, am I to take that as poor performance—a poor opinion of my service?"

Bexley rolled onto her side and propped a hand under her head without speaking.

"It is bad news then?" I asked.

"While the queen can be mercurial in her humors, she is a generous and sympathetic monarch. Before Easter this year, she held Maundy while we were at Whitehall."

"What is Maundy?"

With her pride clear, Bexley explained Maundy was the ceremony where the queen washes the feet of the poorest, most wretched women in the kingdom, like Christ did for his disciples at the Last Supper. As she begins, it is read from the Bible:

'If I then, your Lord and Master, have washed your feet, ye also ought to wash one another's feet. For I have given you an example, that ye should do as I have done unto you.' To seal the blessing, the queen draws a cross with her finger on each foot.

"And does this help the washed?"

"Yes, she provides them with care and alms to raise their prospects. Our queen also lays her hands to heal the sick."

"What were they healed of?"

"The King's Evil, Mistress." Bexley took a pause, no doubt from my look of confusion. "Have you not seen it in Ireland or Scotland?"

I asked her to describe its appearance. From what I gleaned, the disorder causes some kind of swelling around the neck with ulcers on the skin, which might be a few things, including a type of TB.

"That is most charitable."

"It is more than that. It is her sacred pleasure, as an instrument of God, as she performs such duty from what is foremost in her heart for her people."

I sat up in bed, pushing the covers to my lap. A sense of relief coursed through me.

"Thank you for telling me of such intentions."

Bexley sat up to join me.

"Our queen is of the truest heart. We are blessed to be in her service, and you will soon see that for your own."

"Mistress, I only want the queen to smile kindly on the people in Ireland. I only desire a lasting peace and ways to please the queen to ensure that possibility."

Bexley just stared at me. "Such an important task has been entrusted to you."

"Do we not all want peace?"

Bringing her knees to her chin from under the sheets, she hugged her shins.

"Mistress, the queen would not make war on her own people." And then in an almost imperceivable whisper she said, "Our Majesty is not anything like her sister, Bloody Mary."

"The last queen?"

Bexley moved closer to my ear. "She married Spain and the burnings never stopped."

"Were they strictly of her people?"

"Of her subjects, yes. She imprisoned Kat, and Blanche Parry as they served Her Majesty when she was still the Princess Elizabeth. And Mary kept them all in the Tower."

"Bloody Mary shut Blanche, Kat, and her own sister in the Tower? Do they not torture people there? Did they torture Kat?"

Bexley pulled her shins even closer to her body.

"I pray they were spared that horror done to them. Not either has ever spoken of it. It was said Queen Mary put the good Princess Elizabeth into the same quarters as her mother, Anne Boleyn, when she awaited her beheading at the king's pleasure."

"How did Her Majesty and the rest survive it?" I asked.

"With her good wits and her innocence."

Bexley then came close and whispered, "All but one raven took their leave from the Tower, weakening Queen Mary's reign."

I turned this piece of information over in my head. A flicker of a memory arose.

"Is the story that if the ravens all leave, the king or queen will fall?"

"The English monarchy itself will cease, leaving England weak and vulnerable to be ruled by another country," Bexley said, her face taut and her tone foreboding.

The hair on the nape of my now precious neck stood up as Bexley wiped her forehead with the backs of her fingers and placed her hands on her cheeks.

"I am sorry to speak of such things so close to slumber and on your first night. Mistress, please do not tell anyone what I told you."

"I shall not if you advise me on how best to raise myself in our monarch's good esteem."

Bexley held my gaze as a smile opened up across her face.

"Be of use to her… regale her with lore, especially of love. If she puts to you a question about the virtues of Robert Dudley, extol on his wit and manner. She has great appetite for what blooms in the heart and for what burns down below."

Bexley giggled which assured me that what I thought I'd heard, I'd heard.

As we lay back down onto our pillows, I wondered how to accomplish any of Bexley's suggestions. Unable to find a sliver of calm, much less drift into sleep, I thought about life back at Dunanynie. Then I began thinking about my mother.

"Pray tell, are you still awake?" I asked.

Bexley lay silent but shifted slightly.

"I am neither awake nor in slumber," she said with somnolence woven in her voice.

I turned my body to face hers. As if in slow motion, she did the same.

"Have any other ladies served the queen from Ireland?"

Bexley yawned and propped her head on an elbow.

"In my time, you are the only Gael."

"Have any Gaelic ladies visited court?"

"None that I witnessed. Let us speak in the morning. I shall have my wits better about me anon."

With that she lay her head back down and shut her eyes.

Would I ever find my mother here? While I was hopeful in chapel, my gut rang with what my heart didn't want to acknowledge. I struggled to breathe quietly through my cold tears. I wondered if her spirit was firmly connected to the twenty-first century, or could she protect me here? No matter what, she should be able to guide me, right? I fell asleep setting my sights on at least finding the 'pious wizard,' be they a man or woman.

I didn't have much time to congratulate myself for making it through the first day. With the pomp of the prior day's service, I was able to fade into the background, save for the looks to size me up and thankfully a few expressions of welcome.

Seated next to Kat in a bright room near the queen's chambers, I took to some needlepointing, attempting to be subtle in imitating the other ladies around me, grateful for Mary and Siobhan who had showed me how to make a stitch.

Kat leaned in toward my ear. "We are to take supper with the queen this evening."

"Shall it be with all those dishes of fish?" I said with hope.

"Oh nay, last eve was but a fasting day," Kat said.

"Forgive me, but we had so many courses."

"Yes, but they were not of game or meat. This night we will have deer and wild boar, perhaps swan."

"All of those animals?"

Kat looked at me. "And then some, Mistress."

My stomach turned in both queasiness and horror.

CHAPTER EIGHTEEN

As evening set, the queen rose from her elevated seat and led her ladies into a deeper chamber where the silver and glass had been set. I received my instructions and took my lowly place furthest away from her. I didn't mind once a servant placed a small loaf of bread in front of each of our plates, along with gooseberry jam and butter. I'd enjoyed the butter that morning. It sat well with me and having the loaf meant I would not starve. The relief allowed me to lean back in my chair and notice the lightness of mood and chitter chatter that flitted around the room.

Elizabeth signaled she was about to speak to us, just as the servants stationed behind us were poised to deliver the first course. All heads bowed but eyes remained on the queen.

"Oh Lord, bless these gifts, that they may do us good, while we live to praise thy name divine."

The queen commenced with taking the first sip of wine. I must have been too slow to drop my gaze right upon her, as the other ladies had done. She lifted her chin and looked directly at me down the length of the table. It was impossible to look away.

"Mistress McDonnell, do Irish necks not bend during grace?" she said.

THE COMMON HOURS

"Please forgive me. I am still wet behind the ears."

It was as if the room was flash frozen. The queen pinched her eyebrows together and with exaggeration wrinkled her face, mocking my slip of tongue. Her jester joined in by wetting his hands in a goblet of mead, then wiping it on the sides of his head as he walked around tittering. The slaps of howling laughter made my face flush, yet I kept my chin up. Still smiling, Elizabeth spoke above the roaring.

"Consider yourself advised that a lady of the court knows not to stare too long at her queen."

"Your Majesty, I was staring at the sun, so beautiful yet so powerful," I said.

"Mistress McDonnell, you address me as if you were a royal suitor."

Another spray of heat rose up in my face. I thought complimenting the queen was how to disarm her. Elizabeth cackled, and a few of the ladies took their cue and merriment began to surge in another wave. The queen raised the corners of her mouth not so much to offer a grin, but to show me her snarl.

I sat upright in my chair, gazing down on my plate, hoping the moment would pass. With a quiet voice, Blanche Parry who sat next to me, offered a few scraps of conversation while delivering a platter requested by another of the ladies.

For the next course, scorched pink flesh was transported to my plate, still on the bone of a creature that had likely been roaming the woods just past the palace gates. Maybe it took its last breath as recently as this morning.

I moved the utensils over the segment of the animal, making it look as if I was fully participating. Blanche asked me if the boar of Ireland tasted as tender. I knew well enough to answer, no.

I gave silent thanks when the queen pushed her plate forward to end the course. After the third dish arrived, my stomach only grew in queasiness. I meted out my loaf of bread and chewed slowly. Anytime I could be seen chewing an actual morsel of food, helped me feel like I was pulling off the masquerade.

Again, I cut into the new animal on my plate and moved around the pieces, hiding some under the larger slabs of meat. This kingdom for a salad, I thought.

Without a word to me, Blanche rose from her seat and spoke something into the queen's ear. Just then, the fourth plate arrived, and the queen fixed her eyes on me. I gulped my wine and hoped I had not again inspired her ire.

"Mistress McDonnell, pray tell why you have scarcely taken one bite of this God-given bounty?"

I froze.

The queen released her own utensils to the table with a clang and pushed her plate away with disgust. She then curled her finger, beckoning me to stand before her. With unsteady feet, I made my way to face her.

"Your Majesty, like Jesus, I do not partake in any food of the flesh. In His example, I am nourished by the bread and fish."

"You dare liken your being to that of Jesus, son of God? Yet you do not strike me as a woman of great piety. You are of mine past enemy and fresh to my court. How do I know if your aim is to make an end to me?"

A gasp and a cry went up from the group simultaneously. I threw myself down on my knees, my heart pounding for its life.

"I did not wish to offend or cause injury to you, Your Majesty."

"Then take from my plate and show me you harbor no sense to cause me harm."

I stood up obediently.

Kat showed me her knife and set it down next to the queen's plate of venison.

I steeled myself to not flinch as I took the meat to my mouth. It slipped past my lips and onto my tongue. As my teeth sunk into the tender flesh, I scanned the faces of the ladies in my purview, to get their read on the queen.

I swallowed, and she motioned for yet another bite. I complied, heart still beating fast and stomach forgotten. She stared down at me maintaining an angry silence. Finally, she spoke.

"Still standing, but not much in the image of Christ."

"No, Your Majesty, not at all. Your reassurance of my fealty comes first."

The queen tilted her head.

"And so much for your immortal soul," she said laughing. The rest of the ladies tittered, the strain on their faces apparent. Here in the Elizabethan reign, only the queen could make a joke about one of her subject's souls, and then only in docile and loyal company. Now as I stood, I was not sure what lay in store for me, my body, or soul.

CHAPTER NINETEEN

Early the next day, Kat accompanied me on a trip to meet with one of the queen's trusted advisors. As the carriage lurched over the rutted path, it felt like a palm-sized rock sat at the bottom of my stomach, which I believe was the animal flesh lying there undigested from the night before. Diverting myself, I gazed out the window into the forest. For a few seconds, I could deceive myself I was in Maudslay State Park, back home in Newburyport, anticipating at any moment that a hiker would walk by with a Nalgene water bottle carabinered to an L.L. Bean backpack. Oh, to spy a logo again.

The door to the carriage swung open. A young footman secured the livery steps and extended his steady arm to assist Kat and me out onto the grounds. I took sight of Mortlake, a sprawling house of dark wood and stone imbued with large, latticed windows which cast off a pale light in the overcast morning. Kat guided me toward the entrance.

"This is the house of divinely inspired study. Its charm is plain to behold," she said as a striped tabby cat, long in whiskers, approached us. I bent down to let it sniff my hand and it pushed its silken face against my fingers. After several strokes, I could not help but laugh as the cat disappeared under my skirts. A whinny from one of the carriage horses flushed the cat out, and it sprinted into the cover of a flowering bush.

The rounded arched door of the house opened slowly, allowing more of the light to spill out and greet us. Once inside, a young man named Daniel took us to a small room, paneled in deep brown wood. He placed a pitcher of ale onto the table closest to Kat. Upon being asked if she or I would desire some, Kat refused. But as soon as he took his leave, she stood up and poured us both a frothy cup.

As we sipped in silence, she studied me with soft eyes. I looked down and was happy to see my fidgeting feet were undetectable under my skirts. Daniel returned moments later; the master of the house, Dr. John Dee, was ready to meet with us.

We followed Daniel down a hallway, my steps unnaturally small across the storm-gray stones. Cold moisture formed under my arms. While the momentum of my skirts seemed to carry me forward, I was still not sure what awaited me through the course of this encounter.

Daniel gave a small knock on the wooden door and then worked the iron handle to give us access. He announced us to the tall, slender man standing there, dressed in something which reminded me of academic robes. Both his hair and beard were dark and close-trimmed. His eyes were round and a pleasing dark blue. He seemed no more than a handful of years older than me. Not so scary, instead I'd say, kind of cute.

Dr. Dee bowed his head and bade us welcome. Kat announced who I was, and once I'd spoken to reciprocate a greeting, his eyebrows rose and he stood frozen for several seconds. I shot a look to Kat, thinking I had breached some protocol, but she remained as if nothing had been amiss. Instead, she exited with Daniel, and I was now alone with Dr. John Dee.

Through the sizable window, the morning dimmed, and a steady rain began to chime against the leaded glass. Dr. Dee remained looking at me, taking me all in, a slight smile on his face. I found myself fiddling with my necklace, under his gaze. It was a relief when he turned to light a few more candles, and I noticed the multitude of books stacked up and down on shelves of oak. They seemed alive with their offerings of rare knowledge. Then, a fear that I'd be overwhelmed, possibly trapped, thundered across my mind. To retain my calm, I focused on the odors of parchment and ink intermingling with the wood burning in the hearth.

"Mistress McDonnell, you hail from Ulster in the queen's domain of Ireland?"

"Aye, Dr. Dee, the Route to be more exact."

"And your family, are they strong and determined?" he asked.

"In what manner do you mean?"

"Do they swear fealty to the land?"

Despite his interrogation, his voice had a lilt, as if he was playing at his role. Like his questions, was this a deliberate way to ensnare me?

"My kin honor the land."

"And Sorley McDonnell, is he not a Scot usurping Irish territory?"

"He considers himself a Scotch Irish, the Irish being out of the love in his heart. His wife and offspring are Irish, and he prides himself in speaking the native Gaelic." I stopped. In this time and culture, I might be building the wrong case for me and my family.

Something sparked in his eyes, like he was ready to pounce.

"Your speech rings of a strange intonation, sounding neither Scotch nor Irish," he said.

My throat went dry.

"Dr. Dee, I am sorry if my speech falls unfamiliar onto your ears."

He stared into my eyes as if looking for something. Given the circumstance, that should have been where he probed and pushed, but instead, it seemed he was trying to see me, not as a potential antagonist to the crown as he was charged to do, but just as a person. Through this act of kindness, I saw a softness in him.

I wanted to give him a compliment—telling him "Nice robe." But instead, I glimpsed toward his worktable, where several large maps lay unfurled and clearly under study. He followed my glance.

"Are there other countries whence you've spent your days? We could take sight of them on my maps."

He lifted the top one and placed it at the end of the table. Underneath was a chart of Europe and Russia. He was watching my eyes, looking for where they would land, so I made sure to sweep my gaze over the entire region before looking back to him.

The map at the end of the table then curled under itself, making a paper on wood scraping sound. The action caused it to roll up and spin toward the edge of the table. I caught the thing before it fell onto the floor.

"Like a cat," he said as he smiled. "I am obliged for such quickness."

"I feared it might roll toward the fire. I am sure it is a valuable piece of your work."

As I offered the map back to Dr. Dee, caught up in his gratitude, his hand grazed my fingers. I aimed my gaze downward, unable to make eye contact with him being so close to me. He said nothing but took the map to the center of the table and secured the sheet, revealing a visual of the New World.

"What say you, Mistress McDonnell?"

I heard the passion in his voice.

"It pleases me to behold," I said with sincerity.

He leaned over the map and motioned for me to join him. He pointed out the Spanish territory of Florida and how it came to be discovered. I have to admit, I did not recollect this historical knowledge going in. He was teaching me.

"And what is known about this land?" I asked, pointing to the arm of a future Massachusetts Bay Colony. He paused and brought his head closer to mine.

"It is not yet claimed."

"Perhaps England is considering it for its own colony," I said.

His mouth fell open. But then he smiled, and I laughed in relief as his eyes remained on me.

"Aye, we are of the same mind," he said.

"Yes, there is great bounty and beauty here. There would be great riches to be had for England."

"From what power, Mistress, do you portend to have this vision?"

I swallowed. How could me as Mistress McDonnell know this?

"Why else would you, Dr. Dee, a man of letters, desire England to expand its realm there if it were not a land of great abundance?"

His look turned skeptical.

"Pray tell, what makes you designate this particular northern territory?"

The adrenaline kicked up in me and out the words came.

"Dr. Dee, in my homeland, the elders say our own Saint Brendan discovered the northern land but never claimed it for Ireland. Would it not be England's to settle now?"

His eyes narrowed in thought.

"Would somewhere along this east coast be the best place for England to colonize?" I asked impulsively, hoping to help my ancestors by diverting English interests away from Ireland.

My question misted the room. Even the fire seemed to contain its roar to small hisses and cracks. Dee gazed at me with intrigue but took a step back and ran his ring finger and thumb vertically down his chin. A small pang thudded in my heart, as he rubbed his beard in the same manner as Daideó.

"I have my own God-given thoughts on the matter, Mistress McDonnell," he said, not offering anything further.

We sat on either side of our proverbial chess table.

"A kingdom made up of islands does not leave much room for expansion. The New World is vast, is it not?" I said, inadvertently resting my finger on the south. It was a challenge to maintain my bravado knowing colonization also hurt so many people.

"Spain claims that for their kingdom, and for the old religion." Dee spoke low in his throat. His stare became more probing.

"What is said in Ireland about the Spanish?"

"Nothing, but I can tell you Ireland only wants to cultivate goodwill with her new queen."

"Have you ever spied there, a ship with King Phillip's flag?"

"I confess, I have no knowledge of King Phillip, is he the regent of Spain?"

Now his stare bore into my eyes as if he was inspecting my soul. We stayed like that for a while. His expression softened.

"It would be prudent for our discourse to change to more docile topics," he said quietly.

I could not let the conversation rest there.

"I know my loyalty will continue to be tested."

"At court all can be suspected," Dee said.

"Am I suspected?"

"Nay."

"Then why am I here unchaperoned in this room with you?"

Dee broke into a laugh and looked upward as he placed his hand back on his beard.

"Your tongue is blunt and lacking reserve, Mistress."

"I choose to speak from truth, dear sir."

From the glint in his eye, I'd say I was impressing him. If it helped to remove any skepticism about my intentions, I was not sure. What was clear, all hinged on what he saw in me.

CHAPTER TWENTY

Kat informed us the queen would not be dining with us that evening, so we took our meal in a chamber separate from the queen's apartments. Tapestries depicting courtly love shone with vivid flows of leafy greens, apple reds, and moonlight silvers, as they hung across the chamber walls. The images were a catalyst for conversation that ambled from plans for a future masque, to comparisons of who had the finer calves among the younger male courtiers. I wasn't interested in who or what they were talking about so I remained focused on the story illustrated in the tapestry, wondering what it would be like to have angels in plain sight while wooed by a warrior prince.

My mind flashed back to the afternoon's encounter. I waited for something to happen as a result of my time with Dr. Dee, but no one confronted me, and not even Kat said a word. Replaying my performance, it was a challenge to let it go. As the hours passed, I became more unsure of the imprint I'd left on him, and ultimately the queen, through his report.

The next day, Kat asked me if I had written my kin in Ireland to 'dispatch the news of my safe arrival.' She was kind enough to supply me with a white feathered quill, which caught Bexley's eye.

"That's a swan quill. It's what the queen herself chooses to make her mark."

They expected to see my gratitude for being bestowed with such an honor, but I worried about what became of the swan. Kat also gave me an inkwell and several sheets of a thick, textured paper that smelled of vegetation. I took myself and my writing tools over to a window illuminated by muted rays of sunshine streaming through the passing clouds.

After I set to work, I confess my instant frustration at having to stop the flow of words to frequently ink the nib. There are few things as irritating as the scratching sound of a quill's sharp tip when it runs dry. To quell my annoyance, I tried to think of it as a mindfulness practice of sorts, noticing how the ink soaked into the dimpled surface of the absorbent paper, yet skipped over the occasional hair-like plant fiber embedded into the body of the sheet itself. Wishing I could just type, I fantasized about the reaction I'd receive pulling out my phone and letting my thumbs fly across the keys of the glowing screen. My hand felt for the plastic and glass slab hidden in my petticoats. Since I was denied the luxury of being alone long enough to draft the letter first with keystrokes, I decided to blow this quill writing business off for now, composing the letter later.

After a few days, I started to exhale a little more. As it was a busy week legislatively, we ladies of the court saw little of the queen until one afternoon when she sat among us as a duo of her favorite musicians played. One plunked the strings of his lute, and the other bowed his rebec, a precursor to the violin. It was nice for the first minute and then, after that, the restricted notes and whiney pitch made me pine for my iTunes.

"With what kind of ear do you deem our courtly music?" Elizabeth asked me.

"It is with a sweet ear," I said.

"Sweeter than the Gaelic scores?"

Truth was, my Irish music experience comprised mostly of U2 songs.

"I wonder how it would be to intertwine the English and the Irish," I said.

The queen let out a loud guffaw. All stared at me, waiting for me to elaborate or take it back.

"Your Majesty, perhaps it would make for a complementary pairing."

"Tut, tut, mixing will degrade the better sound," she said. To which the other ladies rejoined with polite laughter.

I think she enjoyed baiting me, to see what I would do. I shrugged as a way of acquiescence, and Elizabeth regarded me with a mix of annoyance and fascination. All I wanted was for her to like me. And when I say me, I mean me, a McDonnell of Ireland.

CHAPTER TWENTY-ONE

A chill took up in the air as I placed a shawl around my shoulders. Through the gloomy corridors, barely touched by the sun's late-day rays, were single candles placed in the darkest spots to light the way for the coming and going councilors and clerks. I overheard very little, but it spawned my wish to see the queen in action. Instead, I passed a maid finishing her duty of deadening fires in chambers abandoned for the day.

From around the corner, one of the queen's councilors made his way toward me with fast and flopping steps, holding a couple of scrolls under his arm. He gave the slightest of bows with stoic expression and it struck me wise to return to the other ladies. Upon entering the chamber, no one stopped what they were doing to greet me, so I took it upon myself to announce well wishes.

"How now, ladies, as the sun hath blessed you this day, may the moon follow in her example."

Bexley giggled and Blanche tsked, but I did see a small smile slip across her face.

The growing coolness of the evening air settled into the edges of the room, and I was glad to be near the fire. Finding my needle, I took up embroidering the collar of a freshly sewn linen shirt. Around me, the conversation rose and fell, with moments of near quiet. Blanche chose one of the moments of silence to share.

"The Spanish ambassador emerged none too happy coming from the queen's chamber. Best you all take heed, methinks it has left the queen in a foul mood."

"When was this?" Bexley asked.

"A tick after six by the clock. The queen attempts to keep Spain in abeyance, but King Phillip will only wait so long on the queen's promises to commit."

"What will King Phillip do?" I asked.

All stopped.

"You jest, Mistress McDonnell."

"Nay, I do not possess any knowledge of the King of Spain," I said, realizing this was the second time I'd heard this guy's name since arriving.

The ladies looked at each other.

"'Tis the Inquisition we all fear, lest not the queen."

"The Spanish Inquisition?" I asked.

A few of my companions barely nodded as if saying something out loud would unleash the evil right there in the room. Even the moon hid itself behind a cloud.

Lady Sidney began to bite at her nails as she squinted at me. Bexley leaned toward my ear.

"They take up to persecute those of our religion."

"Will Spain invade?" I asked, my own fear rising.

"The queen has night terrors of the Inquisition coming to English shores," Blanche Parry finally said.

Lady Sidney could not cross herself fast enough. Bexley followed and kept her chin to her chest.

"Why do they think they have a right?" I asked.

"We are no longer a nation of the old religion, and they say our Sovereign Lady is a heretic. She is nearly alone, in standing for the Reformation," Blanche said.

The conversation ceased as the fear billowed up between us all. In my knowledge and recent experience, I never perceived England as anything but a powerhouse, or better yet, a bully, before hearing this. But we were all vulnerable, including Ireland.

Kat walked into our presence all smiles until she caught sight of our collective cower.

"What's all this?" she asked.

I looked around at the anxious faces.

"We were sharing stories of past woe," Lady Sidney said as she peered right at me.

Why are we lying to Kat? I wondered.

"May God keep you on this cool summer night," I said to change the mood.

Kat's smile returned. Taking the cue, each of the ladies resumed with their card playing or sewing as lighter conversation began to jangle around the room.

Extending her hand, Kat reached out to inspect my work. She was quick to hand it back. "Your fingers still do not take so friendly to the work of the needle, Mistress McDonnell," she said.

Who the hell cares? I thought, thinking about Spain.

"Yes, Mistress," I said.

"You shall keep at it," she said with a hand on my shoulder. I took in the best inhale I could manage.

"So, there is hope?"

"There is always hope," Kat said.

Inspired but more compelled, I wrote my kin to warn them about Spain while also producing a message that would build trust with the queen. My goal was to convey we were all on the same side.

Dearest Daideó and Maimeó,

May this letter find you in God's blessing and good keeping. As I dispatch this unto you, it is from good cheer and fine health as I take up my responsibilities at the court of our most serene majesty, Queen Elizabeth. Her fine ladies have introduced me to the proper etiquette of the court as well as gowns and hoods of the English and French fashion. The queen herself is a magnificent embodiment of a monarch much in the image of her father, King Henry VIII. As I hold gratitude for my place here, my hope is to remain an obedient servant, as you wished for me to undertake and to impress well upon those we provide peace with, across all of the Kingdom.

With an urgent invitation, I was taken to sit with the realm's leading mathematician and man of letters, Dr. John Dee, to his home called Mortlake. Our discourse was to do with navigation and the creation of maps. All of which I most enjoyed.

My honorable Daideó, we should take to heart that the Spanish engage in the Inquisition, as it is holy in their eyes to torture their own subjects if they do not practice the old religion. The queen strives never to allow such barbarism to set foot in England nor any shores of her realm. You would be best to take up guard from such invasions, even if they come from solitary men. My prayed for hope is that you shall never witness a Spanish Galleon in Irish waters and that English land shall never be besieged by the men of those Galleons.

In your next correspondence, pray tell of the health of our kin. Methinks the summer is warmer here in London as the sun shines most days. Perhaps it is pleased to have such a true-hearted queen as our Majesty on the throne. That is at least what the ladies say, and I would agree.

Your Most Loving Garinion,
Lindsay

CHAPTER TWENTY-TWO

The opened letter fell to Dee's desk. He placed a hand to his bearded chin as he sat back in his chair. A smile formed around the corners of his mouth as he reread the contents.

Later that day, upon entering the queen's privy chamber, Dee took note of the collection of councilors assembled around the long hardwood table. All gave a respectful nod as Dee stood. Once the queen acknowledged him, he bent into a deep bow before taking his seat.

"I trust Blanche has delivered you all correspondence penned by our Irish Mistress," she asked, wasting no time.

"My cousin has done well in her duty, and Mistress McDonnell appears most gratified to be in your service, Your Grace."

Elizabeth surveyed her privy council, resting her gaze on Cecil.

"She must hold the knowledge that her letters will not pass from this court unread," Cecil said.

Others nodded.

"Sorley Boy McDonnell would certainly warn his granddaughter of such a possibility," Cecil added.

"Are there any passages that tell of Ireland?" another councilor asked.

"She informs her kin to be wary of the Inquisitions put forth by the Spanish. She is aware of their purpose and severity and Your Majesty's striving to prevent the realm to fall to such persecution," Dee said.

"So, she tells of our underbelly?" the queen snapped.

"She warns of the underbelly being shared with Ireland," Dee said immediately.

"Master Dee, what do you faithfully make of her intent?" the queen asked, folding her arms.

John Dee paused, which brought more eyes to fall onto him. "Thus far, her intent appears to be a mission of amity and a true olive branch from the McDonnells."

"If it be so, we have not yet identified Shane O'Neill's intentions," Cecil said.

"Or if they are closely in league," Walsingham added.

"Master Dee, does the mistress say anything else?"

"She is intrigued by my studies on navigation as she took pleasure in viewing a map of the Americas."

"Most would show interest in a map of the New World if they had seen it before," Walsingham said.

"Whence should she have seen it before? Does Ireland or, worse yet, her kin in Scotland take to their own navigation?" the queen asked.

"Your Majesty, there was an exploration taken by the Irish monk, Brendan, centuries ago. Perhaps, she is familiar with the lore," Dee offered.

"I charge you to maintain your eye on the mistress. Perhaps the Irish and Scottish are looking to expand their domain in the New World," the queen said.

"All the more reason for England to claim it first," Dee said.

The queen tightened her fingers around her still folded arms.

"There is one last thing to report. Mistress McDonnell does write of you being, just as your father, a glorious example of a monarch."

"Then she is well educated," the queen said, setting off laughter from the rest of the group. This all brought a slow smile to the queen's face as Dee let out a controlled exhale of relief.

❦

I waited too long to send my kin my first letter—for which I was chided from both sides. Kat said my delay was 'not considerate of relieving my relations of their worries,' and Mary echoed that sentiment with more bite in her response to me: "Your hand at the direction of your head shall engage in correspondence at the frequency befitting to our kinship, lest you forget us." Contrary to her thinking, I'd never disconnect from them. To prove that, at least to myself, I imagined the impact of my letter delivered to Dunanynie. It ended up, I wasn't too far from the truth.

❦

Mary ran through the courtyard as soon as Sorley emerged on his horse under the arch of the gate tower. She pulled a folded parchment packet from her skirts.

"At long last, a letter from our lass?"

"Aye," Mary said, handing it to him.

Noting the integrity of the seal, Sorley looked back at his wife. "Have you not read it?"

"I waited for you," she said.

Sorley inspected the seal and pointed to the excess of wax. "See here, this has surely been read and the contents reported to Elizabeth," he said.

Sorley broke the seal and handed it back to her. The two retreated inside Dunanynie and moved to the closest room away from any other ears. Mary began reading the letter aloud.

Sorley focused his eyes on the wooden planked floor beyond his boots. Mary stopped and regarded her husband after reading the part about Dr. Dee.

"You know of this man?"

"Aye, he serves the Queen of England well," Sorley said, gaze still affixed to the floor, waiting to hear more of the letter.

Mary squinted at her husband.

"Mark these words, this John Dee has made an impression," she said.

Sorley's head shot up. He looked straight at his wife, incredulous. Mary gave a catlike grin and continued reading. Sorley cursed after the direct message regarding the Spanish. He asked her to reread that part.

"What do you make of it all?" Mary said.

"What does your belly tell you?"

"The queen and her court have our Lindsay's ear."

Sorley deepened his stony expression.

"And what about Spain? Is this to be believed, husband?"

"The English aim to prevent any foreign alliances," Sorley said.

"Do we have a friendship with the Spanish?"

"Not we McDonnells, but I know not what has been forged in Edinburgh. Perhaps a Spanish king ravishing on the spoils of England herself would not give us much interference here."

Mary grimaced. "Not at first."

"Of more import, is our lass being used so soon against us?"

Mary began to wring her hands. She closed her eyes as if trying to find some solace. "Is she safe?"

Sorley stepped over to his wife.

"We pray and trust that the forces that brought her to us, also keep her safe—we also pray she remembers our cause."

CHAPTER TWENTY-THREE

Early one overcast morning, the queen took her usual walk around the gardens with us ladies in tow. Today she would not be granting any audiences in the presence chamber or at meals, which meant we all could dress in simple gowns. Despite it being an 'easy day,' my thoughts circled around the wish to shed all these layers of fabric to don a pair of leggings and go for a run. I fantasized about breaking free, earbuds in place, blasting my tunes. Without realizing it, I was quickening my stride and walking with a bounce in my step.

"Pray tell what brings such gladness to your face," Bexley said while nudging me from the side.

"Oh, it is a bit of a secret," I said as she strode alongside me.

She took me in, deciding whether I was serious or kidding.

"Mistress McDonnell, come walk by me," the queen said, stopping our procession.

Bexley let out a few giggles, to which the queen smiled back at her.

"I venture the queen will want to talk to you about that secret," she said under her breath.

Maybe this was an opportunity to lay out my case for compassionately colonizing the New World, diverting resources for such efforts in Ireland. Or maybe a chance to move into Elizabeth's good graces. I strode as fast as I could to the queen's side. As I curtsied, I almost lost my balance.

"Take care, Mistress, you needn't turn yourself into a horse running sideways."

She looked ahead and then back at me twice, as if to bait me into something she was conjuring up. Even quicker, she pulled her skirts up past her ankles and began to sprint. It was like she was inside my mind. I followed as she dashed from the prim garden and onto the bridle path. I wanted to overtake her but grasped the wisdom to stay a stride back. Plus, it was not easy to move with speed in these squared-off shoes.

Stopping short, she chuckled at my French hood coming loose. I tried to re-attach it, but it wasn't going to happen with any grace.

"Let it be, it is just us ladies," she said somewhat out of breath.

Relieved, I pulled the sagging ornament from my hair.

"You run like that of a boy," she said.

"You run like that of a girl, Your Grace."

As soon as I heard myself, my arms tensed, as if they could swat the words out of the air and back into my mouth. Yet Elizabeth let out a deep belly laugh and clapped in applause.

"Maybe you would best serve as a counterpart to my jester, Mistress," she said.

A sincere thank you was all I managed to say.

"You do not mind being cast as such?" she said.

"No, I rather appreciate it. There is nothing to say that what a man does, a woman could not also do."

"I am living proof," she said.

Damn straight, I thought.

"Yes, Your Grace," I said.

At this point, the queen's ladies caught up to where we stood. Kat stared at the queen with concern and confusion.

"Mistress Lindsay and I were pretending to be boys, she thought it would please me," the queen called out in a jubilant tone.

I wasn't sure I wanted the credit for the game, but she used my first name, that's something.

"And Your Grace, how was it?" asked Kat.

"I believe I won," she said as we continued to walk. I stayed next to her, waiting for what test would come next. The other ladies kept a respectful distance.

"Mistress, as you said, you see a woman being on par with a man?"

"Some women might still be greater," I said.

She took it to be a compliment to herself, placing her hand to her chest.

"Would those greater women need to harness themselves in matrimony to a lesser man?"

"Only if she desired the union," I said.

Hope sparked from her serious eyes. "Mistress, what do you think would become of those women who do not desire the union?"

"Your Majesty, some women would retain a blessing to be independent. Perhaps they are already made whole in this life and not in need of a union at all."

"Ha, and what about bearing children?"

"Your Grace, I am surprised you entreat my opinion."

Irritation flared across the queen's face, but it did not deter her from pressing the conversation.

"And, Mistress, what do you think of marriage for yourself?"

"I would want a marriage of equals, or else I do not wish to marry."

The queen stopped in her stead and looked at me dead on.

"A marriage of equals? God's teeth, it is never to be that way. That is like a spider and a fly coupling and the fly thinking it shall rule the web with the spider's consent."

I remained silent as she began to talk again, citing all the reasons to dispel my theory. After several moments she prodded me for a response.

"Your Majesty, I have seen pairings where the husband rules at times, and the wife rules at times."

"Does the wife not always have to obey the husband, no matter her station?"

"Nay, not if her station is above her husband's."

Elizabeth pushed out a loud sigh.

"This is the way it is done in your homeland?"

In that moment, I was excited, thinking I was feeding her an alternative view that would please her.

"Well, in Ireland, we are guided by the ancient Brehon Laws. If a woman is unhappy, she may divorce her husband and keep the lands she brought into the marriage and—"

"I am aware of your Brehon Laws!"

I dropped into a curtsy. "Your Grace, I am sorry, my response was in hope of assuring you, not provoking distress."

The queen kept walking, not acknowledging my apology. We remained in a tremulous silence until I gradually fell back in step with her, waiting for her rebuke.

"How is the marriage between Sorley McDonnell and Mary O'Neill? Did she not understand herself to be a princess as her father had been the King of Ulster?"

I bit my lip, unsure what answer she really wanted to hear, surprised she would acknowledge Maimeó's royalty.

"Go ahead, tell me," she said with a note of impatience.

"They seem to rely on each other's good words, letting those words have influence on matters."

The queen coughed and cleared her throat. "Does she ever fall into discontent?"

"Perhaps, but I believe there is love and affection between them after many years of marriage."

Elizabeth did not seem to be wearing her proverbial crown as she rounded her shoulders and kept her head down. Instead, she was simply a young woman pondering her future.

"But what of childbearing?"

"Your Grace, do you ask for me to answer from my own counsel?"

"Yes, Mistress."

"Please forgive me, but in my heart of hearts I fear that in bearing a child, it might be my end."

Elizabeth leaned into me and grabbed my arm.

"No one would venture to speak a thought so unnatural aloud. How dare you hold such notions in your conscience," she said, smiling with intensity.

"I do not wish to offend," I said, confused of where to go next.

"A breath of spring air shall never offend, not my sensibilities anyway," Elizabeth said.

I nodded and performed some kind of hybrid curtsy bow. She shook her head.

"Mistress, you are a bit of an odd duck, but you have opened my eyes to a new view," she said, walking forward with an energized pace.

The ladies were trailing us, and I wondered how much was being heard. Kat gave me an encouraging smile.

"Mistress Lindsay, I will hold you to these standards, unless it serves me to have you married for a future advantage."

I knew who the hell she thought she was, but it boiled me alive to think of her being able to dictate my life in such an intimate way. I had no words as we continued our walk. In truth, I was also growing weary of being her direct company. It's hard to breathe around such a personality backed up by her position in life.

"Your face reveals you, and it is none too pleased," said the queen.

I wondered how much trouble I was in now.

"Mistress, you take me too much to heart. Although as your queen I could, I would never sanction a marriage without knowing your kin's appraisal."

CHAPTER TWENTY-FOUR

When I looked down at myself, I saw the bodice of my favorite green gown and its accompanying sleeves, but I was wearing my jeans. I remember liking the contrast of where the top of the bodice met and overlapped the waist of the denim. Studying my reflection in the looking glass, was it possible that I was now taller?

I left my chamber to find no one was in the passageway, now lit in a pale golden glow which became tinged with an emerald green as I progressed. Once I came to a heavy iron door, carved with serpents and spirals, I hesitated. The handle was warm and felt right in my hand. Yet the door would not move, and I thought, do I really want to go through? Before I could decide, the door opened from the other side.

Once past the threshold, I was in my garage, back in Newburyport. My Prius was there and standing next to it was John Dee himself, dressed in his long black scholar robe. The car fascinated him.

He said, "A chariot?"

I said, "A Prius."

"My lady, you are versed in Latin."

"What did I say?"

John Dee swept his hand toward the car. "That this is a first, a *prius*."

I joined him by the car, and pulling up on the handle, initiated the two-part percussive sound that bounced off the garage walls. Then I closed the door again and turned to John.

"You should know how to gain your own entry." Taking his hand, I guided him through the lift of the handle. His eyes shone once it gave way, and he swung the door open.

"Do you want to go inside?" I asked.

"To take a journey with you?" he said.

We were now almost touching, and he did not move away to a more proper distance. I placed my hands on his chest. "Before we go, John, what's under the robe?"

His arms encircled me in a gentle embrace while he backed me up against the car, our eyes locked the whole time. I brought my lips to meet his and we fell into a kiss, soft at first and then with more urgency. He stopped and looked back into my eyes; a warm smile broke out over his face.

A not so far off crow of a rooster brought me back. My brain processed where I was—in my bed at Whitehall Castle. Which strangely enough sounds more like the dream.

I closed my eyes to bathe in the fantasy and the bloom of the first crush I'd had in years. My stomach flipped by the intimacy expressed. I fell back asleep, because the next thing I knew, Bexley was shaking me awake.

"Lindsay, we have much to prepare today, you must wake up."

I remembered we had the masque and revels that evening. As we both crawled out from under the covers and made the bed together, I suddenly needed to ask who would be in attendance. Later, I mentioned to Kat I had never witnessed a masque and asked what to expect.

"We shall be the audience for a play, for Her Majesty's entertainment."

"Is it perchance by Shakespeare?"

She peered at me with a side glance.

"Who pray tell is Shakespeare?"

Shit.

The fleeting thought that my mother's travels had erased Shakespeare's ascension flashed across my awareness, but then I chastised myself for not remembering my literary history very well. This was only the start of Elizabeth's reign. Much was yet to come, starting with tonight.

It was now after dark and the other ladies and I found our places in line behind those nobles carrying sizable lanterns, each holding a host of lit candles. The musicians ahead signaled the start of the procession with fluted high notes. We ladies attempted to stifle giggles of excitement. It triggered a memory of a school Halloween parade, the year I was a southern belle, complete with satin and lace over an enormous hoop skirt and the same rising anticipation.

The queen assumed her position behind us, with Kat and Blanche taking up her silver-and-gold-threaded train. Her gown was burgundy adorned by pearls sewn across the squared neckline and golden embroidered crosses framed by silver threads on her sleeves. She wore swooping ropes of pearls which reminded me of the portraits of her, yet to be painted.

Lutes sounded in harmony as we proceeded to walk through the courtyard and into the great hall. The nobles nodded their heads to the music as we entered the room. As those carrying lanterns moved across the threshold, the space began to glow, marking the queen's entrance. All those around us bowed or curtsied deeply as Elizabeth passed them. She favored some with a bit of a smile. She was already masterful in teasing her courtiers' appetites for a spellbinding evening. At last, she took her seat on a throne sheltered by a glittering canopy made to match her gown.

The nobles with lanterns spaced themselves around the room, while a few took the candles from within and extinguished them, much the way the lights go out just before a movie starts. The music lifted, and the remaining lit lanterns were set around the stage where a single actor soon emerged, dressed in a green striped jerkin and matching hose. Branching off his cap reared a black feather nearly two feet long, which set off his shoes, too large for his feet. His appearance prompted laughter across the audience. Watching the queen, I was glad to see her pleased with it all.

A few moments into the performance, I scanned the onlookers for Dr. John Dee, wondering how it would be to lay eyes on him in real life. I worried I'd made him cuter in my dream. My stomach flittered as I caught sight of a long black robe. But it wasn't him. I checked myself. Maybe he wasn't coming and maybe I should just chill out. My eyes then met Lord Candleford's, a thick smudge of a man who spent his time petitioning the queen with many a tedious request. His tendency to strut in and out of her presence chambers annoyed me, his excess of testosterone ever apparent. He was tall, which made my height regrettable, as it gave us something in common. Here at the festivities, he stationed himself across from me and took the opportunity to shoot me a look—one no doubt meant to set me afire with lust.

I dropped my eyes to the floor and moved closer to Bexley, who was beside me.

"Lord Candleford has you in his sights," she said.

"From which I shall retch," I said into her ear.

She laughed and, to my chagrin, peeked over at him, which made me want to kill her.

"Dear Bexley, pray stay with me."

I hoped she would act as a shield.

As soon as I got used to the idea that Candleford would approach me at some point in the evening, I spotted John seated three people over. At first, he was stoic in comparison to everyone with merriment in their eyes. He sensed my gaze and bowed his head, as a greeting, but I looked away. When I ventured a glimpse of him again, he wore the slightest trace of a smile that mesmerized me. He was as fine-looking as I had dreamed, which set my nerves cranking up again. I sat back further in my seat, so he would not see me. Of course, I wasn't sure he would gaze over again. I might be making much ado about nothing in my own head.

The play began with two princes and a princess walking along the shoreline. One at a time, the waves took each prince, leaving the princess on her own. When she realized it was she who would rule across the land, a magical sea nymph sprung up from the water and two ravens came to perch on each of its shoulders. Rising from the shifting sapphire water, the nymph promised to bestow wisdom and a strong army upon the princess so that she could be a good queen for her people. The deal was, she had to take a royal husband, in order to receive all these endowments.

"And let the ravens be your oracle, for as long as they fly in your sights, your people will worship you as their queen."

"But do I not have you, o wondrous nymph, as my oracle?"

"The ravens see and hear all that transpires about your kingdom. They will ensure your safety, as will taking a husband."

No sense of amusement transmitted across Elizabeth's face. I bit my lip as I stared at her. Eventually, her eyes caught mine and she bit her lip back to me. I wasn't sure what it meant as she did it calmly and went back to watching the production. Fortunately, it soon ended, and the dancing began. We were now entering the revels.

Bexley handed me a small mask, and I joined in as the crowd took to wearing their own masks before lining up to dance. I merged into the line with the other ladies, happy I hadn't messed up that part of it. A line of men formed across from us. They too wore masks, but I recognized those with more distinguishing body types from the queen's privy council. As we came together, placing our hands against those of our male partners, I searched for John Dee, but he was not at his seat.

"Mistress McDonnell," whispered my partner.

I saw right through the mask and into the eyes, of who I was not sure. I played with the idea of ignoring the greeting, as it outed my identity in this game. Averting my gaze only raised my awareness of his fingers ever so slightly grasping mine through the dance.

I looked at my partner again, and like a trumpet blast, I realized this was John, in an astounding disguise, resplendent in a doublet of sky-colored silk.

"Dr. Dee," I whispered back before I could think.

He bowed his head in a nod. He appeared so different to me. Why didn't I notice his attire earlier?

"You are like a chameleon, dear sir," I said.

"Dear lady, a chameleon is not a creature familiar to my mind. I pray it is not too ignoble in your eyes."

"No, it has a tendency to enchant any who might look upon it," I said, regretting in an instant how dumb that sounded. But I thought (or at least hoped) I saw a bit of a blush come to the outer edges of John's face, not hidden by his mask.

We rounded the circle and said nothing, perhaps not knowing where to take the conversation from there. With just a few seconds before switching partners, I managed to thank him for the dance and then moved on without looking back, but God I wanted to keep him in my sight. The next man, I could not make any eye contact with—I barely laid my palm against his. Instead, I went through the motions, turning and whirling while my insides did the same as I recalled John's touch. Hoping I would find him at my hand again, my heart fell when Lord Candleford with his undeniable swagger took up as my partner. At first, he did not say anything as I went through the dance as stiff and cold as a barren oak in winter. He cleared his throat to signal his authority. He told me he had been watching me since I came to court.

"Yes, Lord Candleford."

He took that as an invitation to run his fingers across the squared neckline of my gown. From instinct, I threw his hand off me and removed myself, stepping backward, and then turning to reach to the furthest edge of the hall, wondering if anyone witnessed the breach and if I'd be blamed. But now very alone, I sensed I was in more vulnerable territory and huffed back toward the glow that whirled around the queen. Thankfully, she soon ended the dance, and to my stark surprise, issued me a nod of acknowledgment. This gave me the courage to look around, but I did not see the predator anywhere.

Bexley came to my side, grabbing my hand.

"Methinks you have spurned the lord. Was it your intent?"

The line across my chest where the predator's fingers touched still bore the sensation of his violation.

"You saw what transpired?"

"I spied he was your partner as we twirled, but by the next spin, he took his leave with haste."

I wanted to tell her what happened, but the words died in my throat. Bexley leaned into me.

"Lindsay, you are not the first to turn the man away."

My tears started to rise. "He is vile."

She nodded.

"But have I made trouble for myself or my name?"

"Had the queen bade you to show him favor?"

I shook my head.

"As I thought, as she would not, for she finds him to be a gnat. And if you did his pride any injury and that keeps him from court for even a day, Her Majesty would offer you a word of genuine gratitude."

My relief won out over anger I had done any of the *injuring*.

Bexley led me back to our seats. Soon the same actor that started the masque came out to recite the epilogue. The queen now wore a more genuine smile, although I suspect it was because the damn thing was over.

Several more of the lamps were extinguished, leaving just single candles placed around the perimeter; the great hall immersed with an air of intimacy mixed with shadow and the unseen. I hoped the predator was really gone for the evening. When more wine was poured into our goblets, I was eager to partake. Once served, the fair-haired Lady Sidney hooked her arm into mine and asked me to stroll with her through the crowd.

We stopped across from her brother and my scornful carriage mate from my initial arrival, Lady Skew. The conversation was quickly taken up with the performance of the masque.

"Have you danced in the revels?" asked Lady Skew.

"That she did." Lady Sidney answered for me. "And Lady Skew, whence is Lord Skew this festive evening?"

She pointed across the crowd to a group of men standing in a circle. This allowed me a moment to scan the hall for John. Curiously, I did locate him in deep conversation with the queen's head of security, Francis Walsingham, and now he was in his black academic robes. But how...

"Mistress McDonnell, how are you finding being away from your native northern lands?" Lady Skew asked with astonishingly kind eyes.

"It remains an honor to serve Her Majesty, yet I miss my family a great deal."

She lifted her eyebrows. "You speak with such plainness, Mistress."

"She merely holds two minds, Lady Skew," Lady Sidney said.

I thought it was the appropriate thing to say—honor for queen and kin.

Lady Skew nodded and took a sip of her wine, as we all did in the awkwardness of the moment.

As the music sprinkled with quick notes set a playful tone, the queen paired with her favorite, Lord Robert Dudley, and glided around the periphery of the room. He wore a silvery gray doublet and jerkin with small white ruffles about the wrists and collar which seemed like he had been topped with dollops of whipped cream. His colors against the queen's burgundy, made more sumptuous by the evening lighting, were a striking complement. The two took everyone's gaze out with them to start the dancing at the center.

Captivated by his queen, a sly smile bloomed across Lord Robert's face. Elizabeth matched his gaze. The whole crowd looked on, but only some approvingly. All the women anyway.

And then my eyes found John, standing at the inner edge of the circle. He had his hands clasped in front of him as he watched the dance. And almost as if he was waiting for me, he shifted his gaze to find mine. He smiled with only his eyes. Realizing I was near beaming, I turned to view the queen, keeping him in my peripheral vision.

Another councilor of the court approached him and said a few words by his ear. John nodded as the queen waved more of the group to come into the center to dance. Lord Robert held her other hand in his, high above their shoulders, as if co-hosting the event with her.

Those around me moved out and formed several circles. Lady Sidney grasped my hand and brought me into hers. Gaining a sense of the steps took up my attention, but once we were in full swing, I sighted John talking more intently with the courtier who was beside him earlier. My stomach dropped yet again, thinking he was prevented from joining us.

The queen's laughter rang out as she, Lord Robert, and a few of the other nobles passed a humorous exchange between them. Surveying the crowd, the queen sauntered over to our group.

She placed a hand on my arm, so as to have me break the circle and allow her in. My group was giddy as the queen twirled with us. At times, she clasped my hand tightly and I wondered if she'd witnessed Candleford's act. Once she spun herself out of the circle, we continued on. But her spin turned into several, as she was likely becoming affected by the wine. Lady Sidney and I caught each other's eyes as we offered an arm here and there to safeguard the queen, in case she became too dizzy. She shook us off and flew over to dance with another group. Throughout the dance, the whole court was laughing and sharing smiles, taking boundless pleasure in engaging with the queen.

When the music shifted, I decided to take a breather and get my bearings, as the wine was having some impact on me as well. Once off the 'dance floor,' I took up by a nearby table, plucking grapes from the platter to give me the closest thing to hydration that wasn't alcohol. Lady Skew waved to me. Apparently, the queen choosing to dance next to me raised my status instantly. As I strode over, my heart jumped realizing she was talking with John.

"Mistress McDonnell, shall I acquaint you with Dr. Dee?"

I was going to say we already knew each other but John said, "It is a pleasure to learn your name, Mistress McDonnell."

Lady Skew was pleased with herself.

"Dr. Dee administers to furthering the learning beneficial to the realm," she said.

"Yes, I have heard," I said, turning to John. "Dr. Dee, your studies are in mathematics?"

"Yes, and navigation, astronomy, and also astrology. He read the charts for our queen to find the most auspicious day for her coronation," Lady Skew said.

I smiled, most impressed.

"Dr. Dee, you are a man most rare. I do not think I have ever heard of so many disciplines of knowledge residing within the same mind," I said.

"Have you not?" John said, playing.

"Nay, sir."

"Behold, I suspect Dr. Dee's contributions will ensure the forthcoming prosperity of the kingdom," Lady Skew said as she spread her arms wide.

John laughed and rested his eyes on me.

"So you bring us our future then?" I said.

"He certainly can tell you what the stars portend," Lady Skew said.

Lady Sidney approached us. Leaning in close, she said Catherine Knollys had twisted her ankle in the revels, and would I now accompany her to prepare the queen's bedchamber?

I hated her timing. But here was a sign I had earned their trust—the queen's trust.

John raised his eyebrows as I explained a need to depart. I wasn't sure if it was authentic surprise or play acting on his face.

"Adieu, Mistress McDonnell. I trust our paths will converge again."

I wanted to linger in John's presence. But instead, I gave a brief curtsy and joined the side of Lady Sidney as we passed out of the great hall.

"The queen is quite merry and full of love tonight," I said.

"Aye. Methinks the wine is stronger than we are all accustomed."

We both giggled as we hurried toward the bedchamber. At the door, Lady Sidney signaled to the waiting servant to stoke the fire. She then called in another and pointed to the bed. I clapped a hand over my mouth to see this servant roll across the queen's mattress. I waited for Lady Sidney to chastise him.

"It is to make sure no weapon remains hidden among the queen's bedding to harm her person."

The servant jumped from the bed and proceeded to look under it.

"It is clear," he said while retrieving a closed silver pan, inscribed with the queen's crest and attached to a long wooden stick that hung by the hearth. He handed it to Lady Sidney who then gave it to me.

"I know not when the queen shall retire, but we will warm her bed now, in case it falls soon."

"Shall I just slide this up and down the sheets?" I asked.

"Yes, but at an even pace. The queen detests hot spots next to a cold one."

I nodded and hoped I was up to the task. I started to move the bed warmer steadily across the mattress. Lady Sidney directed me to go slower. Upon hearing Elizabeth's voice outside the chamber, anxiety rushed through me in cold sparks.

Leaning on the arm of Lord Robert, the queen entered through what looked like another passageway, circumventing the guards at what I thought was the only door. Kat and Blanche followed. None of this was unusual to them.

"Mistress McDonnell, you venture into my bedchamber?" Elizabeth asked.

"Lady Knollys has become indisposed," Lady Sidney offered.

"And there was no one else?" the queen said.

All remained silent.

"Bess, 'tis fine," Lord Robert said, looking me over. I was grateful to him.

Elizabeth waved it off and told Robert to shield his eyes. He walked over to a chair he greeted as a familiar perch. Dutifully, he turned to look out the window to which Kat and Blanche flanked the queen and peeled her out of her outer evening attire. Lady Sidney gestured I should continue with the bed warming, which I did, trying to keep a slow pace, despite the holy shitness of the situation.

As Blanche undressed the queen, she handed the ropes of pearls to

Lady Sidney, who almost appeared burdened by their weight. The queen put her hand over the pendant she wore, telling Kat she would keep it about her neck.

Both Kat and Blanche placed a long white gown over the queen's shoulders as she stood. Kat finished by tying its shimmering red ribbon about the queen's bosom.

Uncomfortable, I cursed inside that I should have left the side of the bed facing the queen to warm at this point in the process. I did steal a glance at Lord Robert, who was like a contented cat, in his chair. At one point, he poured himself whatever was in the flagon on the table next to him and drank it with relish.

"Sweet Robin, have you grown weary in wait?"

"No, Bess, never," he said.

Elizabeth told Kat and Blanche they were not required to accompany her to bed that evening, to which they curtsied and made their way to exit. I tried to catch Kat's eye, but she remained focused on the floor ahead of her.

Lady Sidney placed her arm on mine, informing me I'd completed my task to satisfaction. I offered her the bed warmer, and she placed it by the fire. During those long seconds of her walking to the hearth, I was certain I'd never be able to meet the eyes of the queen or Lord Robert again. Why was I being made privy to this? Again, Lady Sidney placed her hand on my sleeve, prompting me to follow her out.

"Good night," Lord Robert said, beginning to rise. Elizabeth ogled him, appetite whetted.

I could not leave fast enough. As Lady Sidney pulled the bedchamber door shut, I heard Lord Robert comment that they did not need the bed warmed. No sooner had we taken two steps when Elizabeth's angry voice ricocheted off the walls. Lady Sidney stopped, and we listened. When the nature of the argument became obvious, Lady Sidney cast a hard eye on me.

"They fight of this all the time. He fails to understand the queen will not sport him her maidenhead."

"But are they not already lovers?"

"Lovers yes, but not in full congress."

Lady Sidney glanced toward the queen's bedchamber as things quieted.

"She is most fearful of becoming with child, more than I have ever seen in a woman."

The revelation pinged at my heart.

"It must be very difficult to be the queen," I said.

"Being a queen regent and no less the daughter of King Henry," she said.

Hurrying to take my refuge for the evening, I met up with Bexley, who was leaning against the threshold of our shared bedchamber, all grins in her nightdress and robe.

"Did you most enjoy the festivities tonight, Mistress?" she said.

"I did. And how did you find the wine?"

Bexley stepped back and closed her eyes, contentment washing over her face. She swayed and opened her eyes wide. We both laughed.

She clumsily helped me undress and then bounded into the bed. I took the liberty of closing the bed curtains and blowing out all the candles; however, the flames in the hearth looked like they were still jumping with exhilaration from the evening's revels.

Over the last few nights, Bexley and I had told each other tales. I most loved to hear hers, rich with her perspective of life in these times, being a daughter of a noble family from Cornwall. We bonded over each having lived near the ocean and sharing a penchant for 'taking ourselves into the water.' While she had never been in past her knees, she became fascinated with my ventures to bathe my whole body. For tonight's tales, Bexley wanted to talk about sex.

When she was thirteen or fourteen, she walked up to her favorite ridge perched by the sea and shore. Down below her, she found a handful of young men, one being a stable hand for her family's horses. They were sitting on the beach, wet from their swim and naked in the sun.

"Have you ever spied a man unclothed," she asked in a loud whisper.

"Wait, pray tell, did the boys on the beach see you?"

"You will think me sinful," she said, covering her face.

"It is natural to want to look."

She remained silent while she propped herself up on an elbow and leaned closer to me, a whiff of alcohol on her breath.

"I crept down, at the risk of breaking my neck, to hide behind a rock. There I watched, thinking God would surely pluck me out and drop me down the hill at any time."

"And did He?"

"Nay, He did not."

"Do you suppose, He wanted you to see what might be pleasing to your eyes?" I said.

"Mistress, what wickedness runs through your mind that you should speak thus?"

"Mistress Bexley, you have broached this subject of conversation."

She lay back down.

"And I shall ask you again, have you ever come upon a man unclothed?" she said.

I threw the blanket back and told the truth by lying.

"Upon walking through the forest, I came upon a young man and a lass in the act of love. As he withdrew, I saw the most shocking sight," I said, actually recalling me and my high school boyfriend discovering the thrill of sex in the woods by his house.

Bexley put her hands to her mouth. I had overwhelmed her imagination. She remained wide-eyed and speechless for several seconds.

"I think I should fall into a faint, never to be revived, if I came upon such a display."

"My heart did beat so fast," I said.

She started to giggle, volume increasing into a belly laugh. She then whispered, "Knowing what happens, you will perhaps be that much more prepared for the marriage bed."

Oh jeez, I thought.

Turning to prop my elbow under my head, I couldn't help but slightly change the subject.

"Did any particular nobleman woo you this evening?"

"I could not see most of them through their masks to recognize who they might be."

"Yes, and they would not know it was you under your mask either."

She sighed and closed her eyes. As I tried to think of something else to ask, her breathing deepened. Lying back, it felt like I'd lived the ups and downs of a year in just one night: vice and virtue, repulsion and romance. Becoming fully aware that my shoulder was touching hers, I fell asleep pretending this was John next to me.

CHAPTER TWENTY-FIVE

As the next day passed, the energy around court was muted, almost introspective. This pleased me as I was left to my own thoughts. Wondering how to write home about it, I decided any mention of John Dee might be best left out.

While my promotion to the queen's bedchamber was likely a one-time necessity, I pondered if it was worth including. On one side, it tells my kin that I am trusted, and on the other, it relays to the crown I am honored by the trust. Or will it look like a disclosure of infiltration? I decided to forgo writing altogether as, for all I knew, that was just a show, a test of my true loyalty.

I sighed back into my sewing, which was going better than usual. As I was only two of the ladies running a needle, I sat by the bank of windows, trying to gain as much light on my work as possible, given the cloud cover. We, or at least I, did not see the queen all day.

We ate our suppers with subdued conversation, and in contrast to the night before, the palace was like a university library during finals. Alive with people, but all quietly focused on their tasks. Soft footfalls, book pages turning, and utterances merely above a whisper remained the backdrop. As I was close to retiring, the queen summoned me to her bedchamber. A blaze of worry burned through my stomach as I made my way. I massaged the webs between my fingers to help myself stay in control. Kat met me at the door and granted me entry.

I curtsied to Elizabeth, who wasn't paying any attention, while her hair was being let down by Lady Sidney.

"The queen most liked your bed warming and asked you to perform your duty for her tonight," Kat said.

"Oh, I would be most happy to serve Her Majesty."

Taking up the handle of the pan from the hearth, I began my slow, methodical run up and down the sheets. There was little dialogue save the queen speaking in low but neutral tones to the ladies dressing her for bed. She did want a certain nightcap to wear.

"The green—it is most soft," she said, pointing to the heavy dresser of drawers where such items were kept.

After the ladies finished, Elizabeth came over to feel the bed.

"I should like more warmth, Mistress McDonnell," she said as she dismissed the others. Kat remained but Elizabeth told her specifically to take her leave.

"Your Grace, did you not want me slumbering here with you this eve?" Kat said.

Elizabeth placed her hand to her head. "Yes, of course, but I shall be alone with my bed warmer for a spell."

"Your Majesty, I am most honored you are pleased with my warming technique," I said after Kat left.

"Technique?" Elizabeth laughed. I placed the pan to my side.

"Mistress, I suspect you bore witness to a most private matter last night," she said.

I nodded slightly, not wanting to commit.

"Kat wanted to relay my message, but I thought it would endure in your mind with greater fortitude if you received it straight from your queen. You may be asked about my private doings, perhaps by your own kin, but you will not offer anything but discretion. Your words shall serve to quash gossip and conjecture, leaving those that venture an inquiry to know only that their monarch is just and pious."

I nodded.

"And if you ever betray your queen, you will be punished and sent back to the McDonnells under a black flag."

"My discretion is guaranteed, Your Grace."

She leaned in. "Now, pray tell me what is said about Lord Robert about the court?"

"It was a reserved day. I think the court was much recovering from the strong wine of last night," I said.

"Strong wine, it was," she said, touching her forehead. Her face softened and she asked me how I found my first revels.

"Your Majesty, it remains a mixture of pleasure and pain."

She was not surprised.

"You dispatched of the knave well. Not all my ladies defend their persons with the quick thinking of a tested warrior."

Her praise meant the universe to me, and it almost righted my world, but it burned in me to ask if he would be punished. She chose to ignore the emotion on my face. Even in a place where a woman is in charge, the acts of sexual misconduct get swept out with the cinders and the ash. What made me still sadder was I, coming from centuries later, did not find this way of handling the situation unusual.

"How did you receive the masque itself?" she asked.

I paused, picking through my words. "I wondered if it was to Your Majesty's liking."

"Hmph, and why would you wonder?"

"It seemed that the princess, chosen last, was in requirement of a husband?"

Elizabeth pulled her chin in and squared her shoulders.

"I did not care for it," she said.

"And, if you permit me?" I paused.

The queen gestured for me to continue.

"Pray tell, why would the princess need a magical creature to bestow upon her the wisdom to rule. Hadn't she not been wise enough to survive her brothers? Did she not already have a store of wisdom?"

The queen laughed in clear delight. She leaned toward me. "Yes, she was the survivor and chosen one in the end. But a little magic is something all sovereigns would welcome," she continued in a lighter tone. "Do ye mistress understand a thing or two of magic?"

Where was she going with this?

"Not of magic but of better ways to do things."

"Such as dispensing with the unwanted advances of a man?" she asked.

"And inspiring those that are desired."

A small, tight smile escaped onto the queen's lips.

"Mistress, are you speaking of that which should never pass from a maiden's mouth?"

"No, I am speaking of love and its expression without want of finding oneself with child."

Elizabeth's mouth dropped open.

"How would you behold such things, you are but a maid, are you not?"

"I am. But the knowledge is shared from older women."

That and my own obsession with birth control as getting pregnant was never in my plans.

"You do confirm your Irish folk are heathen—what would spur such discourse with a maiden?"

"I have been privy to talk about women believing they are not ready for the blessing of a child."

I pressed my toes against the bottom of my shoes to find my grounding, but I had already lost my footing digging a profound hole for myself with each sentence.

"What is this better way?"

I tried to clear my throat, which only produced a look of impatience on the queen's face.

"One way is to employ what is known as a condom. It prevents the man's sperm from entering a woman's quinney, so no baby can be formed."

The queen huffed and sniffed.

"As marriage is in every one of my councilors' minds, would it not serve a regent to have access to such devices, so as to not have to rule from within the confinement of childbirth?" she asked.

"Yes, a regent should take reign over her own person—for the good of her country."

There was a pause, as a tornado of energy grew between us.

"What does this device look like?" she asked.

I motioned with my hands and tried to find the century-correct words.

"It is a bit like hose or a glove."

"Made of leather?"

"Made of the entrails of a sheep," I said.

"Mistress, pray tell how such a device may come into the possession of a virgin sovereign?"

"It would have to be made."

She straightened up. "Then I need you to make it!"

The command fell on me like an iron cage sprung from the ceiling.

"You'll have what you need in the catery," she said.

I was helpless.

"Your Majesty, what is a catery?"

The queen walked in front of me shaking her head. "You know of such a thing as a condom but not a catery?"

"Perhaps we Irish would refer to it by another name," I said.

"It is where the meat is cleaved and kept. Downward, within the palace. You can ask for your sheep innards there. Tell them it is wanted to make a unique glove for one of the queen's ladies. Do not tie this to me."

"Yes." It was all I could say.

She then told me to box the thing up and deliver it to her as soon as possible.

CHAPTER TWENTY-SIX

Imagining the new horror show I'd managed myself into, I found my way into the palace kitchen and asked one of the cooks the way to the catery. She stared at me in my finery, confused why a woman of my station would take the journey down into the bowels of the palace.

"I know you—you don't eat the beasts," she said.

"It is an errand for another of the queen's ladies. But it will be a surprise gift. Please keep my inquiry to yourself," I said.

Leaving the warmth of the kitchen, I started my descent into the underworld. Voices soon met my ears, which was some relief as it was too dark to discern the correct time of day. With small steps, I trod down the passage; a smell of raw meat came into my senses—the stench reeking of hell on earth. Before thinking about aborting the task, I was almost run over by a blond man wearing a leather apron emblazoned with drips of blood. He looked equally shocked to see me. "Ye lost your way, lass?" he said, recovering before I did.

"I need to find the catery—for some sheep bowels."

"Who sent you?"

"I require them for a surprise gift of gloves for one of the queen's ladies."

He scratched his head, and some blood made it into his hair as if he had suffered his own wound. He followed my eyes and tried wiping his head with the back of his hand. Nausea was rising.

"I could butcher one fresh—"

"No!"

Just then, two men carried in an enormous wild boar, its front and back hooves tied to a pole. They were struggling with its weight but stopped short at the sight of me. The blood pooled on the animal's side, flagrant in its fresh redness.

My stomach lurched. I turned and vomited, getting some down the skirt of my gown as I could not move it out of the way fast enough.

"God dammit! These stupid dresses!" I yelled in frustration. I wiped the vomit from my dress with my bare hand and noticed the bottom of my gown was wet from whatever was all over the floor.

Trying to regain my calm, I turned around slowly to find the men with the boar gone from view.

"What else have you for intestine?" I croaked.

"My lass or, pardon, my lady, down here be no place for you."

I agreed while not having the strength to correct his etiquette.

"Let me hear what else you've got in your store and I'll move on."

"Closest thing be a couple of lambs butchered yesterday." My heart burst right at that moment. "Or I provide the harvest from that boar ye just met."

I glanced upward to hold back the tears.

"We be cleaning them up for you, wash them out—there'd be no blood," he said in sympathy. "I be delivering them up to the kitchen two days hence."

"Any sooner?"

He paused, poked his head back into the catery and said, "By the end of tomorrow."

"You are most kind and productive," I said. He smiled and gave me a quick bob of his head.

Escaping the smell of blood and opened animal carcasses, adrenaline fueled me back through the glum passageway. It hit me as I ascended the steps: I had two problems, the matter of my gown, and how was I going to make a freakin' condom?

My mind was anything but present, but I found my way back to the kitchens. The cook who had directed me looked me up and down as I emerged.

"Ye had a rough time of it then?" she said while pouring water from a nearby pitcher over a linen cloth. Without missing a beat, she proceeded to wipe down the sick. I had a memory of my mother doing the same thing when I was a kid, only yelling at me because I managed to dump a whole bowl of unwanted oatmeal, complete with blueberries and maple syrup, down my Easter dress. What she was really stressed about was needing to tell my father she wasn't into the Catholic thing anymore. "Sometimes you just have to suck it up and do what you don't want to do—you don't turn yourself into a martyr over it!" I kept telling her it was an accident and that I didn't know what a martyr was.

As the cook shifted back to survey her work, we both agreed her cleaning had been successful.

"Don't think I can help ye with that mess," she said, pointing to the line of stains along the bottom hem. She wanted me to look but I just nodded and thanked her for her assistance. I told her that there'd be a parcel for me coming up from below, and I would check in late tomorrow.

Scurrying through the palace, I dashed through the back hallways back to my own chamber. I prayed that the mucky stench was not too strong anytime I passed another soul.

Once in my chamber, I found Bexley there. She saw the strain in my face and asked me what was out of sorts. I motioned to my gown and that I needed to change.

As she helped me, she asked how I wetted the bottoms of my gown with such—

"Slime?" I said.

"Is that Gaelic for filth?" she said after a hesitation.

Once I was free of my underskirts, Bexley held one of the offending garments up and away from her.

"We shall send them to the laundress. Once when I had been full of mud after riding, she did a fine job restoring the cloth and Kat was none the wiser."

It was a relief to know Bexley had her secrets from Kat and was willing to help me keep a few of my own. One thing I can say about court life, it is more political than anything I had ever encountered firsthand. To not have alliances is to find yourself sunk because you could not make it on your own here. Often, I bore witness to contests between those vying for the queen's ear, and that was just at meals. There was art and skill to work your agenda while appearing like you had the Kingdom of England at the forefront of your heart.

It made me homesick for Ballycastle. I thought about my grandparents and what they were doing, thinking, feeling. I sensed they were praying for me because there was a warmth rising in my solar plexus. It was as if Mary was right there with her hand on my stomach.

Dearest Daideó and Maimeó,

I send you love and blessings from where I write, in the south. The queen honors me with her company and I have taken to new activities at her wise counsel. In the last days, we held a masque, and I had the honor to partake in a courtly dance called a revel. It was not what I would call a wee celebration, as we also feasted and were most merry.

As my tenure at the court progresses, I realize myself as an instrument for amity, and as such, trust that our kin and neighbors live within continued peace. Please take to heart that your forthcoming correspondence brightens my days even more than they are already blessed.

Your loving Gariníon,
Lindsay

Dearest Lindsay,

As you partake in such festivities in serving Her Majesty the Queen, we remain gratified that you are our noble representative. Your honor and propriety reflect well on Ireland, and we bid that you continue to be our pride and the Queen's obedient lady-in-waiting.

Since all is at peace, it is our hope you shall return to us. A sojourn to be with kin would fortify us all. I entreat you to write us the word, if that is your desire, and we shall petition the Queen for such a visit back to Ballycastle.

Thanks be to God and Her Royal Majesty,
Your Loving Daideó and Maimeó

The package arrived the next day, as promised, wrapped in dark gray linen and held with twine. The cook took it from out of a cupboard upon laying eyes on me.

I thanked her.

"Mistress, were ye able to clear the stains on yer gown?"

"Aye, my hope lies with the laundress."

Within the folds of the linen lay several pink membranes. I gave them a sniff and found the smell to be neutral. The intestines were rubbery and cold, but clean. I marveled at how long they were and then felt bad remembering *what* they were. Poor lambs.

Intuiting my need, the cook grabbed a knife from the counter by her side.

"'Tis sharp," she warned while handing it to me.

I took out the membranes and cut them evenly. It was smooth work.

"Ye have done me well with this tool."

She regarded me with amusement and offered her help, should I need it in the future. Back into the linen package the condoms-to-be went. I sought to find my needle, thread, and something softer than twine to secure them given the sensitive place they would be serving. I tried to shake off where my mind brought me, realizing I was thinking of the queen's boyfriend's dick. This was a duty. It was my job. Get over it.

If I can say it here, the ladies of the court thought Robert Dudley quite handsome, a definite hottie, but I found him overdone and a little too smooth. But he had a way with Elizabeth that gave her something nothing or no one else could. She let down her guard with him, a state not easily embodied by her. They'd known each other since they were kids and had both survived the harsh politics of the earlier Tudor times. Jesus Christ, they both had parents who were beheaded at the Tower.

Seeking the privacy of the bedchamber, my heart raced. 'What ifs' clouded my mind. Once over the threshold, I grasped under my petticoats and pulled out the linen parcel. No sooner had I unwrapped the package and laid out my tools than an urgent rapping sounded at the door.

I threw everything back into the linen and shoved it into a drawer, surmising it would be fine to leave the various needles out exactly as they were. It was no sin or crime to be sewing in one's bedchamber.

Opening the door, I saw a royal page. He bowed his head and handed me a small bundle of letters, tied together with red ribbon.

"Mistress McDonnell, I deliver unto you, your correspondence."

I thanked him, but he remained.

"Do you require that I dismiss you?"

"Mistress, it is not unusual for a response to be written upon receipt and shortly thereafter posited back in my hands to deliver."

"Oh, I did not know this," I said, irritated. "How shall I call for you, if I require such service?"

He gave me simple instructions and I waved him off. It was a little bitchy, but he was gruff. Once closing the door, I untied the red ribbon and assessed its appropriateness for use in my sewing project, then laid it several inches from the needles.

The first letter was from my 'father,' Alastair McDonnell. I thought how clever, of course he would be writing to me. In a neat and disciplined hand, like Maimeó, he described daily life back home, as if I had lived with him as my family. He made mention of what my siblings were up to and inquired how I was finding being away from home.

Upon taking the next letter, a distinct J and a D lay embedded in the seal. My heart beat up and down my chest as I opened the fine and soft parchment.

Dearest Mistress McDonnell,

I pray this finds you in joyful spirit since we last exchanged well wishes.

My fond hope is that you shall consent to join me in future days at my home at Mortlake. Since your last visit, my library has acquired two newly minted maps of the Americas methinks you shall take great pleasure in laying your eyes upon.

Your Humble Friend,
John Dee

Like anyone would, I reread the letter and imagined John writing it at his large wooden desk. Or maybe he wrote it outside under a tree. Or maybe he wrote it in bed. I'm an idiot. His intention is to keep his eye on me for the crown.

I worried John was waiting for an immediate reply. Exhaling, I remembered playing coy was probably perfected here in the Tudor royal court. Maybe it was better to make him wait and wonder.

With a burst of energy, I picked up all my sewing and proceeded off to the privy. Keeping myself from running, I passed a few known courtiers and then Francis Walsingham walked into my path and gave me a slow bow of the head.

"Mistress McDonnell, Kat Ashley speaks well of you as the Irish addition to the queen's household, yet we scarcely have had a chance to acquaint ourselves."

Kat speaks well of me. I hoped it was true.

"I shall favor an opportunity to speak more at length, but I am on an errand," I said.

He regarded me while tilting his well-plumed hat back onto his head, resulting in his stance looking that much more dramatic.

I wanted to tell him I believed he did a fine job guarding the queen but that might invite questions in his mind as to why I had even taken note of such protection.

Dropping into a curtsy, I hoped to end our exchange.

"Take good care, Mistress," he said.

I caught his glance as I stepped into the privy. Good, I hope he sees where I am going. The last thing I'd want is his suspicion on me.

Once secure, I began my work, hunched over and focused. Placing the ribbon inside the seam took a surgeon's hand and a chess player's patience. But once I struck the first stitch, I was thrilled to find this 'fabric' so yielding. With the first one done my adrenaline rushed. I slowed myself down to try out the ribbon cinching, encouraged by how easy it returned to its original state. I got to stitching the second condom thinking, if I presented two, the queen would be most pleased.

My bladder made it known I had legitimate business here, so I multi-tasked. When it came to wiping, I laid my work across my skirts, being careful to keep the needle far from the body of the condom. The idea of a pin prick anywhere except the opening sent a chill up my back and into the base of my skull.

Now I know how these things work, but Elizabeth wouldn't. I pondered drawing up instructions but decided we'd be better off if I could teach her face to face.

Elated at my entrepreneurship and path to the queen's favor, I admired my work, holding both finished condoms up for inspection. Folding them with care, I placed them back into the linen parcel, for which I expressed gratitude, given it was doing such an amazing job protecting this whole undertaking. Back into my petticoats, I found a more secure place to keep them, now that I had privacy.

That night, the queen decided she would dine with her ladies in her privy chamber. No doubt she wanted an update on my progress. I decided a change in gown was unnecessary and that the parcel was where it should be. I practiced pulling it out discreetly as I sat. Could I really slip this to her? She's a smart lady, she'd give me a way.

Once in the chamber, the lights were more muted than was usual. The days were not as long as they had been in high summer and the clouded sky ushered in a pall of melancholy. But for me, I felt as if I was about to walk through a golden door.

When the queen greeted me, she commented on my beaming countenance.

"It has been a most productive day, Your Grace," I said.

A broad and sweet smile bloomed. She had never smiled at me quite like that before.

"I will be glad to hear of it after we dine," she said.

I curtsied very deeply, taking in her positive favor. This will surely bode well for her view on us McDonnells.

As the meal was served, the ladies and I engaged in continual but mellow chit chat. During the sweets course, Lady Sidney shared a story of how her brother, Lord Robert of all people, had tripped over his dog, losing the fine cap off his head, only to have the dog then snatch it up in his mouth. Lord Robert had to coax the animal to drop it, only to find it devoid of its fine feather and quite saturated with dog spit. We all enjoyed a long and full belly laugh, including the queen, who had to wipe the tears from her face.

After we consumed the last course, the queen pronounced her wish to retire early and asked both Lady Sidney and me to attend her. No one else. Catherine Knollys, with her ankle still healing, bit her lip. I wanted to reassure her, but she didn't look at me and it was just as well, because maybe becoming the queen's preferred bed warmer was the most fortuitous thing to happen for us McDonnells.

As we followed the queen into her bedchamber, I searched for the silver pan, the new tool of my trade. Lady Sidney proceeded to draw down the bed and she signaled me to help her ready the queen.

"I shall prefer to don the nightgown with the gold embroidery. It was a recent gift."

Sidney smiled knowingly, and as she placed the gown over the queen, I visually checked with her to see if I should take down the queen's hair. She handed me the brush. I was nervous to pull too hard, so my brush strokes were light handed.

"You'll never keep the tangles at bay, stroking thus so. Fragile, I am not."

Glad for her feedback I applied more pressure. Within minutes I had her tresses smooth and gleaming through the many waves of curl. Sidney gestured I should braid the queen's hair while she obtained a night cap.

"No, I shall like to keep it loose this night," she said raising a hand.

With my fingers I commenced with fluffing her hair up. I caught her amused eye in the looking glass.

"I thank you for the tireless effort, but all is fine," she said.

She dismissed Sidney but said she had one more task for me to complete. Once alone, Elizabeth came up close to me, her eyes round and happy.

"I have a parcel for you here," I said patting my hip. "My apologies for digging through my petticoats."

The queen laughed. "Thank the Lord for our petticoats and farthingales."

With a touch of ceremony, I presented one of the condoms to her. She held it with delight mixed with bewilderment.

"Your Majesty, may I instruct you on the use of this vessel? Methinks it would work best to roll it up and then have... Lord Robert roll it down on the inhabitant of his codpiece."

Elizabeth giggled.

"Gracefully expressed, Mistress Lindsay," she said. "As a maid, tell me again how such knowledge comes into your possession?"

"Ah... well, having pondered its utility, that appears to be the most effective method."

She nodded, willing to believe anything I might tell her at this point. I was offering her a new freedom and its possibility intoxicated her.

Taking the second condom, I showed her how the ribbon, if pulled gently, would then secure itself. "Lord Robert might be advised to monitor its tightness."

Elizabeth took the second condom and again giggled. I did too. This was so delicious.

"And you told the servants in the catery this was to be part of a glove?"

"I told them it was to be part of a gift for one of my fellow ladies."

"A *fellow* lady indeed," she said.

I nodded.

"Your Majesty, are you confident in the use of these vessels?"

"Yes, and there is my sweet Robin himself to consult."

She placed the condoms in a drawer.

"Mistress, we find the blessing to possess such a cunning device from your far-flung piece of my realm, as is Ireland."

"Those Irish, inventive and practical," I said, nearly forgetting myself.

"Glad I am queen of such people, as much as I am able," she said, looking flattened.

I wondered if she held some regret. That could be good.

"Your Majesty, I am honored to represent a people who are fortunate enough to be within your sovereignty." I hoped she would believe me. Before a few weeks ago, I wouldn't believe me, but standing here, in alliance with this young woman, I mostly meant what I said, a future war of independence withstanding.

"Well, off with you, it is time we all retire," she said.

I curtsied and exited the room. Closing the door, I heard her laugh in pure delight.

After returning to my chamber, Bexley helped me undress. As she brushed my hair, I reveled in how proud Sorley and Mary would be of me, securing this level of confidence with the queen, assuring us peace and compassion. I was finally on track to elevate the standing of my family.

I then pondered on my response to John's note as thoughts of him set off electricity throughout my insides. I imagined the map he wanted to show me, and in order to fall asleep, I named off the eastern states to get my mind to calm down. After New England, I got as far as Tennessee before crossing the twilight and falling into slumber.

A persistent tickling in my ear lifted me out of my sleep. As I opened my eyes, Kat was crouched next to me, by the bed.

"The queen beckons you to her chamber," she whispered.

I pushed myself up and swung my legs to the side of the bed. "Has something happened?"

"Her Majesty says it is a matter between you and she."

With trembling hands, I accepted the robe Kat handed to me. The cold stone slabs of the passageway passed under my bare feet as I followed her in haste to the queen's bedchamber.

Kat took me through the secret passageway and entered the room first. The queen was sitting on the bed, shoulders rounded, and hair hanging into her face. She raised her head and pushed back her hair to reveal eyes large with fear and wet with grief. My throat tightened, and I almost forgot to curtsy. As I did, the queen spoke.

"Kat, we are to be alone with Mistress McDonnell."

Kat narrowed her eyes as she held my gaze. Her face pained as she bowed her head and backed out of the room. She closed the door gently behind her.

The queen wrung her hands as the tears poured down her face.

"Your wretched instrument of sin will make an end to me," she said in a gravelly voice.

"What happened?"

"You will not speak and you will not inquire."

Instinctively, I fell into a low curtsy. I stayed there as the queen whirled around the room, whipping her robe skirt and grabbing at her bedcovers.

A pillow hit my head; its contact was both rude and jarring. I picked it up and looked at the queen. That act had her fly at me, stopping short as she came up to my face.

We stared at each other. I should have averted my eyes but instead I peered into hers and saw a young woman afraid to her soul, for her life and legacy. Her face softened its anger but melted into pain.

"Let me help you," I whispered.

She grabbed my shoulders, and we smacked foreheads as she tried to shake me. Her face reddened, and my shame swelled across my being. Who the hell did I think I was?

My tears only intensified hers. She slumped to the floor, burying her face as she sobbed into her hands. I lowered myself down and sat with her.

Regaining some control, she scowled at me, anxious for some deliverance.

"It slipped from him as we culminated," she said.

"Oh."

"I am ended," she said.

"Please forgive my inquiry, when are your courses due?"

"Five days hence," she said after a few seconds.

"Then you are not going to be with child."

"How can you portend to know such a thing?"

"It is less likely when a woman is so near to her courses."

"But what if—what shall I do?"

She was asking from vulnerable desperation. I answered from newfound hope.

"We will pray for the running of your courses," I said.

"Prayer will give some comfort and pull in God's grace."

"Your Majesty, may I inquire about the condom?"

Elizabeth closed her eyes hard. Keeping her eyes shut she waved me on.

"As it slipped off, was there… some of…?"

"Yes, some in, some out."

"This is good news! It bodes well as there is less of the substance of danger. Perhaps it is just a spider and not a snake."

The queen blinked. A few tears fell from her eyes as she sighed and fell back onto the floor, staring at the ceiling. After several long moments, Elizabeth thrust her hands out to me, indicating a need for assistance to sit back up. I pulled her almost out of a dead weight. On her own, she rose to her knees and thumped me on my shoulder.

"We shall pray now," she commanded.

I followed her in putting my hands into prayer. This time I found myself silently speaking to a God I left behind in sixth grade, asking for compassion, asking for safe deliverance, and asking for wisdom.

Elizabeth interrupted my prayer. "We ask God to take mercy on an act that sins against Him."

"God is an exemplar of forgiveness," I said.

"This will not go well for you here if God ignores or punishes me."

"Your Grace, you were expressing love."

"And such expressions have consequences," she said.

CHAPTER TWENTY-SEVEN

The whole next morning I busied myself to mask my nerves and exhaustion. A few times I sensed Kat's eyes scrutinizing me. Despite meeting her concerned gaze, I decided to disclose nothing. Not even to her. I was afraid of her judgment of me, and the queen. Elizabeth could also kick my ass or worse.

Around midday, the queen emerged from meeting with the privy council. I jumped upon hearing her voice. Out of the periphery of my vision, I saw Kat startle as well.

The queen swept into our room, motioning with her hand for us to stay seated as we were. She surveyed us, stopping for a half second longer on Kat but avoiding eye contact with me. The queen forced a smile to most of the other ladies and inquired on Lady Knollys's injury.

"The ache lessens each day, along with the swelling, Your Grace."

"Good, good, I decree no one shall have to endure swelling or any such regrets from that night's festivities."

My stomach burned. I imagine hers did too.

Elizabeth turned and left the room with a rustle of her skirts, her dress a declaration of her state duties. Kat's eyes were tense, as she shot a look over at me. The ladies returned to their sewing, but my fingers struggled to keep the needle tracking in a straight line. Oblivious, Bexley began to hum part of the song from the masque. A song about romance which brought me back to my own situation.

I questioned everything I was feeling and doing. The butterflies for John were shamed away, and what would Maimeó and Daideó think if they knew I was making condoms for the queen? Sucky ones apparently. And I was no closer to finding my mother. I had pushed it from my mind for other priorities.

As my hands wove the needle and thread through the sleeve of this most unfortunate shirt, a dam formed in my throat. My plan had not only failed but was making a mess.

A hand on my shoulder had me drop the needle into the folds of my kirtle.

"Mistress, come with me," Kat said.

I was a bit lightheaded, like the way it is before hyperventilating, but I needed to find the needle. I did not want it lying about causing more damage. Kat's eyes clouded.

"Up with you, then," she said.

Her tone caused a few of the other ladies to take notice.

"I've dropped my needle," I said, hearing the strain in my voice.

Lady Sidney pointed to my belly. "It is in deep, do not let it pierce you."

Finding the eye, I pulled the needle from the fabric of my bodice and with shaky hands placed it into the shirt. Exiting behind Kat, we moved through the halls in a charged silence. Kat looked askance at me.

"Mistress, walk like one of the queen's proper ladies."

I raised my head and tucked my chin but remained staring straight ahead. I swallowed hard.

"Kat, are you most vexed with my conduct?"

"I am."

Kat led me into a scantly utilized passageway, where the walls were bare and there was nothing to deaden our footfalls as they echoed. We descended a set of winding stairs and pushed on through another passageway, this one still more cold and murky.

It was a small respite to reach a door to the outside. The cloud-muffled sunlight promised some hope.

"No one shall hear our words out here," Kat said.

I nodded.

"Mistress McDonnell—"

"I cannot disclose anything about the queen," I said, finding my voice.

"Her Grace has told me," Kat said.

"What news then?"

"The queen does not yet bleed."

"Is she having symptoms—signs of her courses coming?"

"She complains of headaches which would be expected, but she does not sleep, and as such, I cannot say her accompanying headaches originate from her courses."

Kat glowered at me hard and grabbed my arms.

"Above all else, the queen cannot suffer through bearing a child." She paused. "As you possess the knowledge of prevention, Mistress, do you also possess knowledge of the dark arts?"

"Does the queen ask this of me?"

"I ask," Kat said through her teeth.

"Do you realize what you are saying to me?"

Kat's face stormed as her eyes jetted out tears.

"Our queen believes herself to be short on this earth should she ever be with child," Kat finally said, her voice cracking. "You well know, Mistress, that she is given constant counsel to marry and issue an heir yet cannot without heralding her own doom. And you have offered Her Majesty false hope."

"Oh Kat, I only wished to help her. She loves Lord Robert and ached to be with him."

"It is a sin!"

"I think it is love."

Kat shook her head.

"Then she should be condemned to live without love?" I asked.

"It is her almighty soul that will be condemned." Kat then broke off. She didn't seem to know what to do with her hands and arms.

"God would not have placed her on the throne through all adversity to then sink her fate," I said.

Kat scrutinized me, eyes like slits. "Mistress, you speak with convenient bending of God's intent. God holds an anointed queen to higher standards."

Her words landed heavy.

"She should be happy." It remained my only defense.

"The crown never resides in happiness. It is an illusion," Kat said.

"But she could be a fulfilled queen."

"You will not say that if she seizes all of Ireland on her way to fulfillment."

"What, what do you know?" I said, as a prickling burned down the back of my neck.

Kat set her jaw.

"She would not do that, the queen is loath to make war," I said, my voice quavering.

"Mistress, you are correct, war is not the way of this queen. I speak from anger." She then folded her hands in front of her.

"Mistress McDonnell, methinks it best if you occupy your time away from court—"

"Pray tell me what you mean?"

"You serve as a reminder to the queen of her indiscretion. If she is with child, her wrath will surely be visited upon you."

Coming back into the palace, now bustling with domestic activities and those that run the country, Kat and I walked with no words passing between us until we reached my bedchamber.

"Mistress, I will assist in packing a trunk and securing a carriage for you."

"Where am I to go?"

Maybe I should return home. My breathing quickened as my mind took a panicked run into how I'd fucked things up so badly.

"Dr. Dee has taken up the task. He will be holding conference with an assemblage of men of letters and their wives. He thought you could well assist him."

Oh God, what does he know?

I looked at Kat for a long time, formulating my question.

"Am I his charge?"

"You are Her Majesty's servant and by proxy his servant," she said.

"Servant?"

"That is all."

"And the queen? Is she informed of this decision?"

"She requested your subtle removal. It is too disquieting for her to lay eyes on you, yet she does not want anyone to be the wiser."

Through all this crazy-making, I would end up spending time with John Dee.

Kat took a few gowns and packed them with care as I tried to help. A blip of consolation registered when she chose my favorite green dress.

"Shall I take my sewing with me?"

"I think not, you will be occupied with Dr. Dee's demonstrations to his guests, as he assures me in his letter."

We fell into a quiet lull as we continued to pack, draining off some of the tension.

"Kat, are you most disappointed in me?"

She ceased her task but did not look up right away. Her eyes went back and forth as she seemed to be putting together her next words.

"Mistress, I am distressed to see Her Majesty in such knots of despair. We are wondering if our trust was ill-placed."

I lunged toward her and took one of her hands in both of mine.

"You were so kind to me from the beginning. That meant so much to me and to think that may be lost. You understand my intentions were to help."

Kat's expression betrayed a small sense of warmth.

"Pray she bleeds and never venture to help again," Kat said resolute.

I kissed her hand and she pulled it back.

"Mistress McDonnell, get your cloak and do your penance."

Early the next morning, as I boarded the carriage, Kat saw me off with a simple adieu. As I settled in for the short ride, I had to calm my escalating anxiety and find my true bearings. After all, a failed condom does not a bad person make.

CHAPTER TWENTY-EIGHT

I remain grateful that, at the time, I was unaware of what was unfolding back at Dunanynie. Riding through the mantle of an early morning fog, Gillaspick McDonnell arrived at the castle just after dawn. Sorley met his young, yet shrewd nephew at the drawbridge gate.

"I can tell by ya face you got nothing good to tell me."

Gillaspick shook his head and slid down from his steed, giving its reins over to a stable hand but telling him to keep his horse close.

"Out with it, lad," Sorley said as they walked to the castle keep.

"We spotted Shane and his men setting off to find their position of attack," Gillaspick said.

Sorley ran both hands through his hair and kicked the dirt.

"Damn him! What he fails to realize is that if he breaks against us, he weakens Ireland."

"Aye, Uncle. He's playing right into English hands."

"The fires have been lit to signal my brother James across the sea?"

"Aye."

"So we square off for the sport of that English bastard, Sussex, in the Pale. We be damned if the queen herself ordered this," Sorley said.

"You think—"

"Sussex takes his own liberties, but God help us if…"

Sorley stopped. He didn't want to hear himself finish the sentence.

※

I wished I was going to Mortlake under better circumstances. I see that it is a twenty-first-century value to believe in the fulfillment of full on, romantic love, and I was wearing modern bias as blinders.

As the carriage entered onto the estate, my palms became wet. I hoped I didn't seem the mess I was inside, especially to John. As we came to a stop, I made the decision to act with confidence. I am the queen's lady sent by the Chieftain Somhairle Buidhe McDonnell. I deserve to be here. When that didn't work so well, I resorted to the mantra Julia reminded me of, back at Bonamargy. "I am that I am." It helped me to take my ego and fear out of the whole equation. I just am—no judgment.

As I alighted from the carriage at the hand of the royal footman, John burst out from the manor and greeted me. He bowed his head and took my arm before I could curtsy. Although maybe I wasn't supposed to.

"My dear mother and I are most fortified by your presence," he said.

Mother?

In the house we went. Its mixed scents of parchment, fire, and warm wood was familiar to me this time. He was familiar to me, and a welcome sight, but I had to be on my game.

"Dr. Dee, have any of your esteemed guests yet arrived?"

"All are due this afternoon. We have arranged a reception prior to the evening meal being served."

As we walked through the entryway, the servants stood in a line and each curtsied or bowed as I passed, as if I was the queen. At the end of the line stood a well-appointed but older woman.

"Mistress McDonnell, this is my mother, Mistress Jane Dee."

I curtsied.

"We welcome thee and offer gratitude to the queen for dispatching your presence to grace our upcoming festivities," she said.

"It is a pleasure to serve," I said, feeling false to receive such a positive welcome.

From there, Mistress Dee led me into a sitting room where elderflower tea and seedcake were waiting for us.

"Is the tea much different in Ireland?" Mistress Dee asked.

Yes, when I don't burn it to the sides of the pot, I thought.

"We may be more inclined to drink it cold."

"Cold?" she said.

"Yes, it can be quite fortifying," I said, actually talking about the twenty-first century.

John waited for his mother's response.

"Should thee prefer your tea cooled whilst at Mortlake?"

"I am happy to drink it warmed by the fire and in your good company."

She looked at John and shifted her eyes back to me. I interrupted our exchange upon noticing a blond-and-black tabby cat sleeping behind John's chair. I wondered if it was the same one I'd encountered on my first trip to Mortlake.

"Who is this magical creature?" I asked, hoping to get a chance to come closer. John peered around him.

"This is Percival, he remains a good friend," John said as he reached down to run his fingers over the cat's head.

"Like any good knight of the round table would be," I said. "May I?"

John nodded and I reached across to allow Percival to take in the scent of my fingers. He rubbed his whiskers against the back of my hand, the soft fur of his face welcome against my skin.

"Doth thou show all felines such favor?" Mistress Dee asked.

"Aye, I had a cat named Merlin."

She smiled but John stared at me, his mouth slightly open.

"Good name, yes?" Perhaps you wish you'd thought of it first, Dr. Dee?"

John closed his mouth, looking tongue-tied.

Changing the subject, Mistress Dee told me about Mortlake's herbal gardens and the flowers to be picked and placed about the house before the guests were to arrive.

"Mother, Mistress McDonnell, given the hour I shall attend to my maps in preparation of sharing them with our scholarly guests."

"I pray you will allow me to look upon them as well," I said.

Earnestness took over his face and what I hoped was a hint of desire in his eyes. Mistress Dee informed me I would find my trunks in my bedchamber. It hit me I would be spending time, at night, under the same roof as John. It's Elizabethan England and I am sleeping over at John's house. I must be blessed.

"Mistress, will you be taking any prayer?" John asked.

"Now?"

"Or anon, before preparations begin," Mistress Dee said.

"We have several places of solitude for contemplation, including the church, yonder from the garden wall," John said.

"I shall like to be introduced of the places fit for contemplation." His being religious might have dissuaded my feelings in the past, but here it made me more crazy about him.

"Dr. Dee, do you take prayer alone?"

His eyes warmed. "Shall you like to join me?"

"I shall."

"It is in the dawning hours of the morning. I fear that may be too early for your liking."

"I find those early hours steeped in the stillness required to feel the spirit."

"The Holy Spirit?" he asked.

"Yes, of course."

Instead of leaving, he remained with his mother and me to discuss the itineraries of the coming days. As he referred to the plans, drawn up on sheets of parchment, I listened to his voice, masculine but with sweet tones which sometimes belied an excitement. I could tell he loved his work.

"Dr. Dee and Mistress Dee, for this first day, what duties shall I perform?"

"Attend to the guests as they arrive. Inquire of their sojourns. Then, entertain the wives," Mistress Dee said.

"Do the men go off to another room to talk of science and mathematics?" I asked.

"Aye, that is usually the course," John said.

"Do you not think women capable of participating in such conversations?"

He was stumped for a few seconds.

"Aye, you are accustomed to being in the company of our brilliant queen," he said.

"Who demands conversations of wise substance and meaning," I said, exaggerating.

John placed his hand on his heart. "Mistress McDonnell, I desire to behold how the parley delights ye when it turns to navigation to the New World. But I fear the wives may not share the desire to converse thus so. Nor will their husbands appreciate such mixed comradery."

"So regardless, I am to attend to only the wives?"

"Aye," he said, his brows rounding with a hint of worry.

That afternoon as the carriages began to roll in, I found my duties came naturally to me. Most of the men were older scholars, dressed in robes similar to John but stout in their figures. The wives were of various ages. A couple were second wives. They were also of different stations, some dressed more richly, but above all else, they were kind in their demeanor.

As we split up, as John said we would, I settled in with the feminine set. Our conversation centered around life at court as they wanted to hear about the queen's gardens, her meals, and her moods —and what I knew about her taking a husband.

"She should marry soon. It will help the country to settle," Mary Stukely said.

"Not if she takes up with a Catholic," Jane Tyrburne responded.

From the beginning, I liked how these women got on. Less concern for finery and places in society, as it is at court, and more inclination toward intellectual pursuit. Late in the afternoon, most of the women wanted to read. I appreciated the quiet occupation, as it gave me a chance to wander the house, asking the servants about linens or fires and, if near the kitchen, of meals. The cook willingly obliged my request for more vegetables but said I should not take in too much of the lowly foods. The first night, despite being a seasoned sixteenth-century vegetarian, I was not quick enough to prevent the serving boy from heaping a steaming lamb shank onto my plate. Waiting until all the others were served and eating, I motioned for the boy to return to my side and asked him to remove my dish and replace it without the lamb. From the other end, John took note and cocked his head to one side. I smiled and returned to my conversation with William Stukely, a scholar residing at Oxford.

"Not to your liking?" Stukely asked.

I might have lied or made up a story, but instead I just said, "Nay, it is not."

John caught my eye again, looking concerned. But I was drawn into the billowing debate that started when William Stukely asked about my surname.

"Mistress, with a name like McDonnell, do ye hail from Ireland or from Scotland?"

"My family lays claim to both," I said.

He frowned. "And ye serves the Queen of England."

"She is also the Queen of Ireland," his wife added.

"We hope for a peaceful Ireland under the queen's rule," I said.

Surprise flashed across the men's faces.

"I hardly think that remains possible," Dr. Sharpe said.

All eyes went to him.

"Pray tell what you see as the obstacle," I said.

"Mary of Scots hath laid claim to the English throne and demands to be Elizabeth's heir. She has her Scots set up there on the north coast."

Was this true?

"I know there have been squabbles—" I said.

"Squabbles? My dear lady, I'd say some significant battles and likely more to come."

"What causes you to say that?" I asked.

"The English crown wants to colonize Ireland, and the Irishry don't want their land taken away by either the English or the Scots. The chieftains—"

"How do you solve that one?" William Stukely asked.

John was reading the discussion on my face.

"Mistress McDonnell, how fares the exchange down there?" John called out in a light-hearted voice.

"It is lively, Dr. Dee," I said.

"And how fares thee at your end?" Dr. Sharpe asked.

"All is well and invigorating but I trust not as rousing as yours, sir," John said.

"Perhaps it is merely a need for more wine," Dr. Tyrburne said, to which everyone laughed. I wished John to stop interceding; this was critical political information.

Several of the male guests poured themselves more wine, and the overall conversation shifted to mundane topics.

But Dr. Sharpe turned to me confidentially and said, "Perhaps Lord Sidney being sent to Dublin and the Pale will solve the problem of peace."

A cloud of heat rose in my gut.

I stared at Dr. Sharpe; his sloped nose and direct style underlined the appropriateness of his name.

"Heaven knows the tenure of Sussex hath been a vile yet impotent show."

I knew little of Sussex.

"Whence is Sussex now?" Stukely leaned in and asked Sharpe.

Dr. Sharpe eyed me as if I might answer.

A hand on his shoulder caused him to look up. It was John.

"On what subjects do you converse upon to rouse vexation across my hostess's face?"

"We only venture some words on the English interests in the western domain," Dr. Sharpe answered. "Mistress, my apologies if we hath caused you worry."

I smiled, aware of all the eyes turned toward me.

"All is well. It appears that talk of the state of the country is inescapable around such learned company," I said.

John then raised his goblet to the whole table. "God save the queen and bless all her loyal subjects."

The group lifted their goblets in accordance. Dr. Sharpe added, "Above all, those scholars." The group concurred.

"I welcome—we welcome you here to Mortlake for the bounty of knowledge that resides at this table. We look forward to ideas spawned and the plans sprung from our time together," John said.

With that, the evening wound down as the guests made their way toward their rooms. John, his mother, and I became a receiving line as each couple bade us thanks and good night.

After the room cleared, I was unsure what to do. What I'd hoped would be an evening of catching each other's eye and sharing smiles had me instead uneasy about Lady Sidney's husband and Lord Sussex. John's micromanaging made it worse. Was it that the conversation appeared like it was vexing the shit out of me, or was it something else which motivated John to shut it down? The electricity between us diverted into the ground.

"Mistress McDonnell, how did you get on with the wives?"

"They are all lovely. We got on quite well. And you with their husbands?"

"I believe these days will prove beneficial for the country."

"How so?" I asked.

Surveying the room, he searched for words. He seemed satisfied with not finding them, producing only a tight-lipped smile.

"It remains to be seen."

This was not playful; it was not flirty; it was evasive.

"Mistress, what did the ladies inquire about pertaining to the queen?"

The dining table scraped along the floor as the servants moved it to sweep the rug underneath. I was inclined to not answer, but I couldn't play that game, not here.

"Dr. Dee, what is your concern?"

My tone was undeniable.

"Mistress, your duty prevents you from revealing most of what you witness regarding the queen."

I straightened my shoulders and took in a deep breath. "Dr. Dee, I am quite aware of my duty in regard to discretion. You should have no care."

A flash of anger came across his face, which annoyed me even more.

"You should understand, the queen prefers descriptions of the grandeur of her court to be circulated and consumed. These ladies are a most willing audience," I said.

"You are irked by my cares."

"Perhaps it is the manner in which you express them. You should have faith in me by now, otherwise why would you call upon me of all the queen's ladies?" Hearing myself, I realized the distrust woven into this whole English court experience was wearing on me. John did not flinch.

"I am a devoted servant toward the protection of the crown. I act from that motivation, and you should be glad," he said.

"Then we are the same," I said, holding my gaze. "If that is all, Dr. Dee, I shall retire to my bedchamber."

He said nothing.

I marched past him and out of the room. While I was so pissed, I still craved he say something.

CHAPTER TWENTY-NINE

As I made my way up the stairs, my stomach soured, and it was more than what had transpired with John. My gut told me Sussex and now Lord Sidney were at the center of trouble for my family. I held hope this would unite the O'Neills and McDonnells, but nothing could have been further from the reality playing out up north.

"Och, what does it say already? Spit it out, man."

Shane waved his free hand as he held a letter in the other, his eyes drilling down the paragraphs.

Without lowering the parchment, he addressed the few at his own roundtable of men.

"Elizabeth requires we take Dunluce Castle from the McDonnells to show our fealty."

"So we can deliver it into English hands?"

"It will be for us," Shane said, as he pushed back on his chair and stood up. The other men followed with yells and claps. After a moment, the room quieted, in anticipation of Shane's next words.

"We'll have to fix a better way to slide around Sorley and James McDonnell."

"I'd say start praying for favorable weather on this round."

"We will not forfeit our advantage."

"Surprising them is the only way. We must prevent him from signaling the Scotch Redshanks to join the battle," Shane said.

The men rolled into silence as a serving boy entered their company with a tray of mead and ale. Once he'd refilled tankards and left, conversation rumbled up again.

"But what if the crown courts the McDonnells to challenge us at the same time, stacking them for a victory?" one of the men asked.

"The crown fears a Scottish foothold more than the Noble Irishry," Shane said.

"Then we need to execute soon."

"Or wait, and watch and plan," Shane said. The other men came in closer, seeing he was onto something.

My chamber was a welcome respite from the tide of the first scholarly evening. A dull headache was now maturing into a pounding pain. I think I drank too much. I'd have to be more mindful.

A gentle knock at the door ramped up my heart, thinking it was John coming to make amends. But it was a maid named Anne, dressing me for bed.

"Am I the last of the ladies?"

"Yes, Mistress."

"Good, it should always be that way," I told her.

I tried not to let my arms flop as she did her duty. Kat told me she liked it when the queen lifted her arms and intuited the flow of the dressing or undressing.

As Anne left, I took my single candle and moved it over to the bed where the blankets were already drawn down. Laying my head on the pillow and burrowing down into the mattress, it was like a warm envelope. I told myself to resist becoming accustomed to it as there was no joy spending my first night under John Dee's roof. At least lying down allayed the ache in my head. Thoughts drifted to the queen and the current quiet crisis. What if she was pregnant with an heir? Perhaps then she could marry Robert Dudley. Maybe she would be grateful. Or maybe he'd demand to be made king. What would change toward my family? Ireland? The New World?

Not sleeping was not an option, and no matter how much I thought about these things, nothing would get solved tonight. I took all the worries and gloomy feelings and imagined putting them in boxes of mother-of-pearl. I focused on benevolent forces and empowered energies transforming them. With that, sleep came, although it felt brief upon waking. Looking toward the window, I wondered what I would be encountering this morning, gray with a soft rain.

Good, the negative ions will give us all more clarity. I vowed to be clearer in my thoughts and emotions. Surrendering to that awareness was like hitting a reset button.

I approached the window, registering the contrast of the upstretched trees next to the flowing grasses of the meadow adjacent. A brown-speckled rabbit, hopping high, disappeared into the woods. I wished him safe there. Once deciding this view was as good as any to take my morning meditation, I dragged a chair over and sat cross-legged. I thought today, I'll even place my hands in mudra—all spiritual luxuries I did not usually have while appearing to pray as a devout Christian at court.

As I moved into my practice, it surprised me to access peace so quickly. My mother, Dorje, and the Buddha Amitabha came into my awareness. In barely a whisper, I uttered Om Namo Amitabha Budhaya, asking to connect to the wisdom in knowing these past times and staying in this past as my present.

Upon opening my eyes, the familiar sight of John's black robes appeared on the path below my window. I startled.

"Good morrow," he whispered and bowed.

"Good morrow, I returned, remaining low so he could only see my head—after all, I was in a nightgown.

"Are you most vexed with me?" he asked.

I paused and shook my head.

"Then this day is already more blessed," he said as a broad smile broke across his face.

His exuberance made me laugh. I mean who would ever say this stuff in my time?

I hadn't noticed he had a flower tucked in his sleeve. "I picked this for you," he said, assessing how to give it to me.

I decided to rescue him. "I shall look for it when I see you next. Have you taken your morning prayers?"

"Aye, and have you?"

"Aye, and it was a most fulfilling connection with the Divine," I said smiling at my own way of sharing my truth.

John stared at me. I wasn't sure if it was what I had just said or if something else was happening.

"'Til we break our fast?" I said.

He gave a quick bow of the head. "Til we break our fast." He stepped back and walked away. Through his image in the window glass, I perceived his glance back in my direction. Maybe he could see my reflection, as I now stood in my light gown. But, as he was about to round the corner, one of our guests met him and the two greeted each other. With a jolt of energy, I leaped across the room. A small knock came at my door. It was Anne come to help me dress.

All set for the day, I descended the steps down to the kitchen. The cook showed me the ingredients for the day's meals. Being prepared were oatcakes and two different berry jams. She named them for me and instructed a young girl to take them out to what I call the Little Hall (little because anything after Hampton Court or Whitehall was going to feel tiny).

Conversation rose as the group gathered in the hallway. I greeted them all, inquiring about the quality of their slumbers and early morning activities. Apparently, a few of the men had been for a walk in the woods already. I appreciated this group would likely not be going out for any hunting.

John entered, passing behind me. As I had my hands clasped behind my back, I felt a brush of something soft. He placed the promised flower in my hand and stood next to me, announcing that we would be taking breakfast before the scholars (men) would meet in his study and laboratory. I told my women that we would decide our morning activities after we ate.

John and I stayed outside the door as the guests filed in to take their seats around the table. I ventured to bring my hand around and smell the flower. It was a sweet scent that I wish I could bathe in. I stopped a maid passing by and requested she place the bloom in a vase.

"Mistress, where shall you like it?"

"Perhaps in your bedchamber?" John said.

He waited to see if I agreed. I told the maid my preferred place was next to my bed, aware of John taking note before we slipped into the Little Hall.

CHAPTER THIRTY

Toward the end of the third and last day, John and his mother found me just as a note, waxed shut with Kat's seal, was delivered into my hand. Was Elizabeth late and I banished? If that were true, I might be taken from here immediately. I much preferred it here at Mortlake. John's mother was pleased to forfeit the hostess duties to me, only making appearances from time to time. She also approved of most of my decisions relating to hospitality, although I was mostly following her schedule of menus and John's schedule of activities. It's possible she was tolerating me and had to defer to my role given my status in the royal household. Maybe I was being paranoid.

Inhaling, I tried to pick up any residue of energy vibrating from the parchment. Serious was the only tone I perceived. I undid the seal.

Mistress McDonnell,

It is with a happy heart that I take up pen to inform you of the joyous course of our matter, now in flow here at Whitehall. Our Lady Sovereign is of the mind to recall you back to court upon the discharge of your duty to Dr. Dee's proceedings at Mortlake.

Joy sprang up through my body, so much so I danced a little in place. Turning around, I found Mistress Dee looking at me, amused. "The happiest of notes hath surely found its way to this house. Pray tell what tidings hath been bestowed upon thee."

"It is good news from court," I said.

"Not a note from a suitor, then?"

Her comment threw me, especially saying it in front of John, so much so that a flush of warmth came into my cheeks. I know she saw it. An impish smile played across her face.

"The mistress hath received a note of good tidings but she will not say if it be from a suitor."

"I should not be in want of a suitor's note coming from court."

"It would not please you?" John asked, looking into my eyes.

I tried to read his intent. "While I remain here, it would not."

"Perhaps there is a nobleman in Ireland or Scotland from whom you would most like to hear?" Mistress Dee said.

"There is—there are—my father and beloved grandfather."

Mistress Dee exchanged looks with her son.

"Mistress McDonnell, thou honor them well with thy devotion," she said.

"They are great men of heart."

"Then thou art blessed."

John was gazing at me with a soft pensiveness in his eyes. His mother intertwined her
arm around his. Reaching out her other hand, to my surprise, she took mine in hers and brought us into the Little Hall.

An abundance of candles flickered in unison around the room, their light playing onto the walls as twilight fell outside. Small branches of evergreen and willow were placed in sweeping bundles across the table, weaving around the glowing candles and bouquets from the garden.

"Art thou pleased? Methinks this evening should be one that inspires greater merriment," Mistress Dee said to John.

"Aye, Mother, well accomplished."

Both turned to me with the same expectant look on their faces, so identical I couldn't help but chuckle. I wanted to tell them how cute they looked, but you know, sixteenth century.

"One cannot be other than merry in this room, that I have already begun," I said.

Mistress Dee patted my arm. "And there shall be a surprise that I will tell not even the pair of you," she said.

John grinned at me. "Then we all shall be the beneficiaries."

She bid us to ready ourselves for the evening while she was to attend to all the details. Back in my room, I found my heart pounding once I'd chosen my best gown. I knew what I wanted to have happen tonight. What I was not sure of was Mistress Dee. Was she trying to marry me off to someone back home or did she see some future between John and I? As Anne helped me assemble myself, I decided to be bold.

"The household is in good spirits this evening."

"Aye, Mistress, it is so."

"Do festive nights happen here often?"

She stopped arranging my hair to consider the question. "Not like this evening. Dr. Dee entertains guests, but they are occasions to show his books."

"Have there been ladies that come to meet him?"

Anne giggled. "It is always scholars."

That was a relief.

"Mistress, I dare say that Dr. Dee has courted none a lady since I arrived to employment in this household."

"Oh?"

"It seems his desire is to court only that of his beloved studies."

She'd confirmed my unexpressed fear.

"Anne, you heard him say as much?"

"It is clear by his pursuits in service of Her Majesty. He is solely devoted to his studies and royal duty."

I sat sorry I'd asked. Anne continued with my hair as I questioned what I had been perceiving. Perhaps John acting interested was solely to get me to trust him, as he keeps watch on me for the queen. And his mother may have been complicit, finding out how my future looked back in Ireland. A boiling of humiliation and anger rolled through my body. My breathing took on a heaviness, like inhaling through mud. Looking up, I hoped the rising tears were not noticeable to Anne. I tried to slow down my breathing, my thoughts now moving to how to get out of this evening. Could I feign feeling sick?

Dismissing Anne to be alone to collect myself, I paced around the bed. The lone bloom, John's gift from the morning before, stood leaning in its vase. The white, creamy petals pulled me to touch them, but I stopped myself. Instead, I snatched the vase to put it out of my sight, as I unraveled into the red of anger and the black of shame and loss.

In an impulse, I threw open my door to summon Anne to take the flower away, but there was John, walking down the hall.

"What is to befall that flower, Mistress?"

"It causes me to sneeze," I said, thrusting the vase toward him.

John took a half step back yet grabbed the vase in his hand.

"Then the offending plant will be taken hence and the wretch who offered the mistress such a gift shall be sent to his perdition."

With exaggeration, John extended his arm, holding the vase as far from me as he could. He tried to stifle a smile.

"You are acquainted with this wretch then?"

"I am," John said maintaining a serious countenance.

"Before you punish him, I should like to know his true intention in bestowing this gift to me."

"Oh, you do not already know?"

"I suspect it resounds in obligation," I said.

John tilted his head, now placing the flower behind his back.

"Obligation, Mistress?"

"Duty," I said, hearing my voice roughen.

"Then perhaps it is not given from such wretched a man as we suspect. Perhaps he is answering to a higher calling."

So on edge, I couldn't decipher what he was telling me. I wanted to say, WTF John. I wanted him to speak American and just tell me what the hell is going on between us—or what's not going on. Instead, I searched his eyes. We were at an impasse.

"Dr. Dee, it is time we attend to the guests."

John brought his shoulders back. "Yes, our guests will be in want of their hosts."

What does he mean OUR—these are HIS guests. Still with one hand behind his back, John offered his other arm to me. I stepped back.

"It is best I am free to move about the guests unencumbered. I thank you not to extend your hand but instead to put it to use to rid me of that vile flower."

With that, I surged down the stairs, catching myself from tripping into a tumble halfway down. I dared not look behind me.

Entering the Little Hall, Mistress Dee motioned for me to stand at the seat beside her. John took his usual place at the head of the opposite end. Soon, each couple came in, dressed in a higher level of resplendency than they had all visit. The men bowed to John, his mother, and to me, with ceremony. Joyful exchanges were shared among all the guests. Quite sure I was baring my teeth like a caged wolf, I willed myself to look gracious.

The servants, conducting themselves almost as if they were part of the royal household, paraded showstopper dishes before laying them on the table before all the guests. I felt left behind as the verve in the room kept rising. It was not until the second course when Mistress Dee called on John to make a toast that I could lay eyes on him. Raising his glass upward, John gazed at all those gathered, save for me. Right then, I damned myself for noticing how fine he appeared in his light blue doublet that set off his eyes.

"With God's help, we have assembled hither these past days to extend our knowledge. I thank ye for all contributions." Now looking straight at me, John finished with, "God keep Her Majesty." All replied in kind, including me. John dropped his eye contact, and I wished I'd looked away first.

The conversation at our end of the table was pleasant, even animated, but I was a poor actress.

"A grimness hath taken over your face, Mistress," John's mother said.

"Tonight marks the end of our gatherings. It is with sadness that I spend this last evening."

"Yet, Mistress, you shall return to the queen's service. Is that not something to look forward to with joy?"

I nodded. She saw my time here as temporary. No attachment.

As the night continued, musicians entered the Little Hall—Mistress Dee's surprise. As they began to play, the couples took up with a dance. John made no move to ask me to participate. Instead, the guests encouraged his mother to partner with her son, so they could celebrate their true hosts. Determined to not let one tear flow, I slipped away to the kitchen.

There I pretended to have business thanking the cooks for their service, which only garnered me odd looks and polite nods. Fortunately, it was already late. I just had to make it until tomorrow. Soon, I'd be re-entering court and able to resume my duties, my work there. But none of it was very enticing.

I trudged out from the kitchen into the gardens. The moon was almost full, and it shone a path for me, out of kindness or maybe pity. Sitting on the bench in the middle reminded me of lying atop the boulder in my mother's garden. I closed my eyes and breathed. The open air was a comfort, as I always had my breath. As long as I lived, I would have my breath. I also had the moon, hearing Daideó's words to seek out 'God's glow in the darkness' whenever I felt alone.

CHAPTER THIRTY-ONE

My grandparents' love for me rushed into my awareness in the absence of love I held for myself. My thoughts focused into a meditation prayer of Metta Bhavana—sending them loving kindness and offering it to all those around me. Through my practice, I communed with my purpose for being here.

"We bring peace," I whispered. "All the forces and energies that deliver me to this moment, come with the intention of peace."

I imagined peace washing in and around me, lapping at my toes and then my fingers as I reached down to bathe my hands. Its source poured from my core and my heart, like a waterfall of warmth and luminosity. I could finish my duty here and refocus on my new chance to serve my family and the queen.

With a shifted outlook I hoped to maintain, I took in the fragrances of the grass and night air. As I strode back toward the house, notes of flutes and mandolins wove around me. Once rejoining the festivities, Dr. Stukely took my hand into the dance. As I fell in with the group, twirling and moving through the circle, it all struck me as a delight. How amazing I got to be with these people, so intelligent and now celebrating their time together. Feeling appreciation for being able to kick up my feet in the sixteenth century, I knew, for this moment, I belonged here to take full part.

As the dance wound down, I wondered if I would ever be a part of this particular assembly again. Maybe someday with my mother present.

"Mistress McDonnell, you have been missed," Mistress Dee said as she appeared by my side.

"Have I?"

She gave me a half smile and used her chin to direct my gaze to John. He stood by the mantle watching his guests, his eyes soon finding me. I smiled, testing to see if the ice I'd created earlier would thaw. He gave me a tight grin, which was something, and enough for me to make my way over to him.

As I passed by, my skirts brushed over his foot, and I lingered. Turning, John immediately locked eyes with me.

"Dr. Dee, I was mistaken to say your flower had brought me grief."

John raised his eyebrows in a look of gratitude.

"Its sweet scent is what I shall miss tonight," I said.

"My intention was only to impart that sweet fragrance to your senses."

Heat rose to my cheeks. John broke out into a huge grin as my new rose coloring laid my feelings bare.

John motioned for one of the servants to come over and he spoke into his ear. He did not share why. Instead, he asked me to partner with him for the next dance.

I responded by taking a tiny step in the direction of the group already in formation. As we joined in, I saw a nod of approval from Dr. Stukely.

When it came time to join hands, a wave of energy passed through my body as John and I made contact. Now I found myself wishing I was back in the twenty-first century, not because I wanted to escape this but because of what I wanted to do to him.

As the dancing ended, most of our guests were either tipsy or blissfully exhausted. Wishes for a good night and expressions of thanks resounded, as each filed past us to seek their beds.

"I think all leave our celebration with a gladdened heart," John said to his mother.

"I still can raise the spirits," she said, stepping to the side to regain her balance.

I stooped to catch her arm and she waved me off already taking her leave toward her bedchamber, leaving just John and me among the servants clearing the space.

John nodded to Anne who was waiting to guide his mother to her room. With every second, a deep craving was rising up in me—to lead him outside across the grass, away from the house, pushing him up against the garden wall, taking in the feel of his full body against mine. I wanted to know what it was like to kiss him.

Instead, we stood looking about the room, each directing a servant here and there and finally turning toward each other.

"This is so regrettably the end of the evening," he said.

"Is it, John?"

"For what is left, Mistress—Lindsay?"

Was he leaving it up to me?

"Perhaps we could visit the moon," I said offering my hand.

Without saying another word, John grasped my fingers and led us outdoors, down to the lawn. Our steps along the yielding grass made a pleasing rushing sound in unison. Once we stopped, John raised his gaze to the night sky bespeckled by the hot white stars, while still holding my hand.

"Do you take to studying the moon?" I asked.

"Yes, often—I suspect it has a definite influence on us."

"Which is always changing," I said.

John nodded as he beamed at me.

"It shows us that our lives remain in flux, nothing stays the same," I said.

"As the Greeks say, panta rhei—all is flowing—and from that we pray to God to guide us through," he said.

My heart was opening and a yearning to touch him was taking over. Yet I kept the connection going through our words.

"The moon is nearly full."

"Strange phenomenon happens under a full moon," he said, looking sideways at me. "I often bear witness to that which is unanticipated."

"You see things I would like to see," I said.

John turned to me full on and took a step toward me. "I am blessed from where I stand."

My breath became unsteady. I had never been this close to him.

"What do you see, John?"

"Lindsay," he said, looking into my eyes. He lifted my hand and kissed each of my fingers in slow caresses, his beard smooth against my skin. I turned my hand to offer my palm. He continued, his warm breath reaching between my fingers, into the places that only I touch. It brought me into the most erotic place I had ever been. With my other hand, I ran my fingers down the entire length of his thumb and clasped his whole hand in mine.

I melted from what I saw in his face.

"Lindsay, you quite possess me," he said in a whisper.

"I should like to possess you," I said, leaning a little more toward him, yet John kept our hands between us. We remained looking at each other, our feelings floating in quiet expression for several softhearted seconds.

"Perhaps we shall have the sweetest of dreams tonight," John said.

"Yes, and if it be so, I shall thank the moon," I said.

We remained holding hands as if the connection, long-awaited, needed to just be. Eventually and with lingering steps, we walked back to the house and entered in a silence heavy with a spell of hearts on fire. John took me to the foot of the stairs. I hoped his intentions were to follow me up to my bed.

Instead, he smiled at me and began to wish me a good night, still holding my hand. I could not help quoting what had yet to be written.

"Parting is such sweet sorrow that I shall say goodnight until it be morrow."

"Parting does bring me sweet sorrow, tonight and whence you leave for court in the morning," he said.

"Perhaps you shall find yourself at court anon," I said.

"The queen shall expect to know the substance of our discussions of these past several days, will she not?"

"That she will!"

"Then in haste I go, making my report."

With that, John picked up my hand and gave it a last brush of his lips. I yearned for him to kiss my mouth, but instead, he bowed and backed up toward his study. He made us both laugh as he continued his backward journey around the corner.

Still giggling, I glided up the stairs, rich with butterflies and fireflies moving around my insides. As Anne welcomed me into my room and began to undress me, I looked over at the vase on the nightstand. There was the original flower and it now had another to stand by it.

CHAPTER THIRTY-TWO

Matching John's gaze across the carriage, late the next morning, I felt the fluttering again in my core. I peered out the carriage window, unable to stifle a grin. The sunlight glinting through the trees warmed the moment even more. Coming to a crossroads, our driver yielded to another carriage. A raven perched atop a stone road marker where we stopped. John noticed it too.

"Ravens are my charm of good luck making," I said.

John asked what made me say so.

"They have appeared to me all along my journey, and now as I travel with you."

"And what do you make of this raven?"

"That there is magic afoot and in the air about us, John. It is a good sign indeed."

John lit up, taking both my hands in his. The carriage lurched forward, but the raven did not flinch as we passed. It remained watching us, like it knew us.

"It blesses us as we bless our queen," he said.

He was always thinking of the queen.

"How so?"

Like Bexley's story about Bloody Mary, he explained to me that if the ravens ever left the Tower of London that the English monarchy would crumble.

It was why they still clipped the wings of the Tower ravens in modern day. John said the ravens were not only at the Tower but were in abundance, showing themselves at Elizabeth's castles.

He stopped and contemplated me, gazing soft and long.

"What, John?"

He moved closer. I looked him up and down.

"Kat will have your hide for transporting me without a chaperone, or worse, she'd forbid me from hosting future engagements, if the chance ever arose again," I said.

"She will not be the wiser, and if she was, I shall remind her that it could only be you who assisted me in my scholarly inquiry for the good of the realm," he said in a whisper.

"Only me?"

"Yes, only you."

A blush rolled up my neck and into my face, which only encouraged John.

"I shall speak to the queen and make my intentions clear."

"Dr. John Dee, this is rather untoward, we have not spoken of any intentions."

"I do like how you protest, while the rose in your cheeks shows me your feelings otherwise."

He moved his hand, allowing it to rest against mine in soft contact. He claimed me by crossing his pinky over mine. I had to stop myself from taking his face in my hands and kissing his lips. Instead, I sat with quickening breath and a thumping heart as I averted my gaze out the window. Being a courtly lady, I pretended not to notice the tossing of the carriage which allowed our bodies to come into contact, a half second at a time.

I turned quickly as too many moments had passed where I could not look into John's eyes. I wanted to ask him exactly what he meant by intentions. Did he want to marry me? A hefty bump in the road jostled him toward me at the same time. His lips grazed my cheek. I did not move away; instead, I leaned into his chest and his arms drew me in snug against him. Closing my eyes, I took in the feeling of how well we fit together.

"Dr. Dee, we will be arriving at Whitehall in a short time," the driver called down.

We shifted to sitting side by side again. John caressed my hand and moved back opposite me as we came upon the road leading up to Whitehall.

As we disembarked, John offered his arm to steady my climb down the steps and we strode toward the hustle and bustle inside the palace. Blanche Parry greeted us, noting John and I were arm in arm.

"It is good to lay eyes on you *both*."

"Mistress Parry, I take it that all the ladies are well and serve a happy queen?" I said.

"She is full of vigor, conducting matters of state," she said, her line of vision shifting to the commotion developing behind us.

Spurting from the queen's chamber emerged four men clad in saffron linen tunics, calves exposed. Each wore their hair long to the shoulders and unflinching satisfaction showed upon their faces. I knew they were from Ireland or Scotland, and inside me, the adrenaline rushed.

Last to emerge from the queen's open door was my uncle, Shane O'Neill. Why was he meeting with the queen? John was watching me. He must have known these men were soldiers from Ireland.

"Make way for The O'Neill, as decreed by Queen Elizabeth herself," one of Shane's men announced.

Shane, puffing himself up, proceeded to walk out. I shot over to him.

"The O'Neill is a title that certainly shows evidence of the queen's changing favor," I said.

My uncle stopped as John arrived next to me.

"Niece, you have inserted yourself well within the queen's court," he said, looking at my very English dress.

"And you, ensuring the peace for our northern lands with the queen?" I asked, hopeful.

One of the soldiers sniffed, keeping a stone face. Shane narrowed his eyes as his lips curled above his teeth.

"As are you, Niece?"

"I am always about peace for Ireland," I replied.

"Then keep doing your trusted duty," he said and started on. I was now desperate to know what had actually transpired between him and the Queen of England.

"Will you send good wishes to my McDonnell kin?" I called to him.

Shane stopped and pointed his stare at me. His eyes shifted to John and then he swung back and lumbered out of view, saying nothing. I watched as my stomach tightened with anxiety for my family. In an instant, I felt my failure. Shane created much greater inroads with Elizabeth for his cause, while I likely made things worse for my kin.

I stepped back and surveyed the scene. This man I was infatuated with stood against the backdrop of the courtiers of prickish men acting superior to the unhappy women, bound up and hidden by layers lest they be seen as unworthy in God's eyes. Even for the woman sitting on the throne, a sense of freedom only came in the wee hours of the night.

"John, this is not the day to speak to the queen."

"That is plain. Your uncle has left you tied in knots."

His manner was guarded. I wanted to tell him everything and I wanted him to always be on my side. But he fused himself to England like Daideó did to Ireland. I was like a spider tied up in her own web.

Upon my first encounter with Kat, I told her I was ill. Out of concern, she kept asking me questions. Not feeling well here could mean slipping into death tomorrow. I assured her the queasiness resulted from a particularly bumpy ride to court. Kat placed the back of her hand on my cheek but let me go.

Once released to my chamber, I needed to write to my kin. This was some work, knowing the queen had men shored up somewhere scrutinizing every word. Among the customary compliments, this letter should read as if I was only concerned with the mundane, womanly things of the day:

My sewing is improving as my patient tutor, Kat Ashley, shows me stitch methods of quality and speed.

Through the process, it dawned on me that Shane's visit was public, and I could write about it, like it was the best thing.

Lately, I have seen my esteemed uncle, Shane O'Neill, bid a visit to court. I was most surprised and hoped it forbears that peace has come to live among the English and Irish shores, as the queen has restored his title of The O'Neill. I would partake to imagine that this will not be news to you, as he has surely come to tell you himself. As the queen's generosity and inclination to honor her Irish subjects resounds from her wise heart, I hope you find similar favor.

I'd rather I look naive than deceitful.

CHAPTER THIRTY-THREE

A few days later, with my letter dispatched, I was sitting with the other ladies as two of the court musicians played for us. I was tired and irritable, unable to slip into a peaceful rest over the past few nights. While notes from the virginal played on, I recalled bits of songs from my time. Powerless to raise the volume of Beyoncé or the Beatles in my head, I could not drown out the plunking of the ancient keyboard, yards away.

Bexley began to hum along as her fingers worked her needlepoint. I shot her a dirty look as the small book in my hand fell into the fabric of my kirtle. Digging my nail into its earthen brown leather binding, I traced the letters of Aristotle's authorship, branded on the front. The rest was in Greek, save for an inside placard that read *The Library of John Dee at Mortlake*. I stared at his name. As I wondered why he thought I could read Greek, it remained a consolation that this object ensured some kind of reconnection when I departed too abruptly from him, after the run-in with Shane. But John should have embraced me right then and there, assuring me all would be well. On my own, I needed to focus on gaining back Elizabeth's esteem, praying Shane had not thrown too much shade on the McDonnells but knowing damn well he probably had.

Two maids scurrying across the courtyard diverted my attention to the outside. Despite my low mood, I laughed out loud when one dropped her bucket after stumbling over the cobblestones, inadvertently kicking it into the path of the other maid, who tripped and then floundered across the ground. Bexley turned to regard the scene, which sparked her own mirth. The sound of the bucket still rolling around only made us both laugh harder. My delight seemed to inspire the court musicians, as they began playing an upbeat piece that got Bexley on her feet to dance, while the other ladies joined in. Bexley coaxed me to stand but I had no inclination to puppet my body through a regimen of skips and turns.

Like a lightning bolt, Kat, wide-eyed and tense, blasted into the room, making the music stop.

"The queen has taken ill," she said.

The other ladies rose with alarm.

"What is it?" Knollys asked.

Kat looked around, struggling to push out the words.

"She has signs of the pox."

Two of the ladies fell into tears; Bexley stood still with mouth agape. Knollys placed her hands about her neck and décolletage, feeling for any manifestation of a similar fate upon her own person.

"We progressed here to Hampton Court well before the outbreak in the city. How can this be so?" Knollys said.

Kat shook her head at the stone floor.

"Do her physicians attend to her?" I asked.

"Dr. Burcot is with Her Majesty."

"Then hope is not lost," Bexley said.

"Does she need us to attend to her?" I asked.

A few of the ladies stepped back from us. Kat glared at them. Redirecting her gaze to me, she said she and Mary Sidney had already taken on the duty.

"I will help you."

I heard Bexley gasp.

"I think God shall smile upon us and protect us as we attend to our queen. May He also instill her absolute healing through our vigilance," Kat said.

"God save the queen," Knollys said, and the others followed in near unison.

Kat and I made our way to Elizabeth's bedchamber as her anguished voice banked off the walls.

Inside, the chill of the hallway gave way to heat and a sickly fragrance of too many herbs mixing. A few candles burned about the corners of the room, but many surrounded the queen's bed. There lay the thin figure of Elizabeth Tudor. The curtains were drawn back, and Dr. Burcot, an aged physician of ascetic countenance, sat administering poultices to the red-pussed welts which speckled the queen's face, neck, and hands.

Elizabeth's eyes were wide and weeping.

Mary Sidney met us and pulled us close.

"She bears witness to her marks. She asks if she shall die."

At hearing this, Kat rushed to the bedside and knelt.

"You still recognize your queen through these evil spots?" Elizabeth said.

"Your Grace, you are still a reflection of your truest self, in beauty and in strength."

Elizabeth touched her face, running the tips of her fingers over the pustules on her cheeks.

"No, Kat, those virtues take their leave."

Elizabeth went silent as her gaze shifted and locked onto the floor. A servant fearful of entering used his outstretched arms to offer Mary Sidney a ream of red cloth.

"We are to wrap Her Majesty in this red linen and make sure the heat of the fire remains stoked," Dr. Burcot said, propping himself to a stand, leaning on a wooden crutch.

Kat spoke calmly to the queen, informing her of the next part of the treatment.

"More red upon my skin?" Elizabeth said with rising volume.

I caught the doctor as he hobbled toward his bag at the side of the chamber. "What is this treatment?"

"It will burn the plague from her body."

I leaned toward him, incredulous. "This is to cure the pox?"

He pulled his chin down in a single nod. I tried to read his face on a prognosis, but his expression remained stoic. I chose my words and spoke in a whisper.

"What is the likelihood of the treatments healing her?" I said.

He made the slightest shake of his head. At my shoulder was Kat, trying to make sense of it all.

"Mistress Ashley, would it not be prudent to plan our attendance on the queen? Methinks Lady Sidney shall need to take respite soon," I said.

Kat's gaze narrowed and then she appeared to lose focus altogether, overwhelm playing across her face. I placed my arm around her to guide her out of the room.

Once alone inside another chamber, I pulled her close, as tears streamed down her face. I swallowed and readied myself to tell my truth.

"Kat, Dr. Burcot thinks she may die, so I need your trust to—"

Kat grabbed my arms to steady herself.

"Dr. Burcot told you this?"

"Yes."

Kat crumpled against me. Unable to catch her, we both sank to the floor where she sat looking upward, her face frozen with pain. I crawled over our skirts to come eye to eye with her.

"There is a way to save her, but we must call upon Dr. Dee."

"He is but an advisor on the medical arts, he could not be more learned than the queen's physicians, and what he does know best—it is a dark act to cast the queen's astrology in a time such as this. He will refuse to look to her end."

"God in heaven, Kat—nothing of that nature. He has new knowledge here, that which sprouted from his recent meeting of the great minds of the kingdom."

She peered at me with a reddening about her nose and eyes. A tear flowed down. I took her hand, finding it wet and shaky.

"Yes, he shall be summoned," she said.

Back inside the very warm bedchamber, the queen was lying in her red swaddling, her face pinched through closed eyes.

Kat turned on her heel and spoke to one of the queen's secretaries seated outside the door. She then whispered into my ear. "John Dee is already here. I will have him called."

"No, I shall fetch him. Where is he?"

"By the privy council chamber."

I shot out of the room and flew through the palace. As I clomped along in my shoes, my toes grabbed at the meek insoles to keep them on my feet. Spotting John at a distance, I ran to him.

"Mistress McDonnell—Lindsay."

He reached out his hands to take both of mine. I pulled him into the closest empty chamber.

"John, the queen has the pox, and it is unlikely she will survive. But I can save her."

John's face tensed as his mind made meaning of my words.

"Are not her physicians attending to her?"

"Yes, but I fear the treatment is doomed. John, I have to speak to you in deepest honesty."

He held my hands tighter.

"My calling in my homeland is that of a healer."

John tilted his head toward me and waited expectantly.

"John, my homeland is not Ireland but America in the New World, almost five centuries from now."

It was as if I had opened my chest and given him my heart and lungs. I waited for disbelief to cloud his eyes, but he looked at me knowingly.

"New, England?"

"YES, New England. How do you—?"

"I have been to this New England, in the year 2016."

A cold burn ran up my spine and I was sure my brain had flipped over in my skull.

"You have met another time traveler, then."

"Yes, Sara."

"My mother!"

John gulped down a breath and pulled me down by the hands to sit with him. It dawned on me in full realization, John must be the pious wizard she was seeking.

"What did she say? What did she do?" I asked, grasping his fingers.

John's eyes moved back and forth as he cobbled together the chunks of information in his mind. I kept asking questions.

"To where did she bring you?"

"Her homestead."

"My house," I said. "Did you see me?"

"Your arrival at Mortlake was the first time, but you conversed in a tongue like hers. And when you spoke of your cat Merlin—I had made his acquaintance when he jumped into my lap as I sat at your mother's table," John said, leaning toward me.

I nodded in full, liberated understanding.

"Since first we met and I heard you speak, I wondered who you truly were, then on your second visit to Mortlake, I knew who you surely had to be," he said, his voice tremulous. "But I was already besotted with your grace and intelligence that made you shine as if all the stars had conspired to pour their lights into one soul."

He drew me to him and took my face in his hands. Now no force could stop me. I lifted my mouth to him and we kissed, sweet and full. He kept his hands around my face as we parted and stood with love in our eyes. He released me but I laid my palms on his chest, unable to break contact with him. Finally unearthed, I was fully seen under his gaze, and he was letting me in to witness his innermost spirit. All this was released in the awareness that we were without any liberty to linger.

Concern for his health flip-flopped through my mind.

"John, as my mother conveyed you back and forth, did you feel any pains in your heart?"

"Nay, I was invigored and strengthened." He paused. "Yet your mother became pale upon our venturing to your century. She spoke of being well and only in need of taking a rest."

I swallowed. My mother was killing herself with every journey and so might I. He asked me where she was now.

"She passed away from this earth," I said.

He placed his hands on my shoulders and brought me into his embrace. I sunk into him as it gave me profound refuge. His knowing her, him being the one she sought out expanded my soul. This man was invited into our innermost circle, and he'd accepted. I had tears, but they arose from realizing the benevolence of a holy Source that created this hallowed connection. John retrieved a linen handkerchief to offer me, which brought me back to the queen's crisis.

"John, keep this, you shall need it upon entering the queen's chamber."

"And shall you bring Her Majesty to your time to heal her?"

"I cannot." I paused.

"Lindsay—"

"Smallpox no longer exists then, so I need to bring her to an earlier century, one where I can get the required medicine. To journey, I will need to hold the queen close to me so I cannot risk entering the process in sight of those who attend to her. Neither of us has the authority to clear the room but the queen herself and perhaps Kat," I said.

"The queen is aware of my sojourn," John said.

"She knows!"

"I relayed an entreaty from your mother to the queen. Sara desired to ferry the queen back to her time."

"Why—what did she tell you?"

"To counter the prophesies of Nostradamus, to ensure a long reign, but the queen—"

"The queen did not believe you?"

"Her Majesty did. It was in her heart to believe but her head was not so well made up. Through our discourse, we agreed I would consult the stars to determine the best time for such a journey."

"What if you told her that now is the time?"

Empowered by my own words, I stood up and grabbed John's arm.

"That's it, we must go." But I held his arm firm.

"John, you must place your linen over your nose and mouth as you speak to the queen. You must not inhale any breath expelled from her body. Then go from the chamber and wash your hands and burn this cloth."

John nodded in somber understanding.

As we came closer to the chamber, I composed myself and gestured to John that I would enter first. He complied and came in soon after. All eyes fell on him.

"The great John Dee comes to share his wisdom," said Dr. Burcot.

"I am here to speak to the queen."

"It is not words that will heal her of the pox," Dr. Burcot said.

John ignored him and approached the queen who was being attended to by Lady Sidney. Elizabeth lay on her back, staring at the underside of her bed canopy. Lady Sidney moved aside as she stared at John with hope. He placed the handkerchief to his mouth and kneeled by the bedside. The queen maintained her stare, blinking from time to time. As she let out an exhalation, Lady Sidney clutched her own hands in despair. I found myself pulling on the back of John's robes, prompting him to maintain some distance.

"Your Majesty, it is your servant, John Dee."

The queen turned her head slightly toward John. He spoke in her ear, using the linen more as a screen for muffling his message and preventing anyone else to hear, than as his own shield. At first, she appeared stunned, yet she remained quiet. Soon her face sparked the faintest image of a smile.

"All except Kat, Dr. Dee, and Mistress McDonnell, leave us be."

The group appeared confused; some looked at me. Kat caught my eye and held it for a couple of seconds.

"The queen commands," Kat asserted, which got everyone moving save Dr. Burcot. Kat asked if he would kindly vacate the room for the shortest of spells as Mistress McDonnell attended to one of the queen's more intimate needs.

"Mistress Ashley, we are beyond such modesties given the queen's state," he said, throwing a glare toward John.

Kat moved closer and spoke in a steady tone. "You are in no state to lift her. The queen will be put more into distress if she is to see a breech with our usual care and you ignoring her command. If you are naught to leave, what will she be left to think?"

Good one, Kat, I thought.

The physician considered her sentiment and nodded in agreement.

"I will await on the other side of the door."

"That shall serve us well," Kat said as they parted.

Once we were alone, we all went to the queen who was drowsy and quiet—probably due to the heat.

"Kat, I shall assist Dr. Dee. You need not stay near." But Kat did not move.

Nevertheless, I sat on the bed and spoke in soothing tones, reassuring Elizabeth she was looking better. A slight smile appeared across her face as I pulled her into my arms. John whispered in my ear that my mother took both his hands into hers when they journeyed. I whispered fervently back in his ear to wash his hands and to recommend that all in the queen's service wash their hands, "with heated water and the use of castile soap." Elizabeth seemed to take in what I was saying as she remained staring up at me like a trusting child.

Wanting to put all my focus into the meditation, I instructed Kat to remove herself to sit across the room and turn away as I 'assisted Dr. Dee.' She finally complied.

Taking Elizabeth's hands into mine, I told her to close her eyes. My intrusive thoughts of wondering if this would work began to fall away as the Amitabha Buddha chant played in my brain, and as I thought of my intended date and place.

The familiar chill passed through me along with rapid movement. I stayed focused on the weight of the queen's petite body against me and her hands resting in my own. The landing was abrupt as always, but relief coursed through me once I opened my eyes on top of the billiard table in Mark Twain's study, on August 5th, 1878.

From the hallway just outside his study door, I heard, "Well praise be, another visit from beyond."

I turned to see Samuel Clemens in the doorway, but his smile faded to alarm seeing this red-clad and red-spotted woman in my arms.

"Miss Lindsay, what's this?" Who do you bring here on death's door and looking none too ready to join the Devil?"

"Are you ready for this? This is Elizabeth I," I said.

Sam's eyebrows raised halfway up his forehead.

"Your momma would be proud."

"Sam, you look better than last we met."

"I took well to the remedy you fixed me up with," he said stepping closer.

"But have you been vaccinated for smallpox?"

"Thanks be to God, yes, I have. Is that what has taken over this poor creature?"

A weak voice came from my lap. "I am queen, sir."

Samuel's eyes sparkled.

"Sounds like a queen. I beg your pardon and welcome you to a place I pray will be your savior."

Elizabeth fixed her eyes on Sam, pipe lit in his hand. She followed the white ribbons of smoke as they coasted up to the ceiling.

"I see spirits," Elizabeth said repeatedly, each time attempting to grip my arms.

"No spirits, just a nineteenth-century pleasure of mine."

Sam put out his pipe in haste.

"Nineteenth century?" she asked.

"It's 1878, rightly," Sam said as he stood up tall. She slumped against me.

While attempting to move across the table with the queen, Sam jumped to assist me. I thanked the Divine he was protected.

"I had to come here to you. In my time, smallpox no longer exists, and I would not be able to get the needed remedy," I said.

Sam lifted the queen and carried her toward one of the bedrooms across from his study. I slipped off the billiard table, and with gown rustling, rushed ahead to pull back the blanket and bedspread. Once he'd lowered her body, I covered her and began to remove the red cloth from her head.

"No! That is to heal me!"

I kneeled by the bed.

"Your Majesty, it has done its work."

"Where is Kat? Mary Sidney?"

"They are close by and we will return to them soon," I said.

"Return to them? Where have you taken me?"

"Like Dr. Dee told you, I have brought you to a future time where you can be healed of the pox."

Elizabeth's eyes remained fixed on my mouth.

"Your words do not make sense to my ears."

Sam leaned in.

"And who is this man? Is he to be my physician?"

"I'm proof you have arrived here in 1878, Your Queenship." He raised his index finger and left the room; the crinkling of newspaper pages preceded his return. He presented the masthead to Elizabeth.

"Says it right here, August 5th, 1878."

The queen looked through her swollen eyelids at the print for just a second and then shifted to me.

"I'm very tired, Mistress," she said and closed her eyes. I recognized she was overwhelmed and still feverish.

"I reckon we should take care of these pox, Miss Lindsay. I trust you have a plan."

"Can you recommend a homeopathic physician in this city?"

"I can get my physician here in two shakes of a lamb's tail."

"I need one that practices the homeopathic arts." I was betting that at this time in history, there would be ample practitioners in a city like Hartford.

Sam held up his finger again and went across the hall, back to his study. After several minutes and an opening and closing of drawers, he rushed back into the room holding a calling card.

"My wife utilizes the services of Dr. Jameson. I could send for him."

"I'll go. I know what to do and he can furnish me the remedy as a fellow practitioner."

"Not likely, Miss Lindsay," Sam said, looking at my skirts. "He'll want to see the patient for himself."

"I'd still like to go get him. I need to make sure he brings the right stuff."

Sam pulled the silken rope to summon his servant. After several seconds, there were quick footfalls on the stairs followed by a staunchly dressed young man, appearing at the door.

He slipped a glance at Elizabeth and with trepidation looked back at Sam. He then laid eyes on me. The scene did not compute for him.

"Mr. Clemens."

"George, this is Lindsay McDonnell and her sister, Lizzie. Miss Lizzie has fallen ill, and we need you to take Miss Lindsay here to fetch Dr. Jameson."

Sam referenced the calling card. "He is on Prospect Avenue."

Taking out his pocket watch he noted the time of 10:38 a.m. You should make it there in less than a quarter of an hour. Sam handed me the card and George made haste to ready the carriage.

Sam followed me out to the staircase.

"Please stay by her side," I said.

"I will."

"And you've been vaccinated?"

"You're repeating your questions—and oh good God, yes, I see no need to tempt fate when a little science can keep us well and living."

"Keep a cold compress on her forehead and assure her she is where she needs to be and that all will be well again. She will live."

Sam nodded and returned to the bedroom where Elizabeth lay. As I left, I fought the fear that the sixteenth and nineteenth centuries should never be left on their own to play nice.

CHAPTER THIRTY-FOUR

In true Twainian style, I was told the story of what happens when Mark Twain and Queen Elizabeth I are left in a room together:

"I heard my mistress's assurance, but I remain weak in this pained body," Elizabeth said.

Sam took a chair and pulled it up to the queen's bed. "Well, I reckon that will change once Miss Lindsay gets you the medicine you need. In the meantime, let me introduce myself. I am Samuel Clemens, master of this house."

"Master Clemens," she said.

"It won't be any time at all before Miss Lindsay brings the doctor back. 'Til then, I can sit here with you quiet like, or I could spin you a story."

Elizabeth managed a wan smile.

"It is good of you to take us under your keeping. Pray tell, are we still in England?"

Sam let out a laugh. "Well, it's New England that you find yourself."

"And who reigns here? Is it the English Monarch?"

"Not anymore. We have a democracy with an elected president, Mr. Rutherford B. Hayes, but I'm supposing that I'm not supposed to tell you that."

In fury over this news, Elizabeth motioned for Sam to help her sit up.

"Maybe you should best stay as you are."

Elizabeth glared at him. "It is not your station to tell me what I shall do, Master Clemens."

"Well, I can understand your way of thinking, but the way I see it, until we have the medicine, there's no sense at all in you exerting yourself."

Elizabeth eyed him but relented.

"And you don't have to be queen here. You can take that load off and just get yourself better."

"I am delivered unto this crown by God and will not relieve myself of its burden. Perhaps with your democracy, you have forgotten what it is to be ruled properly by an anointed sovereign."

"Your Queenship, I don't want us to quarrel. Maybe I could share a tale, or I could hear one of yours. Tell me, what do you think of the plays purported to have been penned by the actor named Shakespeare?"

"I have not heard of such a man," she said.

"I knew it!" Sam said, slapping his hands together. Then he stopped short and surveyed the queen's face.

"You are so young, yet."

"My reign is but a few years."

"Damn, that's too early! I thought I had him as a fraud by his alleged patron herself!"

Sam apologized for cussing. Elizabeth's eyes enlarged trying to register his meaning, but given her low energy she waved him off in forgiveness.

"Master Clemens, I say God's teeth to these cursed spots," Elizabeth said, splaying her hands. He glanced at her pustules and checked himself.

"God's teeth? Pardon my smile but is that a true cuss?"

"If you mean profane—it is never for the ears of ladies, children, or any clergy."

"Then who?"

"Men... and I."

"So, a queen can speak profanely, even blasphemously?" Sam said lightly.

"Sir, as queen, the burdens of taking care of my people and my country are heavy. They compel decisions that can save or extinguish. My exclamation lets God know we require His attention."

Sam smacked his lips. He had never heard such a justification.

"I am not in your place. Thank you for the enlightenment."

༄

Dr. Jameson was less experienced than expected, which made it easier to advise him on the best remedy for the situation. My knowledge surprised him, thus earning me instant credibility.

"I would concur, Miss McDonnell. Where have you formally trained?"

"In Europe, under one of Dr. Hahnemann's disciples."

A thrill ran through my body, knowing the prestige this carried in the nineteenth century.

"Oh, I was unaware that such tutelage was being provided to women," Dr. Jameson said.

"They do—they have," I said, a bit unnerved.

Snapping his case shut, he lifted it under one arm and asked us to lead the way.

George helped us into the carriage and off we went, back to the Twain house. It soon occurred to me to lay some proactive footwork.

"Dr. Jameson, the patient may also be under delusions she is royalty."

"Delirium is not usually a symptom of the pox. If I can be indelicate, is the patient also mad?"

"No, but her lady's maid said that upon waking she mentioned being a queen. Perhaps she was feverish and coming out of a dream, which made it difficult to discern reality. As I have been acquainted with the patient for some time, I would say she is quite sane."

Dr. Jameson nodded, his eyes reflecting some inner puzzling.

"Perhaps I should not have mentioned it. I do not wish to predispose your clinical picture of her condition."

Who cares if he thought her crazy. I only needed him to administer the remedy. I would take it from there.

In a quick burst, a dog darted across the road causing our horses to step sideways, rolling the front wheels of the carriage into a shallow ditch. George did his best to settle the whinnying animals and ask about our welfare. With our reassurances, he tried to get us moving again, but one of the axles had broken.

"So sorry, Dr. and Miss," George said, his face appearing at the side carriage window. Dr. Jameson opened the door to join George in assessing the damage. Neither thought they were able to repair the axle without some help. I sat inside, biting my nails. What if Elizabeth was worsening? Without a second thought, I leaned over and opened Dr. Jameson's case, picked through, and pulled out the vial of Variolinum, slipping it into my bodice. It occurred to me that anyone who'd had contact with the queen may need this, including John and me. I asked George to assist me out of the carriage.

While the men were distracted, I walked across the street, out of their periphery, and hightailed it toward the Twain house. I didn't like a doctor who let a little thing like a busted axle get in the way of serving a patient in need. Once I saw the house, I broke into a run, as well as I could in my shoes. Holding my bodice to make sure the vial was secure, I passed a few other ladies, who became most perturbed. At this point, I didn't give a shit.

I reached the house, and I was grateful George hadn't locked the door, allowing me to bolt up the stairs to find Elizabeth, spotted but calm, and with Sam seated next to her bedside.

"Mistress," she said in a small voice.

"You look like you're running from the law and happened upon us while making an escape, Miss Lindsay," Sam said.

Catching my breath before retrieving the remedy, I nodded at Sam's observation. From the vial, I meted out the proper dosage.

"Your Majesty, allow me to place this under your tongue," I said.

"The queen, eager for the promised help, opened up. She jutted her chin out following my instructions.

"How did you convince the doctor to give you this?" Sam asked.

I explained what transpired with the carriage, along with my thievery.

"Oh, I bet they are going to be flaming mad," he said.

"Maybe we won't be here."

"How should I explain it?"

Sam gestured for me to follow him out of the room. I remembered the queen and spun Sam around to face her. I curtsied and tugged down on Sam's arm to do the same. The queen looked at me feebly.

I backed out of the room and saw Sam was annoyed. We moved into his study, and he closed the door.

"I'm not one for bowing to another human being, least of all a queen from a country we had to fight tooth and nail from to gain our independence."

"Did you tell her any of that?"

"No, Miss Lindsay. I know the rules. Although a question about Shakespeare may have slipped from my lips," he said.

"I did the same thing with one of the queen's ladies. So, what else did you two talk about?"

"We talked about cussing."

"Really?"

"We talked about her being out of her own time and what her people would do if they discovered her disappearance. She thought they'd try to get a fake queen. Wouldn't you know, an idea of how to pull it off popped clear into my head, so I told her how I thought it could work."

"When we return, it will be as if we were never gone. Time passing here is independent of time passing there," I said.

"So, I guess she won't require any of my schemings."

Sam walked over to the mantle and started to pack his pipe.

"Miss Lindsay, perhaps this time away gives Queen Lizzie a chance to breathe. Even I don't have to be Mark Twain all the time but you—well you're here, in full duty."

I took in what he said. "No escape," I replied.

Sam sucked in on his pipe, as the tobacco brightened to florescent orange. His taking a long exhale gave me a chance to ponder my own words.

"Sam, do you think there is wisdom in no escape?"

His brows rumpled as he took another puff and blew it out.

"Having no escape means learning what you're made of. Now, *giving* yourself no escape can be a cat of a whole other color. That's when you realize you've got the courage moving through your blood. Maybe it's a bucket, maybe it's a teaspoon, but you've tapped into something that's going to remake you."

We sat in a reflective silence.

"You are a sage," I said.

Sam puffed on his pipe to suppress a grin.

"We should take our leave. I cannot, and I mean cannot, find the words to express my gratitude."

"Miss Lindsay, it is a lovely thing to be in your service, and I have met me a real-life queen. I think there might be some stories waiting to be hatched from that—fiction, of course."

I bowed my head. I couldn't tell him his future, even now."

"Miss Lindsay, there is one thing. I did tell her she could come back with you to visit anytime."

My stomach turned. "Do you think—?"

"I was just remembering a conversation with your momma. She wondered if our human race could avoid a whole heap of suffering by teaching folks from the past about the future."

"Jesus Christ, I don't know, Sam."

"Me neither, Miss Lindsay. And when I say I don't know, my meaning is I do not have the answer."

"It's too much to think about."

"But you may have to," Sam said.

"Yes, but not right now."

He scratched his head and nodded in acquiescence. After pausing, he said my color was off and that I should rest after performing such a rescue of "this royal damsel in distress." I placed my hand over my heart as he opened the door and took a gander down the stairs. The house was still quiet as we crossed over to where the queen was now sleeping.

"You, sir, are my touchstone and I am very grateful," I said.

"On a day like today, apparently there is nothing that cannot happen. I'm glad to have borne it witness. Make sure you take care of yourself."

Sam exited, closing the bedroom door behind him. Watching Elizabeth sleep, I took assurance from the warm glass of the remedy vial hidden against my sternum. I brought my hand to my heart to feel it beating again and assessed my reflection in the nearby looking glass. I'll just rest after this trip, I thought. Grounding myself before commencing the return to the moment we left the sixteenth century I spent a few moments sweeping out the doubts gathering in my mind. As long as I was clear for the next few moments, we'd be fine. I gathered Elizabeth back into my lap and held her hands as I initiated the syllables of the sacred chant in my mind, imagining the feel of the heat back in Elizabeth's bedchamber. Soon, a profound cold blasted through my awareness as I held my breath. The contrast of the warmth signaled we'd made it back.

I opened my eyes, thrilled she was still sleeping.

"Have you taken your due course?"

It was John, standing by the other side of the bed, where I'd left him.

I nodded while easing the queen back onto the bed. Her complexion, while full of pustules was of overall better color. The remedy was working fast. I wondered if the journey back was hastening her healing.

"Kat please join us." Kat turned around. She and John both rested a hopeful gaze on the queen.

"Mistress, surely she cannot be better off than before, it was too small a time to administer to her condition," Kat said moving to Elizabeth's side.

"Kat, look at her. Dr. Dee's plan is healing our queen."

I felt John's eyes upon me.

Kat placed her hand against the queen's forehead. "She is much relieved from her fever."

The queen opened her eyes slowly and took us all in.

"I see the worry has left your faces. Am I dreaming? Will I live through the pox?"

"Your health has begun its restoration," Kat said through jubilant tears.

"Kat, we shall inform those outside of the good news," I said.

"And how do we explain it?" Kat asked as they both looked to me.

"Her recovery has been the collective effort of the queen's good physicians and the prayers that commended her to God," I said with confidence.

⟡

When John readied for his leave, we were out in the open air of the court while a hushed carrying on of the evening business flowed around us. An act of formality was necessary and unfortunate, as I just wanted to hug him to me. Before he stepped into the carriage to take him back to Mortlake, I thrust a small folded parchment into his hands.

"John, inside is the medicine that healed the queen. If you—"

He signaled that he understood.

"There are instructions, place the pellets under the tongue."

He nodded, gratitude in his eyes.

"Sweetest lady, pray next we meet, will you lay upon mine ears the course of your journey to the queen's health?"

"Yes, Dr. Dee, but only if you send word to me, in haste, if my mother arrives once again into your presence."

The apples in his cheeks rose. "It would be one of my greatest pleasures to behold such a reunion."

To use Daideó's words, we would all be sharing common hours. After a day like today, it seemed more possible. Yet, as I watched John's carriage become smaller in the distance, my heart broke a little, wishing I was with him.

CHAPTER THIRTY-FIVE

What I set in a new motion, kept Elizabeth from death. It took me time to realize it was my destiny to change history, as Elizabeth was surely going to die, but instead, she had a long reign to become one of the most beloved queens. Yet before that, and unbeknownst to me, Elizabeth seeded the growing schism of Irishman upon Irishman, one of my family against another. I wonder if she ever confessed to this to God as she plunked her foot down on the neck of her golden goose.

While she lay recovering in her palace, Sorley supervised his troops to be on watch for an attack. On the coast, his men paced atop the hills closest to the sky, ready to set bundles of kindling ablaze to signal the Redshanks, mercenary soldiers waiting in Scotland, seventeen miles across the ocean in Kintyre.

"If it is not the English themselves, it'll be Shane creeping up to battle for the Route," Sorley said. "Worse yet, he will bring combined forces back from London."

"We've got eyes like eagles," said one.

"Aye, and we'll all be in need of your keen sight. I'm sure Shane takes clever cover knowing we wait for him," Sorley said.

Such preparations paid off within the month when Sorley's troops spotted Shane's army across the River Bann. Days of rain caused the river to flood. Sorley believed this would do no more than slow Shane and his soldiers down.

Soon before dawn, to sound the first roar, Sorley fired off the guns. The growing light revealed a deluge of boats transporting Shane's men across the surging river. As it continued to rage, Sorley descended downward into battle, flanked by his newly arrived Redshanks.

Through the clamor, Sorley recognized Shane's top man, one who ate at our table, soon after I arrived. Another of Shane's swordsmen took advantage of that split second, slicing into my grandfather's shoulder, the force dropping him to the ground. Several of Sorley's men jumped to his aid, surrounding him as he regained his footing.

As the battle simmered then fizzled, and despite their casualties, Sorley's forces had slain those crossing from Shane's side. To counter, Shane retreated to pick off the small Scottish settlements that lay west, reporting these successes to the queen.

While the red welts remained prominent on the queen's face, of all her councilors, she only allowed William Cecil to meet with her in her privy chamber. No doubt, he reported on the outcome of the battle.

"Your Majesty, the McDonnells remain fortified, given the loyalties of neighboring clans and their store of Scotch Redshanks. However, the division among the Irish, and those who call themselves Scotch Irish, cannot be undone."

The queen rested her eyes on Cecil.

"And what of Sorley McDonnell?"

"He fought and sustained injury but he outsmarted this O'Neill."

"He lives well in victory, then?"

"He now knows there is an enemy in his own brother-in-law," Cecil said.

Elizabeth huffed. "Do the McDonnells see this threat from its origination?"

"My thoughts are to assess that through Mistress McDonnell. Her letters continue to be intercepted, but perhaps a more direct approach could be undertaken."

"God's teeth!" Elizabeth said.

Cecil stepped back.

"Mistress McDonnell is never to know!" the queen snapped.

"Then we will take pains to ensure that end."

CHAPTER THIRTY-SIX

I thought this was a golden time. I'd proved my loyalty and supreme value to the queen, and all was repaired with Kat. I enjoyed high favor at court, remarkably among the queen's ladies. John had also risen in Elizabeth's esteem and was sent to Europe as an emissary to broker a greater flow of scientific and intellectual information between England and the continent. I yearned for his company, which only made me more lovesick—a happy circumstance and one I believed would be soon remedied with his return.

But I received only a trickle of correspondence. After a longer than normal period of any communication getting through, I did receive an envelope in a hand I had not seen before. The letter explained it was written by a new secretary to my grandfather. It also seemed different, more positive toward Elizabeth with a slight aspersion thrown in about Mary Queen of Scots. Was that to appease the crown or were the tides changing in the Celtic alliances?

I rationalized to myself that my place here at the English court was more advantageous if there were problems with Scotland. Elizabeth owes me and the McDonnells big time. Still, I sensed something else was riding in on a dark wave.

Back when I was in Ballycastle, close to the time I left for England,

Daideó took us on his horse to Dunluce Castle, situated high on an ocean cliff like Dunanynie. He told me how the McDonnells wrested it from the McQuillans while taking over the Route and how it gave us another foothold in overseeing the sea and land.

"Daideó, with all this to maintain, do you ever have any peace inside yourself?"

"My post here is decreed upon me as chieftain. I am grateful, as it was an unlikely honor."

"Why unlikely, you were chosen, were you not?"

"I am the youngest born, the last in line to inherit this post, but it fell to my charge when my older brothers did not care to venture to Ireland."

"Do you regret it?"

"Nay, how can I regret a chance to serve?"

"But you must be weary."

He did not answer right away.

"When weariness comes, I call on the unseen guidance within the trees and of the land itself, and I call on God for sustenance. It is with those allies that we all persevere."

We rode in silence as I pondered what he said. It made me feel ashamed. I always thought the less pain and bullshit, the better.

"Lass, I am sorry you will take to your servitude alone. Even here away from Scotland, I am not solitary in my stewardship."

"I was an only child. I'm accustomed to doing things alone."

After several seconds, he kissed the top of my head, and I relaxed a little against him as our horse quickened in pace. I settled into what it meant to share these mystical, common hours.

"Make sure you keep your senses open to God and the spirits. You must tend to the connection, as you will only hear divine guidance if you have welcomed it in."

"God must have trouble deciding on who to favor as most people pray, yes?" I said.

"Prayer is also to see into your own heart and make alliances with what resides there."

I found this true about meditation. Observing feelings as they arise without the judgment which scares them into hiding, or contorts them into appearing more noble or invulnerable.

As he urged his horse to pick up the pace, the elements of nature all converged with the palettes of sea and sky on our left and the hues exuded from the grassy meadows and forest on the right. After some time, we passed the pillars of Dunseverick, a castle fort where Saint Patrick once performed sacred duties. Daideó told me how ownership went back and forth over the centuries since.

"What if all the clans were all on the same side, and what if England, Scotland, Ireland, and Wales were all united?"

After a moment, he said, "'Tis never the way."

"And if it was, if it could be, would you take that world?"

"Men always have something to battle for, we'd soon find our squabbles in who waged peace the best."

I wasn't sure if he was right or if he could not conceive any other possibility. I wondered if the peace I strove for was even possible. Would I fight for it? I'd never had to fight for much of anything—not to vote, not to say what I want to say, and not to stay alive. These were things I only thought about with passing appreciation. Riding through this land, knowing we could be cast from it as others had been expelled, I realized how much I take for granted in my time.

One night as we prepared the queen for bed, she stood inspecting herself in the glass. Enough time had passed for us all to know that the enduring marks left by the smallpox were likely permanent.

"These are wretched," she said raising her voice in frustration.

"Is there nothing to be done about this marring, Mistress McDonnell?"

I was at a loss. The queen bore into me with her eyes as if accusing me of holding something back.

"Perhaps in time they will fade," I offered.

She stomped her feet.

Lady Knollys cleared her throat. The queen turned to her.

"Catherine Knollys, do you have something to say on the matter or are you just rude?"

"Your Majesty, there are plasters we could apply to your fair complexion as the marks fade," she said.

"I've not needed any such plaster before."

All in the room nodded in agreement.

"One that is said to diminish the spots can be concocted in a lunar cycle's time," Knollys said.

"A month? Elizabeth said pained. "What shall I do in the meantime, hide from my own court?"

"Your Majesty, until the arrival of such plaster, we shall create one of simple lead and vinegar," Kat offered in a soothing tone.

"Lead? Kat, I do not think this is wise, it may disagree with the queen's constitution," I said, alarm rising.

"I cannot abide to be seen like this any longer," the queen said, moving her fingers about her face. After several seconds, she wrung her hands and turned from the glass.

"What constitutes the other plaster?" I asked Knollys.

"Nutmeg, mace, ginger… oil of bevercod, all soaked in wine."

"Your Majesty, I should think this is much better," I said.

Kat directed Lady Knollys to dispatch to the apothecary with discretion.

"I do not wish anyone to know," the queen said.

Knollys curtsied. "Yes, Your Majesty."

Later, Kat saw me grimace as the ladies applied the lead plaster not just to the queen's face, but to her hands and chest. I took Kat aside and asked if all that was necessary. I suggested we dress the queen in her high-necked gowns until the other plaster arrived.

"By my troth, the queen shall not give over her mind. Too soon, the Yuletide festivities commence."

"Kat, I believe the lead to be poisonous."

Kat hushed me. "No lady has ever taken ill from it."

"Kat, I would not say this if I did not know it to be true."

"Perhaps the lead of Ireland is debauched," she said.

"Lead is lead and the poisoning is slow," I said.

Kat eyed the queen, who was now looking at her reflection and smiling."

"This will do quite well," Elizabeth said.

"She is pleased and will not do without it, at least not until the other plaster is delivered to us."

I stopped myself from shaking my head. The queen asked us to survey her newly whited complexion. There were smiles all around and compliments, but it looked like shit to me. The ladies were unsure what to make of my obvious disapproval. They were probably wondering how I was getting away with it.

In taking the queen's usual morning walk, she directed us to the pond garden instead of the usual path on the south-facing side of Hampton Court.

"Your Majesty, it is inspiring to see the water flow for your pleasure," Bexley said.

"It was my father who had all these delights installed."

She lingered by a fountain, looking at her reflection. A Caucasian-colored fish, the size of my palm broke the surface of the pool. I thought its scales mimicked the queen's true complexion while it seemed to mock her as it opened and closed its mouth.

She turned and told us she'd like to walk the perimeter of the back half of the palace. Feeling my privilege, I approached her.

"Your Majesty, may I walk with you?"

Without breaking stride, she gestured for me to join her.

"I entreat you to walk with me in silent discourse."

"I merely intend to make myself useful."

"Mistress McDonnell, I am eternally grateful and in awe of your ability. It has not yet fully come into my mind, no less my heart, what remains possible with your gift."

"And that gift is bestowed on you from my McDonnell clan."

She placed a hand on my arm.

"I thought it was from your mother, Sara, who is from a country that does not yet exist and from a century too far in the future to conceive."

"My mother is a McDonnell, Your Majesty."

"Pray tell, who else do the McDonnells favor with their magical envoys?"

"Only Your Majesty."

"And your mother is not pursuing the King of Spain or your Queen Mary of the Scots?"

"I am the only one. My mother has recently died."

"At someone's hand?"

The question hit my chest like a careless but hard-hitting elbow and an anger rose in me, made worse by knowing I could not express it.

"It was her heart, it stopped beating."

The queen found her compassion.

"For that, I am sorry and wish condolences upon you."

I withheld my thanks for several seconds, but then gave it.

"In absence of a mother, there are others who can provide love and caring," she said, clearly referring to Kat. I nodded, realizing Kat was someone we both relied upon.

"As your mother's daughter, you shall be a great asset to me."

I let my silence stream between us for several strides, determined not to give away any power.

"And what of my McDonnells beyond the Pale?" I said.

"What do you ask?"

"That you command Sussex to let them tend to their lands without interference."

The queen spoke low and guttural while gripping my arm.

"Then you ask that they be given to their own rule, but I am the queen here and the sovereign there."

"They will revere you for it and never do you harm," I said.

"Not now perhaps but—"

"I did not have to use my gift to save you. I am commended by my kin to support your rule but not at their detriment," I said hearing my own strength.

"Mistress, you cannot understand the complexity of the matters, unless you have seen my future and the future of England."

She was laying the gauntlet down. A new challenge to me and another test. I searched my mind for something to hook her.

"Do you see yourself as becoming a great monarch?"

"I cannot fail my people. England needs great care and I aim to devote my reign to being her savior."

"Then a savior you will become. But you must honor all your people to achieve your aim."

"I cannot honor those who plot against me, whether in great or small measure," she said, her eyes wide like two moons, her hands in fists held against her chest.

She stopped walking. "All is in flux in the lives of us princes. We must stand guard to see what is to happen before it takes hold. You would be wise to provide me such counsel."

Elizabeth slipped into the tennis courts built for her father during his early reign. I followed behind, allowing some of the other ladies to catch up.

Once inside, the queen stepped along the bright lines laid out on the court itself as she engaged in a slow, thoughtful walk alone. I took my place with the rest of the ladies in the spectator area. I had a blast of memory from when I was fifteen years old and visiting Hampton Court with my parents. My father had picked a fight with my mother, close to the spot I was now standing on centuries earlier.

"Maybe you could get off your high horse to support me once in a while," he'd said.

"And where's my support, my pats on the back, Dan?"

The tension simmered all morning on the train over; my father threatening to get off at the Wimbledon stop. I was pissed at them for being such assholes that I risked the humiliation of a public scolding by taking a seat on the other side of the train car. I'm not sure they even noticed. I kept thinking what a mess they made of their relationship. Could they ever come back from that? And now standing here, just like then, I had no idea how to play my cards, except I really should know this time. I had the magic, right?

Bexley nudged me and placed her warm hand at the small of my back.

"Lindsay, you look wrung out. Do not let Kat see that scowl burning on your face."

A nod of thanks was all I could muster as I tried to soften my expression, despite the sour jumble churning in my stomach.

Later that night when we were in bed, I asked Bexley why she thought the queen paced the tennis court, as we bore witness. She told me the queen takes counsel by summoning her father's spirit within herself, in the place of his king's sport.

"Perhaps she is contemplating a marriage, or worried about her prospects given her." Bexley finished her sentence by waving her hand across her complexion.

"Have you ever seen a happy marriage?" I asked her after we blew out the candles and lay in the dark, where it was easier to speak from the heart.

"Happy?"

"Yes, where husband and wife enjoy each other?"

She sighed. "Is marriage not to raise your family's standing? Methinks it is the parents who succeed in wedding their sons and daughters into advantageous matches that have then earned a happy marriage, at last."

"What about a love match?"

"I pray they truly exist. But they say happiness is what a man knows with his mistress, not his wife."

I didn't want to talk anymore. The acidity in my stomach rose up again as I rolled into a fetal position. Bexley moved to her side, making sure our backs were in contact, like she always did. After a few moments, I could not stand it and maneuvered closer to the edge of the bed, preferring the chill of the outer perimeter to the warm touch of this deceiving world.

CHAPTER THIRTY-SEVEN

It had been some time since receiving any message from my kin. From my trunk, I retrieved the past letters, bound up in ribbon. I smelled the paper, hoping to get some whiff of Dunanynie. Maybe the scent of the earth or ocean there, like a mix of the right essential oils, would boost me out of my deeply laid rut. The same day I received a letter from John:

Dearest Mistress McDonnell,

As I will likely be on my journey for a period to come, my hope is that you shall receive my heartfelt wishes for a warm and safe harbor from the winter snows. If your dear Sara appears at Mortlake in my absence, my good mother holds instructions to dispatch a letter to you at court.

Upon my return, I will look forward to being invited into your gracious company once again.

Your Devoted Friend,
John Dee

Yes, I was overjoyed he'd thought of my need to see my mother again. I was grateful yet, regarding me and him, we were going backward. *Your Devoted Friend* was not the closing for which I was hoping. I tried to focus on him wanting to get together but I'm not sure how he felt being with a twenty-first-century woman. I attempted to help myself feel better by thinking I had the sixteenth-century equivalent of a fling: a little dancing and hand holding but that was all it would be and it was just as well. Finding a new boyfriend was not why I was here; I should let that part go.

That led to me questioning if I was not doing enough, still failing to intersect with my mother and falling behind on helping my McDonnells. I also wondered if I was in too deep with the queen, if I'd done far too much for her. I mulled over the dizzying implications for modern day. Soon, a foreboding haunted me about my McDonnells. Were they okay? I wished I was with them.

Over the next few weeks, life at court left me with a stomachache as a daily companion. I was powerless witnessing the queen parade around in her poisonous, ghost-white complexion. And my longing for John pushed up into my heart but it left me chastising myself for being selfish.

⧉

Moving through winter, my body was assaulted by the chill of the gray days. My immune system was compromised, and my energy depleted as, day after day, I had to put on a near constant 'professional' face serving the queen while her need to have me in her presence only increased. I hoped for a note to arrive from John's mother, summoning me, but wrestled with how I would ever be allowed to take my leave. By the time of my birthday in late February, the idea I might miss my mother altogether took up space across my heart and thoughts. I made it to early March, when I took to my bed with congestion and a pounding headache, never being so grateful to have a cold, to be able to sleep and take respite.

After I resumed in the queen's service, Kat told me John had arrived back at court and asked to see me. When she found me asleep, he took that to mean my condition was not improved.

"Dr. Dee wore his concern for you plain upon his face. He turned from our conversation a reduced man. He holds a love which flows deep for you, Lindsay," she said, patting my hand.

Love. A deep love. My heart drummed.

"Methinks the queen has taken notice of it and may find this a most agreeable—advantageous match."

For who? I thought. What was there to take notice of—he's been away on her mission.

"I shall want the counsel of my Sorley and Mary McDonnell."

"Aye, but it remains with the queen."

My Americanism was rising. My twenty-first-century inhabitantism was rising. Why does Elizabeth get to decide? Where were John and I and our feelings in this conversation? And, oh God, what the hell are Sorley and Mary going to think?

"Do you desire such a man as Dr. Dee to be your husband?" Kat asked.

Her question rushed through me, awakening every cell I had been willing toward a somber, anesthetic sleep on the subject. This was a secret I did not want to divulge. "Dr. Dee is a fine man of unusual talents."

"And ye has not been betrothed in Ireland or the Scotch Isles?"

Kat endeavored more than a woman-to-woman exchange with me now. This conversation had another audience.

"No, no other betrothals," I said, as an idea sprouted.

"I shall petition for my return to Ireland to take direct counsel with my kin."

Kat pushed back into her shoulders. Her face was unmoving.

"That matter will be decided between William Cecil and the queen. The queen holding the final say."

No escape.

CHAPTER THIRTY-EIGHT

The next day, I hid myself in an herbal garden close to the kitchens. It was a rare moment I had to myself, and thank God, as I was in no mood for conversation. My heart hurt whenever I thought of my family. Something felt wrong and that it was happening right now. But I wasn't sure if taking a trip to see my grandparents was the correct path or a reckless whim to assuage my immediate anxiety.

While I walked the path around the kitchen gardens, a brusque wind took the dead leaves deposited last autumn and lifted them into a perfect circle. The wind also shook the early spring buds flashing yellow and red; it was a reminder that the natural energies could be called upon for guidance. With eyes closed as I stood, I dropped my awareness down into the ancestral connection. Like a roar inside the curl of a high wave, the sound heightened and then calmed. I breathed into the knowledge now illuminating in my mind: My clan needed me.

I checked my pulse—once, twice—had enough time passed for the organ of my heart to heal since journeying with Elizabeth? Checking again, I still couldn't be sure. But I sensed my gut instinct.

In the farthest corner of the garden, I found a solitary bench. It was in full view of many a window in the palace, but I thought that was all right. I didn't need to be hidden as I'd be back in a fraction of a second. I could still do my work covertly, slow and mindful. I was ready. As I breathed, I placed my hand on my heart and shifted into the sacred chant. All neurons firing with the intent to see my beloved grandfather when and where he needed me. The shift took root and into the void I went. This time, it was as if ice was forming on my face and hands, and it took longer. I stayed the course.

I was conscious of arriving on top of Dunluce Castle, engulfed by the screech of sword on metal, guttural war cries and howls born from those being hacked up alive, choked out only by the boom of the guns. On my knees, I clung to the low stone battlement in front of me.

"Where in the Devil's hell did ye come from?" a soldier yelled down.

I turned to find a row of Redshank troops. One jumped on me and brought me down hard onto my belly behind a parapet. His weight was like a boulder and his chainmail slapped hard against my arm and hand as we landed. I heard myself begin to push out a scream but lost my breath.

Gunshot bashed against the castle walls while arrows whooshed above. Several troops ran past us. I could hear the clanging of swords close by, but the Redshank holding me would not yield. A burst of cold sparks sizzled down my spine in a sweat. The stench of burnt gunpowder and bodies cleaved open, oozing blood, bile, and shit, overtook me and I nearly lost consciousness.

God only knows when, but the Redshank loosened his grasp and weight on me. His face, scratched red and smudged in black, tensed in fierce expression. He pulled me up to a sitting position with one hand but penned me in to still be in the cover of the castle wall. My body shook beyond my control.

"Lass, we have a halt."

As the clangs of metal ceased and the guns fell silent, a single bagpipe wailed in the distance. It came closer until it was near underneath us. I kept my eye on the Redshank, trying to read what was happening by watching his face. I followed his line of sight to where, only yards from me, stood someone I hoped was Sorley, but as I got a better look at him, I could only identify him as a McDonnell.

"Surrender now, Gillaspick McDonnell, and give us the castle. It is yours no more," a voice called, familiar to me in its ire.

Gillaspick McDonnell spoke from his gut. "In whose cause do ye fight for, Shane O'Neill?"

"I've got your kin for hostages. Your beloved James McDonnell, Laird of the Isles, and with him your chieftain here, Somhairle. You will all be spared if you surrender now."

The Redshank who had been protecting me stepped back. Several seconds passed and yells in Gaelic sounded across the chasm between the castle and the battleground below. I crawled to my feet. Looking down, I recognized James from the portrait at Dunanynie. Bloody from his shoulder to his chest, he lay on a stretcher of sorts. His eyes were open and moving on a face hard and sad. Gillaspick began pacing and waving his dagger.

I spotted Shane sitting on his huge charger of a horse, muddied with blood spewed across his chainmail, his sword still in hand, dark red with remnants of flesh stuck to the blade. Just like he had the pre-dawn morning he spoke to me at Dunanynie, he placed one hand over a fist and raised it up over his head. He unfurled his fist into an open hand. He was now signaling his men.

I heard my own cry when I saw Sorley being led out with a rope around his neck and his hands tied.

"No, No—what is this madness?" I screamed out in sobs.

All stared at me, including Sorley. His eyes widened, and fear burrowed into his face.

"And a wee lass fights for your claims," the man behind Shane taunted my grandfather.

Shane's men squinted and yelled insults at the McDonnells. Sorley kept his sight on me. So slowly, almost imperceptibly, he shook his head as his eyes welled up. He mouthed, "Go back."

"You all see how gravely wounded is your James," Shane said and paused, as two of his men pushed Sorley from behind, the rope tightening around his neck as he stumbled forward.

"And here your chieftain will be withheld all sustenance."

The anger and terror ripped through me. I turned to Gillaspick. "We've got to save them." I lunged to grab his hand. He pulled back while two arms restrained me from behind. I tumbled out of the grip and took two flying steps to stand back at the parapet.

"Shane, the queen will send the might of her forces down on you!" I yelled.

He locked eyes with me.

"I will let you go, Lindsay McDonnell, if you report back to the queen that I have done her bidding and done it well."

The words rang out like a storm of arrows hitting their target.

"You did this for Elizabeth?"

There was silence. A shadowy smile showed itself in the curl of Shane's lips.

He couldn't be telling the truth—he just wanted Ulster for himself.

"But these are *your* kin," I said, my voice wavering.

"These are *your* kin and best ye raise the gates and relinquish Dunluce."

I shot a look at Gillaspick, who was conferring with the Redshanks around him, and then I looked back to Sorley, only now they were tying a gag around his mouth.

CHAPTER THIRTY-NINE

I had no other contact with Shane before I was brought down into the English Pale and shipped from Dublin. The image of Daideó with a rope tightening around his neck slithered through my every thought. What about Maimeó? And what of James? I was sick realizing my unexplained arrival put us all in greater danger. It was a labor to breathe, and I couldn't tell if it was due to the trauma of the battle or damage I was doing to my heart in taking another journey.

The crewmen attended to me with respect as we sailed south to England, but my liberty was limited, as I always remained in the presence of one or two soldiers. They too, treated me with honor, but flanked my side wherever I ventured, above or below deck. Was I a prisoner or still a golden goose? I had no idea what ramifications awaited. When I thought about Elizabeth ordering the attack, it burned right through my stomach. But it had to be a lie. It was the McDonnells who sent me to her, and I'd saved her life.

The journey was grim and gray while our ship sliced through the jagged waves. I spent much of my time staring at the horizon and praying, asking for help from all I knew, from Green Tara to Amitabha Buddha to Jesus Christ. I appealed to Father Sun and Snake

Medicine to transform this mess. My guards kept watch and would often interrupt my focus with thumps of their feet and yells to the crew and the other soldiers onboard. It happened with such frequency that I wondered if they suspected I was in sacred process and purposely denying me my spiritual connection.

Arriving in late-day London, the soldiers traveled with me after I'd received a fresh gown and a maid to clean me up. Then they brought me to Whitehall—the back way. As I alighted from the carriage there was only Kat, Blanche, and fresh guards there to receive me.

Kat's jaw was set.

"Mistress McDonnell, we are most pleased to see you back at court," she said without a trace of perturbance in her voice.

"How is Her Majesty?" I asked.

Blanche regarded me as her eyes narrowed. "The queen is well and thriving."

"That is good news," I said barely above a whisper.

Kat accompanied me to my chamber, and as soon as she closed the door, she embraced me, then shook me by the shoulders. I laughed to dispel the tension but gave up pretending.

"Kat, how much trouble am I in?"

"There is the report from Shane O'Neill that you showed yourself at the surrender of Dunluce Castle. Yet you were present here that same day at court."

"Then it could not have been me," I offered. "There is no woman who can be in England and Ireland at once, right?"

Kat waved me off.

"Did you arrive aboard a ship sailing down from the Irish Sea?"

"That does not say I was at Dunluce."

"There is talk that you performed an act of witchcraft."

Flashes of scenes from the Witch Museum in Salem hurled themselves around my mind.

"Who speaks the word?" I asked.

"No one claims it," Kat said, which was of little comfort.

"I need to see the queen," I said.

"And she commands to see you."

We walked through the palace corridor with only the slap of our heels on the stones passing between us. I quelled my impulse to ask if the queen was behind the attack. I was fully aware that Kat could not answer me, and it would only put us at odds.

Kat entered the queen's chamber while I waited outside with the guards. Within seconds she exited, taking everyone who was with the queen out with her. Knollys trod past me without acknowledgment. Bexley touched my skirt as she walked by but kept her head down as several men appeared in the passageway. One of them was Francis Walsingham. As the queen's chief protector, he always threw off a sense he had been a dragon in a prior life. With his arrival, I maintained the body language of an innocent. I'd no sooner looked them in the eyes to show I had done nothing wrong when Kat pushed me into the queen's privy chamber, shutting the door behind me.

I met Elizabeth's gaze straight on. She was holding herself upright and stern. I matched her, summoning power in my own stance. Pushing my shoulders back, I did not wait for her to speak first.

"Your Majesty, I implore you to intervene to save my family—both James and Sorley McDonnell are Shane's prisoners.

"You make no demands on me."

"The McDonnells sent me to you, and I saved you from the pox."

"And now there's talk of you being a witch."

There was a pause and then she tore into me. "Why would you let yourself be seen in the afternoon here only to be witnessed at a battle hundreds of miles up there, on the same day? If you are to be so heedless, you should never be permitted to close your eyes again to do your magic."

I put my hand on my gut. "I knew something was going terribly astray. And then I find my beloved grandfather captured by Shane O'Neill. They are brothers-in-law—what would bring them to this carnage?"

"This is certainly not the first time. As much as they ally themselves, they also take to battle."

"My grandfather stood with a rope around his neck, and they gagged him in front of my eyes. Shane threatened to starve him and deny him drink." I stopped as the emotion pushed up into my throat like a geyser.

She remained unmoved, unsoftened.

"You have to help them," I said, raising my voice.

Elizabeth flew at me. "I am the Queen of England and Ireland and do not have to do anything bade to me." She then grabbed a goblet from the table before her, took a swig, and slammed it down on the table.

"Let Sorley McDonnell be parched," she said.

"Then you did order it," I said, moving toward her.

She took a step back. "You are close to the edge, Mistress."

"Then rescue me from it—rescue them," I said, hearing the anger burn.

"God's blood, what would you have me do?" the queen roared.

"If you have so much fucking power, then wield it!" I yelled, throwing my arms out so that my hand knocked the goblet across the room. Upon it crashing to the floor, the doors burst open, and two guards snapped me up. Walsingham came in right behind them.

"Are you harmed?" he asked the queen.

With her face taut and hands to her mouth, she shook her head.

"We heard the threat to you, Madame," Walsingham said.

"I made no threat," I said, arms now pinned.

I stared right at Elizabeth as I had done nothing of the sort. The goblet smashing was an accident. But she said nothing. Instead, she cast her arms up toward me, as if trying to banish me from her sight.

"You can't sweep away your treachery," I said, but I shouldn't have.

The guards tightened their grip and pulled me from the queen's presence.

Elizabeth wrung her hands as she stewed, now red in face and neck.

"But you can save them, you can order their release," I yelled as two guards dragged me out the door. It was like a spear was thrust into my chest, my fear and rage like blood, spilling over the rest of my body, leaving an invisible but palpable trail down the passageway of the palace. I started to weep and hyperventilate. The guards stopped but I heard a voice behind me.

"No matter—off to the Tower."

My brain understood those words but fought to convince itself they were not pertaining to me or my fate. Yet they kept moving me out—down the stairwells, and out to the cold bite of the moon. My brain told me to fight, but it was useless against two guards holding sharply bladed weapons. I could be hacked to death right there on the grass.

Once the guards loaded me onto a long wooden boat, I had the journey by water to realize that, time traveler or not, it was only through my living physiology that I could impact any change. I was no good to myself or my McDonnells, dead in a heap.

The shivering of my own disowned body brought me back into it. The shaking was not from any cold temperature but from its innate fear response. I was going to the Tower. The Mother Fucking Tower. And now the fear wove its way along my nerves and into my synapses. I tried to key into the lapping of the oars in and out of the water of the Thames. But once I closed my eyes, one of the guards hollered, "Eyes Open!"

His voice breaking into my thoughts was stunning enough, and then it hit me. The queen told them to not let me "take my solace" or my prayers, for fear I would make a leap.

A hurricane of energy gusted inside my mind. What if I dove into the water? Black and cold, it had to be better than what comes next. I would swim and swim—unless being so weighted down in all my layers, I drowned. As if validating my conclusion, the boat shook as we jetted past rocks and into the churn of the river rapids. Like being in the belly of the whale, I had no way out. I thought of John. It was here in Elizabethan England where I fell in love. It was in sixteenth-century Northern Ireland where I found my family, my true tribe. And it was there at court, where my soul found yet another home, but as the seconds ticked, I was losing it all.

My tears fell fast. I took in the air of the night, gasping, as it might be the last time I could inhale the night air, out in the open.

The sound of lapping water hitting unmovable rock gave way to the orders blaring from the guards. Then I took in the sight of the man-made mountain of the Tower. One of the guards pulled the boat toward the wooden gate.

"No heads to look down on you tonight," one said, pointing to the top of the wall where there were sharp spikes. "Not even one with his eyes plucked out by the crows."

As our boat skimmed across the water, past the gate and into the moat, I quaked and my teeth chattered. I could still dive into the river and let it wash me away from all this death. Maimeó flashed into my mind. Our hearts must be in sync, as she must be feeling the same profound fear.

Once the guards moored the boat, they corralled my arms, lifting me up and out. My legs were weighted like iron as they brought me up a flight of unforgiving stone steps. The air was damp and laden with wretchedness. How many others had walked this path? At once they deposited me into a cell, or maybe more a chamber, which resonated the same level of doom. One of the jailers remained, taking up guard in the only chair. The heavy wooden door squawked to a slam; it was followed by the rattle of a padlock.

"Am I to be questioned?" I asked.

"You are to be watched," he said.

I realized I had my phone hidden on me. What if—the thought that they weren't likely to strip search me calmed the swell of anxiety. They wouldn't, right?

After several minutes of the jailer staring at me, I attempted to engage him in conversation, desperate to make something shift.

"How long have ye been serving at the pleasure of the queen?"

He did not answer.

After several minutes of tormenting silence, I glanced out the slit of a window. The sun was setting, while black and blue clouds were strewn across the sky.

Sliding down the wall I found my seat on the rough stone floor. The guard's face remained almost unmoved, but for a second or two. Perhaps because I had been one of the queen's ladies just an hour ago, he thought to lift himself from the chair and offer it to me. But if that was the thought, it did not translate into any outward behavior or courtesy.

The silence between us allowed the wails of a man crying out to break in, which sent a cold heat slicing down my back. I suddenly looked at my fingernails and then my hands as if they might be taken from me. After all, they thought I threw the goblet.

After the room darkened through the dusk, there was a clattering at the door. Two plates were brought in with a tankard that had seen better days. It was some kind of gruel and brown bread. I placed it next to me as the jailer loaded up the gruel onto his piece. It was clear his portion was more than mine. He eyed me as he took a swig from the tankard.

"Are we to share that drink?" I asked.

He finished his sips and pushed the tankard toward me. As I drank, the weak mead fell down my throat and into my raw gullet. After eating and our bowls collected, the guards switched. The next arrived with a metal chain in hand. Using his chin, he motioned deeper into the chamber. My stomach rumbled and I was shaking once again. He grabbed my arm, shackled my wrist, and pushed me back.

Letting out the slack, he directed me to sit on the spent hay, littered across a cot.

"There are to be no whispered prayers, only sleep. At the queen's command, if I reckon ye be in prayer or contemplation, I will yank ye down from this cot."

I slowly reclined onto my back, the hay my only cushion.

For what seemed like hours, I contemplated the ceiling, which was a darkened ambiguous mass of containment. I was afraid to close my eyes, for fear of being thrown to the floor. She did not want me going anywhere to anytime. Late into the night, the drowsiness took over and I relented to let my eyes close.

"Bang, Bang, Bang." The sound rang into my cell. My consciousness quickly landed into a shocked wakefulness. The guard smirked at me as I lowered my arm and wrist, pained by being stuck in the same position all night. The banging continued, wood on wood, and it intensified.

"Pray, what is that?" I asked.

The guard only pointed to the sliver of a window.

I leaned over and peered out. From a tree below, a raven with the blackest feathers stretched out its wings. It took perch on a high branch across from the outer wall of my cell. It stared at me, or rather made sure I took in its presence. I wondered if this could be one of the ravens that visited me before.

"Do you not see it?" yelled the guard.

I shifted my view. Down below, men were assembling a scaffold.

"Did ye take sight of the new block?" the guard said, now getting closer to me.

His words did not make any sense.

"It is from a big fat oak, carved to fit the necks of dirty traitors," he said next to my ear.

I spotted the hunk of shaved wood. My face contorted, and through a spray of hot tears, I closed my eyes hard.

"Eyes open, wench," he said in my face, his exhale smelling of rot and invading my awareness like a noxious gas, remaining with me as he returned to his post by the door. He eyed me like he might come back, adjusting his crotch, his lips crimping into a dead smile.

My breathing labored as I couldn't get enough oxygen. I gasped as my throat would barely open. The guard spewed insults but they barely registered; I was too far gone. My arms felt like lines of acid were passing up and down them, searing just under my skin. My heart beating with sharp pains, I thought a heart attack had come to claim me before these Elizabethan fuckers could.

You know what, that would be fucking great. I'll take it. I'll go out like my mother. You're not gonna get me. Ha, ha, ha, you asshole-motherfuckers!

CHAPTER FORTY

Hearing the thunder of my thoughts brought me to an internal precipice. Within my anger, I could tip over the edge or breathe into this speck of power. I chose my own sovereignty and inhaled over and over to calm myself down to a low boil. No matter what, they could not take my spirit. They could not take Daideó's spirit either. I tried to sync with his psyche, sending him a message to hold hope and remember his power from within. I imagined it flowing outward, reaching him, from my cell in the Tower to his in Shane's dungeon, or beyond.

After some time, no idea how long, the dog shit of the jailer guarding me banged his fist twice on the wooden door. The clattering of the padlock followed by the door opening produced the guard from the day before and two others. My thought was they were going to take me, but they stood at the threshold, not coming or going.

The next thing my senses took in was John, my John coming into my cell.

The guards left us, and I rushed to him. His eyes were of fear and love as we embraced.

"You're here, you're here," I kept saying.

He caressed my head and kissed my forehead and cheeks, tears in his eyes.

"My dear, it is you that are still here."

"The queen denies me all refuge. John, this is an awful place."

John held both my hands.

"You should not have to endure such agony."

"Then you know, I did not assail the queen. It was an accident. In my passion, I asked her to undo what had been done in Ireland and pleaded with her on behalf of the McDonnells, but she refused."

"The queen asked for the release of the McDonnells on her behest, as does Mary, Queen of Scots, but Shane has Sorley, still a prisoner."

"He is alive?"

"It appears so, but I am afraid James McDonnell succumbed to his wounds in the battle."

"Oh God," I said.

"Bless and keep his soul," John said.

"Am I to be executed?" I asked, nearly losing my breath as I spoke the words.

John held my hands more tightly.

I pointed to the slit in the wall. John walked over and held his own heart as soon as he saw the grim structure below.

"This cannot be for you. You would at least have a trial."

"A trial? John, they think I am a traitor. And the queen and Kat said there is talk of witchcraft. They could punish me for all of it!"

I slumped down against the wall, and I saw the pain in John's eyes watching me struggle.

"You can take your leave from here, while you are with me—"

"You would come with me," I said.

John took in a great breath and looked back down on the scaffold. One of the Tower's ravens—one of the monarchy's protectors—snatched his attention. He seemed to take it as a message.

"All that God instills in me says I am to stay. This is where I serve, no matter how my love has taken root for you."

He understood the full consequences of me leaving, under his watch. On that alone, I wasn't leaving. God knows what would rain down on my kin if I were to return to 2018.

"John, you and the queen are aware of what and who I am. I came to bring peace for all the kin involved in this struggle. That is what God conspired for me. A word from the queen and all this could be righted."

His mind was searching. An expression of hope rolled across his face. He took a quick look out the window and motioned me to come over.

"A word from you."

With his hands on my shoulders, I gazed out and locked sight on my winged friend.

John spoke in my ear. "You see it?"

"I do, I have been blessed with the ravens my entire journey, but now I fear they remind me that they protect the queen.

"Lindsay, you also keep the queen from harm."

It then dawned on me.

"I shall write her I am a true friend as is the raven that stays here at the Tower, ensuring the security of the Monarchy. I, remaining in the kingdom, ensure the longevity of her reign."

"I will deliver your letter to the queen myself."

"But these are only words—most of which she knows already."

"She does not. Your flight to Ireland set the queen on a course to believe you'd turned against her. And then you contested her, right in her privy chamber."

"I was called to take care of family, none of which I did."

"Your interference beseeches the queen to realize that the McDonnells are not who should be manipulated," John said.

"Can't she leave Ireland be or at least allow it to rule itself as an ally?"

"No, she cannot. Yet it may be the work left for you to influence."

I could now see a path out.

John pointed to the small wooden table where there was a rolled parchment, a quill, and inkwell, reserved for confessions. He placed the only chair beside it for me.

I took to writing, confidence sprouting as the words populated the page. John sat on the cot while I worked. Outside, the banging of boards for the scaffold intensified, and I thought, while I was in my new hope, someone else was at their most dire.

After signing the letter, I asked John to pray aloud with me. We took to our knees, side by side. I prayed a Christianized Tonglen practice.

"God, let us attune to the fruits of this moment, awakening our hearts and senses to the breath. Let us breathe in the regret and fear all around us. Knowing its heaviness and darkness and then breathing it out as clarity, forgiveness, and hope. Let light stream with each exhalation. Let us breathe this way for ourselves and all those who are suffering and in need of redemption."

CHAPTER FORTY-ONE

I sat in the pre-dawn hours of the next morning, beyond rest, convinced I'd hallucinated John's visit after my panic attack. As I pictured John, the images were of his presence here: his beard was longer, his hair was disheveled, and the tension drawn into his facial expressions was unlike any I had ever seen on him, or any I'd conceived in my imagination. His visit must have happened. That birthed a stirring hope for liberation. Enough that I gave myself over to the moment, breathing in the dark murk of uncertainty and releasing it into my cell as clear-eyed faith. The key sounded in the lock to my cell, confirming my belief, but then it crashed against the cold stone floor and the shit stain of a guard staggered in for his shift, and maybe something worse. He approached me and I pushed out a breath that sounded more like a cat hissing. He stopped and waited. I bared my teeth and stared at him, probably wild-eyed. He took the one chair and set it down away from me and near the door.

As time trudged along, my belief bled out of me as I disconnected from my surroundings. A numbness took over my body, which made me wonder if I had already died. A quiet and quick heart attack that stopped the flow of life instantly. I tried not to make that my new intent. I kept telling myself to hold on—for family, for love, and for finishing what I'd started.

Another night passed and I bobbed in and out of my black hole, failing to buoy my belief, becoming lost to myself.

A ruckus rose up in the passageway and the door opened yet again. Things went quiet and then John came through the threshold, tears in his eyes, parchment held tightly in hand.

"You are freed, my love."

I wanted to run to him, but I sank to the floor. All the relentless tension and trauma of living this time-traveling life had sucked the wind from my lungs and the blood from my muscles. John lifted me up against him. I don't remember much of those moments other than the way his neck smelled of his wonderful home, Mortlake.

As he and someone, I'm not sure who, assisted me down the steps and out of my confinement, the crisp air braced me enough to find my footing again. After a few steps, John eyed me, lines of worry across his face.

"Vile, putrid place," he said under his breath.

No words came. I was rendered aphasic; the perfect storm of emotions shut me down. Once we were out of the Tower's yard, John lifted me into a wherry boat to take us downriver. As soon as the boatman pushed off with his oar and we were in the flow of the River Thames, I sought out John's arms and just sobbed. As I calmed myself, he kissed my wet eyes. I remained against his chest.

The rhythmic slipping of the oars down into the water was accentuated by the soft rain that draped over us.

"What now, John?"

"You are released to my mother and myself at Mortlake."

"I am in your custody?"

"Our watch, our safe keeping."

"Will I ever have to go back to the Tower?"

"Not if you stay with me."

John told me that, when he took a private audience with the queen, she was stirred upon reading my letter. It helped that it was delivered by John, who attested to its sincerity and truth. I could only kiss him to express my gratitude and he held me closer against him. His heart beating strong and fast told me he knew how the events could have played out.

"Do you possess news of my kin?"

"Your grandfather remains Shane's prisoner."

I felt distress grab hold of me again. John's face mirrored my anguish.

I wondered if I should believe the queen when she says she has no influence over Shane. No matter what, Elizabeth holds power over my life, yet through all this I have compassion for her and her cause as an orphaned, young, female monarch. I was not sure if it had been conditioned over my months of service or because I could see her brilliance —like a diamond that increases in sparkle the more it is cut—but I believed in her as a person. She told me she was not behind Shane's attack on Daideó's forces, yet he remains a prisoner, as does a piece of my heart with him. Maybe I was asleep at the helm. Maybe I did not speak to the queen enough about the peace in the north of Ireland, but I did not realize what a wildcard Shane had become, so much so that not even she could contain him.

It was then I felt Maimeó in my heart and gut. She is so scared and enraged. Her brother imprisoning her husband. She needs me, and like the ravens at the Tower, my wings are clipped. All the forces were keeping my physical body ensnared and my heart entwined with London. Then I thought of my mother. If she would come back, she'd come back to Mortlake. What would she see now: me here, beside John, holding the truth of what has been put into motion.

"John, will you pray for us all?"

"Let us both pray, united in our message to God."

I took John's hand in my own, and gazed into him, soul to soul. We were together. Not only was I not alone, but we were together. And I was going back to Mortlake, the place where my mother would be the most likely appear in a time journey taken in her past but my future. After all, I now knew nothing was impossible. It was the time to let back in belief. All that comes to us, and to which we belong, flows to us if we create the opening to receive.

THE END

ACKNOWLEDGMENTS

Gratitude to Wendy Kram from LA for Hire for pointing me to who the protagonist needed to be, Terrence Hawkins and the Yale Writers' Conference for recognizing my early writerly voice, Eve Bridburg, Kate Racculia, Matthew Salesses and Colwill Brown at Grub Street, April Eberhardt of April Eberhardt Literary for her pivotal encouragement, Julie Kingsley of The Manuscript Academy, Eric Maisel, Elizabeth Evans, Lesley McDowell from Jericho Writers, Masheri Chappelle of the New Hampshire Writers Project and Portalstar Publishing for sharing her passion on the need for spiritual fiction. My amazing beta readers: Larissa Douglas, Sandra Coppola, Rosemary Lorimer and Patricia Crisafulli. Hollis McGuire and Taryn Fisher of the SBDC for your encouragement and business sense. Kevin Duffy for co-creating the author website. Lynne Griffin for your wise counsel, Kerry Ellis and Sharon Rutland via Reedsy. Dr. Emily Sommerman, Trinnie Houghton, Lisa Stockwell, Michele Lowry, Lynn Hundertpfund, Heather Ramsey and Dr. Jennifer Maher for listening to me share where I was in the writing and all your deep encouragement. Emily Lane for opening up greater possibilities on the spiritual plane and the rest of the Galactic Six and my Celtic Anam Caras for holding space. Dr. J. Michael Hill and The Honorable Hector McDonnell for sharing your passions for Sorley Boy's McDonnell's history. Ancestry.com for helping me uncover the ancestral ties that inspired this story. Dalriada Tours in Northern Ireland and our knowledgeable guide, Arthur Ward through two tours of McDonnell locations. My family: the Jacobsens, the Krohns—especially Marsha and Donna, along with Sammy, June and Stevie for your feline company and my Beloved and fellow writer, Mark Jacobsen, for your perpetual support and partnership…and to the Divine for all of it.

ABOUT THE AUTHOR

DEBRA ANNE LECLAIR'S debut novel, *The Common Hours,* stems from a visceral connection to the Tudor era and the discovery that her own Celtic ancestors tangled with the crown. As a psychologist and coach, Debra is also impassioned by the connection between psychology and spirituality and what that brings to a hero/heroine's journey. She welcomes visitors and messages at her website,

www.debraanneleclair.com

Printed in the USA
CPSIA information can be obtained
at www.ICGtesting.com
LVHW090420291024
794794LV00006B/607

9 798990 582316